THE FIVE

WISHES OF

MR. MURRAY

McBRIDE

Also by Joe Siple

The Final Wish of Mr. Murray McBride

The First Wish of Mr. Murray McBride

Charlie Fightmaster and the Search for Perfect Harmony

The Town with No Roads

The Last Dogs

THE FIVE

WISHES OF

MR. MURRAY

McBRIDE

Joe Siple

**UNION
SQUARE
& CO.**

NEW YORK

**UNION
SQUARE
& CO.**

NEW YORK

First published in 2018 by Black Rose Writing.
This 2025 paperback edition published by Union Square & Co., LLC.

ISBN 978-1-4549-6112-3

For information about custom editions, special sales, and premium purchases,
please contact specialsales@unionsquareandco.com.

Printed in Canada

2 4 6 8 10 9 7 5 3 1

unionsquareandco.com

Cover art and design by Patrick Sullivan
Interior design by Rich Hazelton

*To my dad, John Siple, who taught me perseverance
through the "Never Going to Get There" lesson.
I'll be forever grateful.*

Any magician worth his salt will tell you—there's fake magic, and then there's the real thing.

The fake is how we make our living. It's the magic the audience pays to see, knowing full well it's nothing but illusion and sleight-of-hand. We make hundred-dollar bills disappear. We levitate our assistants. Sometimes we cut an audience member in half and miraculously put them back together.

But the real stuff, actual magic, a lot of magicians don't believe in anymore. They think they've discovered all the secrets and learned all the tricks.

Not me. I've seen magic in my life. The real stuff. I know it exists.

"Prospero, you're on in fifteen minutes!"

It's the man who's been attached at my hip these past few days. His name is Miles, although he refers to himself exclusively as "Prospero's Biographer." I've argued a man of thirty is too young to warrant a biographer, but Miles simply hobbles along beside me in his wrinkled, moth-eaten suit coat, insisting he's the luckiest man on earth to "have access to the greatest magician in history."

It's not true, of course. The "greatest magician" part. Not when there have been performers like David Copperfield and Criss Angel. And has Miles never heard of a guy named Houdini?

"Please, we've talked about this," I say to Miles. "Call me Jason. Prospero is just for the stage." His lips turn down. We both know he'll never call me anything but Prospero. "Forget it," I say.

"Fifteen minutes?" I scan the backstage area. Several people bustle around—one rolls a thousand-gallon tank of water from which I'll inexplicably escape despite three-inch-thick chains . . . another prepares a series of mirrors, angling them until the woman in front of them disappears from view. I know I should finish preparations, but tonight the thought terrifies me. "I can make time for a quick question or two," I say, stalling.

He slaps a hand to each of his pockets—his sport coat, his pants, and finally his front shirt pocket, from which he removes an audio recorder. He bumps the curtain with a stray elbow, sending dust into the air and onto my newly dry-cleaned tuxedo. I rub my nose and stifle a sneeze.

Miles presses a button and the machine makes the same beep I've heard nonstop for the past three days. He adopts a voice reminiscent of a newsman and forces his heavy black eyebrows together. "According to the magician himself, it's the biggest night of his life, less than fifteen minutes before he appears onstage in a puff of smoke. Prospero, Master of the Impossible, the greatest illusionist in history, turns to me and says . . ."

I put my hand over the recorder and angle my lips away. "Please," I say. "Nothing contrived. Tonight is too important."

The crowd continues to file in. Anticipation is building like the arc of a magic trick. I don't wear a watch—I need my arms clear from wrist to elbow—but the buzz of the crowd counts me down to showtime. I peek around the curtain again and stare at two empty seats. Front row, directly in the center, so close to the stage I'll almost be able to reach out and touch them.

"Why do you keep looking out there?" Miles asks. "Is it those two seats again? The reserved ones?"

I straighten my bow tie and replace the curtain in front of us. "Yes."

"Are they for your family?"

I heave a deep, regretful sigh. "I haven't seen my family for several years."

I can tell he's dying to ask why, but he resists. "Then who are the seats for?"

His audio recorder is outstretched and nearly touching my lips. I take a step back, but he leans onto his toes to keep the recorder to my mouth.

"Some very old friends of mine," I say. "They're the reason this night is so important. Actually, they're the reason I first got into magic."

"You've never told me about that," Miles says. "About how you got into magic."

"No?" It's a baffling thought. This man hasn't let me out of his sight for the past three days. He's watched my tricks from every conceivable angle, asked me every conceivable question five times over. We've talked at length about the awards I've won, the masters who've taught me, and the various skills involved with illusion and sleight of hand. Is it possible he hasn't asked me the simplest, most biographical of questions—How did I get into magic?

"It's a long story," I say.

"But the world needs to hear it."

I think about the two open seats, right in front, and realize Miles might be right. Their stories deserve to be told. "All right," I say. I brace myself against equal parts dread and curiosity, wondering if I'll have the strength to finish the tale.

I guess I'll attempt that trick when I come to it.

I ignore the growing murmurs of the crowd and find two folding chairs leaning against the wall at the very back of the stage. I set them up near the curtain and Miles and I sit, our knees almost touching. I try not to worry about wrinkling my tuxedo.

"When I was young, I was blessed to meet an amazing, wise old man and a sweet but feisty young girl," I say. "The man, without my knowledge, taught me what it means to live a full, meaningful life. And in turn, I like to think I might have given him a glimpse into the memory of his youth. The girl . . . well, the girl gave me even more."

Miles's eyes are bugging out at me. He leans forward, probably looking for my love story. A little sex to spice up his book. But what I have for him is beyond such things.

"Her name was Tiegan Rose Marie Atherton. And his was Mr. Murray McBride."

I think back on how it all started. How I met an old man, randomly it seemed at the time, and my life was changed forever.

"I met him on his hundredth birthday . . ."

CHAPTER 1

Murray McBride
Lemon Grove, Illinois
Twenty Years Earlier

Bran Flakes. Every morning for longer than this old brain can remember. Since Jenny died, anyhow. Chalky and bland and disgusting. But I'm not one of those picky folks who need the most expensive caviar for every meal. Never have been.

I stare at the Bran Flakes like they're a worthy opponent. I'll attempt to chew and swallow and they'll try to kill me with a lack of flavor. May the best man win.

It's my birthday—the Big Ten-Oh—which does nothing but remind me I have no one left. No family, except a greedy grandson who rarely visits. No friends, except the grocery checkout clerk with the pierced nostril—a sparkly hoop I can't help but stare at. I'm not proud of it, but I want to include my internist, Doc Keaton, on that list of friends. Why else would he insist on a birthday physical? A glance at the clock tells me I'll be late for the appointment, but what do I care? Get to be my age, and people don't expect much out of you.

I crush my pill up good—I only need one. Not one of those old-timers who has to take twenty pills a day. I mix it into the Bran Flakes and slowly win the battle, though not without a good fight. Guess I'll live another day. Doc Keaton'll be happy about that, at least.

I've been dressed since 4:00 a.m. because sleep doesn't come as easy as it did, once upon a time. Seems backward, if you ask me. A man my age should be able to sleep the day away if that's what he wants to do. Figure I've earned it. And kids these days can sleep like a baby, right when they're supposed to be in the thick of their lives. I once saw a lad—looked about twelve—sleep through an entire Easter Mass. Made me curse under my breath and I had to confess it to Father James later that day. But the good father just laughed. Now I'm not one to question a man of God, but that didn't sit too well with me, to tell the truth about it.

I only live two blocks from Doc Keaton's office, so I'm able to walk there in about a half hour. They put me in a room by myself and Doc sweeps in a few minutes later. Seems happy to see me. He asks how I got here and when I tell him I walked he about bounces off the ceiling. "It's just walking," I tell him. "The day I can't do that is the day I go meet St. Peter."

My legs dangle over the examination table, same way they did at doctor's offices when I was eight, and thirty-eight, and eighty-eight. Same old, same old.

"Surprisingly healthy," Doc says over and over. "Heart of a fifty-year-old."

He conveniently forgets to mention the lungs that are only kept working by my morning ritual of Bran Flakes with crushed, life-saving-pill. Sometimes toast and jam on the side, if I'm feeling adventurous, but that happens less and less these days. Too much damn work.

"I'm thinking of the twenty-second," I say. I don't need to explain. He knows I'm talking about the pill. In truth, I would've stopped taking it a year and a half ago if I didn't feel like I was letting Doc down. I hate to think how bad he'd feel. Probably blame himself. But that doesn't mean I'm not serious about it. I've known for a while I won't live to see the new century. Just turns out I won't live to see 1998. What's the big deal?

"Don't joke about that, Murray," Doc says. "We've talked about this, remember? If you don't take your pill, fluid will build up in your lungs in a hurry. You'll suffocate in a matter of hours. Does that sound like what you want?"

I try to give him the answer he wants. Really, I do. But nothing comes out except a grunt and maybe a bit of gas down below. "What about work?" he says. "Has Brandon been calling? Have you had any shoots recently?"

"A fair few," I say. "A light bulb company a few weeks back. Couple different advertisements for oatmeal. One other, too, but I can't think of it. Oh yeah, shampoo. Can you believe they wanted me for a shampoo ad?"

Doc straightens his tie and stifles a smile. Way I see it, doctors still ought to wear white coats. It's only proper. He eyes what's left of the wisps at the side of my skull. "What did they need you for?"

"Just wanted me to stare at some young lad with thick, black hair. Took about a thousand photographs of me sitting there looking at the fella—told me to act more 'longing.' As if I could look longingly at a man's hair! Then they gave me two hundred bucks and told me I was free to go. If you were looking to convince me not to take my pill, that there was almost a clincher."

Doc puts his hands up in surrender. "All right, Murray. No more shampoo ads. But listen. We've got to get you some socialization. Physically, you're doing miraculously well, but . . ." He looks at me in that way so many people look at me these days. With pity.

"But what, Doc?" I say, daring him.

"How long's it been now? Eighteen months?"

I try to keep my eyes down, but they glance up over my bifocals at the bulletin board Doc has covered with Christmas cards and baby pictures and people's grandchildren. It's a shrine, that's what. Patients sharing their lives with Doc Keaton. Pinned right to the top is a picture of yours truly planting a kiss on the cheek of the most beautiful woman who ever lived. The two of us are right below the headline "LOCAL COUPLE MARRIED 80 YEARS." I swallow hard and blame it on the dry Bran Flakes. "Eighteen months next Tuesday."

"I'm sure Jenny would have wanted you to be happy. To have friends. Have you met a single new person since she passed?"

I pick at the corner of my nose, because I'm old and no one cares if I do stuff like that these days. "There's a checkout clerk at the grocery," I say, studying the fleck on my finger. "She always smiles at me, even when I stare at the ring in her nostril, or when I'm counting out change and there's a line behind me. Why doesn't anyone use money anymore?"

Doc Keaton ignores my question. And my answer, for that matter. "There are organizations for retirees, you know? Or maybe you could join that group that meets at McDonald's for coffee every morning. You get up early enough to get there by seven, don't you, Murray?"

Seven? What I wouldn't give to sleep until seven. I don't know how to answer in a way that isn't insulting to my own kind, so I just tell the truth. "Everyone there is too damn old."

I'm not sure what's so funny about that, but Doc has a good, long laugh. "And you want to be surrounded by youth," he says. "People who are the same age as you in spirit, if not body. Am I understanding that correctly?"

"My spirit's not so young these days," I say. Youth, I realize, was . . . my old brain's not quite as quick as it used to be. *Invigorating.* That's the word. Youth was invigorating.

Doc reaches under his desk and brings out a cupcake with a single candle. He lights it with steadier hands than I've got these days. "One candle," he says. "For my favorite one-hundred-year-old."

It's a nice gesture. He didn't have to do that for me. I could be just another fifteen-minute checkup before he moves on to the next old bag. But I'm not. I actually mean something to him. Still, I can't muster the energy to paste on a smile.

I inhale all the air I can force into my lungs and let it out all at once. It's still not enough to blow out the candle, but fortunately a bit of spit flies out of my mouth and lands right on the flame. "Youth was a long time ago," I say over the sizzle.

My words drift out the window and dissolve into the humid summer air. Clean air, too, since Lemon Grove is a good twenty-five miles from Chicago.

"Well, I have a message for you," Doc finally says. "From Brandon. He says you haven't returned a single call since the shampoo shoot and that it's not polite to ignore your agent. Not to mention it makes me look bad since I'm the one who set you two up." Doc looks at me like I'm a kid about to be sent to the corner. "Although I don't intend to become your secretary, he also says he has something else for you. A community education art class. Could be what you need, Murray. It's today, later on this afternoon."

He hands me a piece of paper with a building name and room number on it, which I take and stuff into my front shirt pocket. "I'll think about it."

That makes Doc scowl a little bit. He leans forward, elbows on knees. "All right, let me give it to you straight, Murray. If something doesn't change—and I mean soon—you're going to die a pathetic old man. Sad and alone."

I'll say this for Doc, he doesn't sugarcoat. I'd have preferred he said something like "You've had a good, long life," instead of "pathetic, sad, and alone." Those words don't sit so well. Actually makes me want to do something about it—I've always been a problem solver. But this problem is a doozy. How can a man as old and washed-up as me possibly find a reason to live?

CHAPTER 2

I think about whether I should go to Doc Keaton's art class later in the evening. I really do consider it. But the thought just makes me tired. And I realize all over again I'm just a broken-down sack of bones. Pathetic, sad, and alone. That's the only thing Doc Keaton got right about me.

So I've made a decision. I'm not waiting around until the twenty-second. If this world's got no use for me anymore then I've got no use for it. Don't know why I've held on this long, anyhow. When Jenny passed, I thought about not taking my pill the very next day. Between her and Doc Keaton, well, I couldn't do it. But Doc would get over it and Jenny's long gone now. Only thing I want is to see her again, and that's not going to happen as long as I stick around this joint.

So I've decided to die. Only problem is, not taking my pill doesn't work the same as using a gun or a rope, and I can't use either of those because suicide's a sin. Guess I still have to stick around until tomorrow, waiting for my body to do the deed. In the meantime, I figure I should do what Doc said, just so I can have a clean conscience about it all. Instead of going back home with most of the day still to get through, I stand outside the clinic and consider what to do with my last hours on earth.

Sure, I could sleep them away and then go to the art class. But I can't help thinking about Doc's whole youth thing again, and it gets me brainstorming ideas. I could volunteer at a place where kids are looking for parents—orphanages, they used to call them. But with just one day left, I'm not going to be anyone's father. Didn't do a very good job of that the first time around, anyhow. I could visit a playground, that'd be nice and temporary. But the phrase "dirty old man" didn't come from nowhere. I could do without the stares from overprotective parents.

Maybe a hospital—the children's hospital. It'll be full of kids with loving parents, so it won't matter when I don't show up tomorrow. And since the kids are all sick, it would stand to reason the parents could use a little support. They just might welcome some help while they sneak a quick nap. I always did enjoy reading, back when my eyesight was better. I never read to my boys, I'm sad to say, but every now and again to my grandkids. Big picture books with beautiful illustrations and funny stories. I especially liked when they got old enough to listen to *The Secret Garden* or *Sherlock Holmes*. Books with no newfangled words or kid's lingo.

'Course, I won't actually go into a hospital room. That's something I'll never do again, and wouldn't even if I was going to live another hundred years. But hospitals have nice gathering spaces now. Real roomy, some of them, with books on shelves and pictures on the walls. I remember that from Jenny's time before she passed on.

So I hop on a city bus and take it toward the hospital. Well, "hop" probably isn't very accurate. I don't know why they make those steps so big. Who do they think is taking the bus, Long John Gee? I lean on the railing and it takes all my breath to get to the top. I wipe my brow so no one sees the drops of sweat and plop down on the first seat I see.

There are two teenage girls sitting nearby. Talking so loud I can hardly hear myself think. Using profanity, too, which never would have happened in my day. I consider giving them a piece of my mind, but then I think better of it. It's my last day on earth. What do I care if the damn world goes to hell in a handbasket?

I try to ignore the girls, and the stabbing pain in my knee every time the bus hits a pothole. You'd think with all the taxes I've paid I could get a decent ride across town. But here I am, dealing with shooting pain because the city council can't get its act together. Some representatives we have.

When I finally get to the hospital I go straight through the front doors and rest my forearms against the information desk, doing my best to look casual, not spent.

"Heart ward," I say to the young woman behind the desk. Maybe she's not young, but she's a good generation younger than me.

"The cardiac floor is on level six," she says, and she gives me a look like I should know it's not called a heart ward anymore.

I do. I just don't care.

I take the elevator to the heart ward and step into a room with paintings of mountains on the walls and a bookshelf chock-full of books, just like I pictured. I don't really have a plan, but near the back there's a little boy, looks maybe six years old, playing a video game on a television set. My television at home is a sturdy, eleven-inch, black-and-white RCA. The one the kid's playing his game on must be twice that size. The biggest television set I've ever seen. Must be a good two feet wide, that thing.

He's plopped on a beanbag of some sort, his legs splayed wide like he's been there a good long time. And as I approach I see he's not playing the video game, he's just staring at the screen. His eyes are half-open—his mouth is, too, with a bit of drool on his chin. And he's holding an oxygen mask inches from his lips, like he fell asleep between breaths. I think about letting him sleep, but it's my last day. I don't have the luxury of time.

"What are you playing there?" I ask.

He jumps awake and slurps the drool from the side of his lip. He cranes his neck and looks at me through big brown eyes. The eyes are normal, but the rest of him looks . . . can't rightly think of the word. Deflated maybe. Like he's a tire that's run out of air. His skin looks almost blue until he sucks another breath from his mask, then it seems to whiten a bit, although it could just be my cataracts. Something in his cheeks makes him seem older than I first thought, but even plopped on his beanbag I can tell he's tiny.

"Shweetness!" he says. His body might look my age—swollen-looking legs and bags under his eyes—but his voice is surprisingly spry. From the beige carpet, he grabs a plastic controller of some sort and tosses it to me. It bounces off my chest and clatters to the floor before I move a muscle. There was a day when I'd have snatched it out of midair, but that was a good long while ago now. The boy looks from the controller back up to me. "Dude, come on. Playing alone sucks. I need someone to distract the aliens."

"The name's not 'Dude,'" I say. "It's Mr. Murray McBride." He tilts his head and the light shines through a space in the shirt of his hospital gown. It catches a scar on his chest that tells me two things: one, this kid's pretty familiar with the heart ward; and two, his body hasn't cooperated right from the first pitch. I shuffle my weight left and right until I'm low enough to sit in the beanbag next to him, then take the controller from the floor. Don't know how I'll get up, but I suppose I'll cross that bridge when I get to it. "This a game?"

He snorts like it's a funny question.

That's me. A regular comedian.

"All-Powerful Gods and Bloodsucking Aliens," he says. "Last year's version."

It's not much of an answer, least not one I can put into any context I'm familiar with. But this here's a skill I've developed over the past many years—if I don't understand something I simply grunt a little and things tend to move along just fine. At first, that made me feel like my hanging around this life didn't matter. No one would even notice if I was gone.

Well, still makes me feel that way a bit, I suppose.

I take the controller and try to make heads or tails of all the nobs and buttons. No dice. There's motion on the television, but I just watch.

"Come on," the boy says under his breath. He's more energetic than I thought he'd be at first sight. 'Course, his energy couldn't have gone much lower than being asleep and drooling in a beanbag.

Near as I can tell, it's a building game of some sort. The kid's moving the nobs on his controller, and a little character on the television starts setting up a shelter, or some such thing. Gold circles and silver flags come in from the sides of the screen and somehow disappear into his character while the character that must be mine stands just as still as I'm sitting.

The kid's voice gets louder the same time a large spaceship drops down from the top of the screen. "Come on, come on, come on . . . yeah, baby! Look at that alien suck out your brain! God, I love this game."

His eyes bulge real sudden-like and he grabs the oxygen mask from the floor beside him. He slaps it over his mouth and the plastic fogs and clears a couple times. After a few deep breaths, his eyes slowly return to normal and his skin gets a little flush to it. He tosses the mask aside like it's not important, snatches his controller, and resumes the game like nothing happened.

Judging by his reaction before the oxygen, he must have done something good in the game. The character that seems to be mine sits with its head cocked to the side while an alien-looking character chews on its hair. A disturbing gurgling sound comes from the television set and then my character's head breaks open and spills liquid goo on the ground next to it.

"A boy your age, you shouldn't be watching this," I say.

"I'm not watching, I'm playing," he says. "Besides, I'm ten years old. I'm not a little kid anymore."

Ten! And here I thought he was half that, little as he is. But now that I see him moving around a bit, ten doesn't seem so strange. It's just that he's little. Almost unnaturally small. A kid like this, I should probably cut him some slack.

"How do you play, anyhow?" I ask.

"You build stuff," he says, and he restarts the game.

"Build stuff? You mean houses and churches and post offices?"

"Holy crap, dude, what year did you come from, 1986?" I should scold him for calling me that word again but he grasps for his oxygen mask, and that stops me in my tracks. He doesn't stop looking at the screen, though, so his hand keeps missing the mask by a few inches either way. I lean over, put his hand on the mask, and he gets a couple good breaths before tossing it just as haphazardly as the last time. It smacks against an oxygen tank on a metal roller— almost like a rolling suitcase—and bounces onto the carpet. "You gotta build bomb shelters and safe rooms and castles you can shoot from," he says.

"Why?"

The kid pauses the game, puts his hands on his face, and rakes his fingers down the swollen area near his eyes. "Dude! The aliens!"

I must still look confused because he sets his controller down and turns his beanbag to face me. He gets a serious expression, like he's about to embark on a wise lesson.

"We're the All-Powerful Gods, okay? But we're not all-powerful in the beginning. We have to build structures that will keep us safe from the aliens. And we have to stockpile enough weapons to shoot them when they attack. Got it?"

Easy enough, I reckon. "How do you win?"

"You have to build a sustainable society, populate your city, and then blast the aliens out of the sky."

"Why don't you start by blasting the aliens? Then you can build your society without having to worry about them."

The kid smacks his forehead with his open hand. "Jesus, dude, don't you know anything?"

"Now see here, I'll not be spoken to like that, using the Good Lord's name in vain. Didn't your parents teach you to respect your elders?"

I'm not sure if it's the mention of his parents or the scolding I gave him, but the boy's manner changes in a split second. "Sorry," he says. We sit quietly for a few moments, and I feel a little bad for yelling at a boy in the heart ward. Especially one who has a hard time breathing. If there's one thing I know, it's the feeling when you can't quite get enough air. "Mom says that same thing," he says. "'Respect your elders.' What's it mean, anyway?"

I wonder how many times he's heard the phrase without a lick of understanding. "It means you should be polite. Use proper names, like 'mister' and 'sir.'"

His mouth turns down like he ate something sour. I don't reckon he likes what "respect your elders" means. I know I should stick to my guns, but I just can't take the sad look he's got. Another breath of oxygen seals the deal. Something about the way he wiggles his face into the mask until it fits just right—or maybe the glazed look he has just before taking the breath. Whatever it is, I can't help but feel for the kid.

"How do you know when the aliens will attack?" I ask.

A little shrug. "Pretty much if you do something stupid."

"Like what?"

Another look of disbelief, but he reins it in quick-like.

"Like spending all your gold coins on guns and ammo. If they see you building a stockpile they blow you into oblivion. Or drop down and eat your brain. And every once in a while they just blast you for no reason, even though you didn't do anything wrong. That always sucks. So are you ready to play again?"

He restarts the game before I answer. This time I mess with a few of the nobs on the controller, but my character doesn't seem to respond. Least, not that I can tell. There's a little chuckle next to me. "Holy crap, dude," he says under his breath.

The alien spaceship returns and immediately kills my character. The kid's whole body jolts and convulses. All the movement makes me worry about him. Is he going to hurt himself? Will he get enough oxygen? His character and the aliens are firing something back and forth when someone calls out from near the elevators.

"Jason, you're discharged. Let's go." An athletic-looking man in his thirties is leaning out of the elevator, holding the door open. I can feel his energy from here, but also his stress. Like he's late for a board meeting. "Right now," he says. It's a demand. A sign of immaturity. A modern phenomenon that no man of my generation would have done. Well, maybe the drunks. "Your mother seems to think her job is more important than mine—"

The elevator door starts beeping. I feel a glimmer of hope when my video game boy doesn't respond. But then the man sweeps over and grabs his shirt just as the kid—Jason, I think the man said—is gyrating with the controller swung up over his head.

"Okay, fine, just let me go," Jason says. When his father ignores him, Jason gives up and pulls his rolling oxygen contraption behind him. Jenny had something similar for a few weeks before she had to stay in bed. The BreatheEasy, hers was. Looks like Jason's model is the BreatheEasy-2.

He walks alongside his father, shoulders so low he looks like a hunchback, the BreathEasy-2 rolling behind him. His father punches the down button rapid-fire, and the doors slide open. They've just stepped in when Jason screams, "Wait, Daddy, wait! I forgot something."

"You can get it next time," his father says as the doors start to slide.

Jason pulls and tugs, trying to escape, wearing nothing but a hospital gown—although he's got some sport shorts underneath. Now I don't ordinarily agree with a boy fighting against his father, but in this case I can't help but root for Jason to win. If I was forty years younger, I'd go over and take the boy right away from his father. Might not be what's expected of a stranger—might not even be legal. But this here's something I've learned in my life—what's right and what's legal aren't always the same thing. And when put to it, a man ought to do what's right. The law be damned.

The little boy's eyes are locked on me. Looks that way, anyhow. And my eyes used to be so good I could see the spinning seams of an eighty-five-mile-an-hour curveball. But I'm old now, my bifocals are hung around my neck, and it turns out he wasn't looking at me, but near me. Somewhere by the television set or beanbags.

"Daddy, please!" he screams. But his voice fades away as the elevator doors come together.

I decide to do something about what's happening here, but the world moves so fast these days. Before I even take a step, the elevator's long gone.

Just as well, I suppose, since standing up makes my head swirl like a roller coaster. I manage to sit back in the beanbag. Fall back, is more like it. Fortunately, it's a soft landing. I pick up the controller Jason was using when his father stole him away. And then I notice a crumpled piece of scrap paper directly in front of his beanbag. And I realize he hadn't been staring at the television set as his father carried him away. He had wanted to come back so he could retrieve this piece of paper.

I consider leaving it here. Maybe his father will change his mind and allow Jason to come back for it. Or maybe a janitor will find it and know who it belongs to, why it's so important. But if that doesn't happen . . . if someone assumes it's trash and throws it away . . .

It takes me a full minute to unwrap the crinkled paper. My dexterity left me long ago. It's a Post-it note with the sticky stuff preventing me from peeling it apart easily. But eventually, I get it open. What I see nearly breaks my old heart.

> Five Things I Want to Do Before My
> Heart Dies and I Go to Heaven
> 1. Kiss a girl (on the lips)
> 2. Hit a home run in a Major
>   League baseball stadium
> 3. Be a Superhero
> 4. Find a Nice Boyfriend for Mom
> 5. Do Real Magic.
>
>   By the amazing Jason Cashman

When I first read the list, I wonder if he'll get to do a single one. Now I don't know his prognosis, but the kid couldn't go more than a minute or two without a dose of that oxygen. Plus, of the five wishes, only the kissing thing seems like it's even possible. Maybe the boyfriend for his mom, but even that seems like a stretch.

The kid can dream, that's for sure. I can't help but think we could have been friends, if we'd been born in the same century. Back when I was a kid, I could dream with the best of them. I still remember that, despite my age.

Recalling those feelings brings on a glimmer of hope. I used to feel hope all the time, back in my charmed youth. That sense that anything's possible. Not only possible, but virtually assured. The knowledge, deep down, that things will work out.

Thinking about that kid, I feel that old spark of hope for the first time in years. The spark of possibility. And I can't stop the thought that at least in some way, everything on this list could happen for him.

I decide right here and now that I'm going to make sure they do. I'm going to take that pill after all and stick around for a while. In fact, I'll be damned if that boy doesn't get each and every one of those wishes before he dies. They're not just his wishes now, they're mine, too.

If I wasn't stuck in this beanbag, I'd find a phone and call up Doc Keaton right now to tell him the good news. His favorite one-hundred-year-old has found a reason to live.

CHAPTER 3

The world has changed a lot from when I was younger. There was a day when, if I wanted to take a boy under my wing and help him out, I'd just knock on his front door and speak to his father about the matter. These days, the world's got so crazy I'd probably be put in the clink for pulling a stunt like that. But I have Jason's list in my pocket, so if for no other reason than that, I have to find him.

I take the bus home and think on it for a while. By 11:00 a.m. I've been awake for a good seven hours and I'm hungry, so I treat myself to a birthday lunch of stove-warmed Chef Boyardee. 'Course, that's all I eat anymore. Just a matter of whether it's ravioli or spaghetti. Today, I go with ravioli. If I heat it just the right amount on the stove, it gets warmed all the way through and the red sauce is bubbly, but not scalding. It might not sound like much to some, but I've never been one of those high-maintenance folk. I drove the same American-made pickup truck for twenty-five years. I used the same Rawlings baseball glove my entire fifteen-year professional career. And the last time I bought a new piece of clothing was 1989—other than a fresh pair of undergarments now and again. 'Course, thanks to that pill I wet my bed so much I might have to take the bus to the clothes store soon. Or get Chance to drive me there.

The doorbell rings, so I shuffle over and peer through the peephole. It's like my thoughts have brought him here; one of Chance's baby-blue eyes is staring back at me from an inch away.

"Granddad," Chance says when I open the door. "You look great. Can I come in?"

I'm not a fan of these here surprise visits. Seems to me a fella ought to respect a man's privacy. Chance claims it's for my own good; I need someone checking in on me now and again. The way I figure, if I keel over and die, no one's going to get hurt by it, so what's the big deal? 'Course, I might have a bit more gratitude if I thought Chance stopped by because he actually cared.

"It's not even noon," I say. "Why aren't you at work?"

He waves me off and is in my living room before I can tell him to go on home to his third wife and leave me in peace. He's got a box under one arm, which isn't uncommon. Might seem nice on the surface, but I don't buy it. Not since he brought over a box of clothes after his second wife's father passed. I ended up taking all but two shirts to the Goodwill. Only the Good Lord knows why he thought I'd want T-shirts that said things like "Take it to the limit" and "I survived the Break Neck Roller Coaster." One of them was even missing its sleeves.

He takes his suit coat off and loosens his tie, like he's planning to stay a while. Then he runs a hand through his curly brown hair, flaunting the fact that he's got a full head of it and I've got more coming out of my ears than on my head. I want to keep standing so he knows I expect his visit to be short, but my knees are killing me so I take a seat on the sofa. He sits in the recliner across from me, puts the box down by his feet, and we're a regular old happy family.

"What's burning?" he says.

I glance at the fireplace, but I haven't been able to squat down and build a fire for a good ten years now. A trail of smoke drifts from the kitchen at the same time the smoke alarm starts blaring. "Dadgommit," I say, because Chance isn't a little boy anymore and he says worse than that right in front of me. I'm never sure if I need to add that word to the list for next time I see Father James.

"Sit down, Granddad, I got it."

I'm not going to lie, I get a little jealous at how easily Chance jogs into the kitchen. I haven't even moved from my spot on the sofa, even though I've been trying. I hear some of those swear words and then the faucet running and the hiss of water on heat. Heavy scraping sends my Chef Boyardee right down the drain. He could have at least saved my lunch.

"See, Granddad," Chance says as he strides back into the room, drying his hands on a dish towel. "This is exactly why we need to get you into a home. It's not safe for you to live here by yourself. For the life of me, I can't understand why you even want to stay. Look at this place."

I swallow all those swear words of his right down my throat, thank Saint Joseph. "You wouldn't understand."

"Try me."

He says those words, but his tone screams something else. Nothing but condescension, that's what. So I don't say a thing. I don't tell him it's because Jenny's gone but her memory is here, all over this place. That if the house is gone, then her past, her history, all the memories we shared, they'd be gone too. It'd be like she never existed, except in my mind, and my mind's not all that sharp anymore. Chance cocks his head to the side, like he knows what I'm thinking.

"Staying here won't bring her back, Granddad."

"Yeah, well, happy birthday to you, too. Or did you forget about that?"

Chance pulls his tie all the way off. "Of course not, Granddad. That's why I'm here." But he won't look at me when he says it, which tells me plenty.

"Well, how do you like that?" I say. "My one hundredth birthday and my only living blood relation didn't even remember.

The only thing that brings you by is to tell me to get out of my own house."

"That's not true. And even if it was, you say that like I'm being selfish. I offered to pay for an assisted living place, remember? Those homes aren't free, you know? I'd be using my own hard-earned money."

"Keep your damn money. And I'll keep my house."

Chance and his money. Always talking about how hard he works. How much money he has. But I see the way he looks at my old baseball things—like they're nothing but merchandise to be sold at the nearest pawn shop.

He looks around my house, scrutinizing it like he does every time. His gaze pauses on a faded picture of Jenny on the mantel and I wonder if it makes him think of his first wife, who he left for a pretty young thing, or his second wife, who he left for his current, prettier, and even younger woman. But his eyes move on to my favorite ball glove—the one I used my entire career. He puts it on and punches his fist into the palm like he owns it.

"Too bad you played ball before the dawn of free agency," he says for the twentieth time. "Those guys these days, they're making a killing."

"I never needed to make a killing. I played because I loved it. Jenny loved it. The kids—your father—loved it. That was enough."

"Yeah, well," Chance says, not bothering to hide his disgust. "They're all gone now and it looks like loving the game's not enough anymore."

I know that look in his eye when he gazes at my glove, flapping it open and closed like he's breaking it in. My only living relative, eyeing one of my treasures, probably wondering how much he can get for it after I kick the can. I bite my tongue so hard I taste blood. 'Course, that doesn't take much these days. When a body gets as old as mine, the skin might look like leather, but it tears like wet paper. Chance seems to have forgotten about me until his wandering gaze lands on the box by his feet.

"Oh yeah," he says. "I didn't forget your birthday, see? I brought you a present." He jumps up from the couch again, but I try not to hold it against him. He doesn't know how seeing that makes me miss my younger days. He extends the box toward me, and when I don't move to take it, sets it on the sofa next to me. "Open it, Granddad."

I scowl at the box, at its slabs of ripped cardboard flaps and wisps of loose packaging tape. Three different names and addresses are scrawled across the side, each crossed out with permanent marker, each with messier handwriting than the last. But to hear Chance tell it, you'd think it has birthday wrapping paper and a cute little bow on top.

Turns out, I don't even have to open it. When I lift the box, only the sides come with it. Some clunky electronic device plunges through the bottom, almost falling off the couch cushion. It's not even in a bag.

"What is it?"

"It's an email machine, Granddad. Old people tend to use them instead of computers because they're simpler—well, I guess it is a computer, technically, but it only has email, so it's simple. I figure you could use it to email . . . whoever. Keep up with the times, you know?"

I've got no interest in keeping up with the times. Chance knows that, just like he knows I've got no idea what this confounded machine does, but I do know I'm not a fan of his tone. I may not always know what his words mean, but I'm smart enough to know he's mocking me. "I don't need it," I say.

Chance looks genuinely surprised, which makes me wonder for a brief second if he actually did bring it as a birthday present. His eyes, made an even brighter blue by his dark hair and strong jaw, nearly double in size. "Fine, Granddad. Do what you want with it. I'm just supposed to get rid of it. Janine and I are clearing out our storage space. Thought you might like it."

And there it is. The truth.

"You can leave," I say. "Unless you have anything else to say to me."

"You really are an old man, aren't you? You didn't used to be like this." We stare each other down for a few seconds and I can see his disgust turn to frustration. In his defense, I do believe he simply can't understand a single thing about me. And believe you me, it's mutual. It was never like that with my boys.

Well, maybe it was. But Jenny and I thought it was important to teach our sons independence. The Depression painted a vivid picture of how bad things can get. So we taught the boys to work hard, get an education, make a life for themselves, and not to rely on anybody—including us. Can't help but wonder now if maybe I should have spent more time telling them how much I loved them. If I had, maybe they wouldn't have been distant parents with their own kids.

I should tell Chance I love him right now. Redeem myself for my shortcomings with my boys. But before I can speak, Chance tosses his hands a few inches into the air, like I'm not even worth an all-out surrender. "All right, Granddad. If that's what you want, I'll go. But the email machine . . . suggesting you move out of this dump . . . you know I'm just trying to do what's best for you."

He grabs up his tie and suit coat and pauses at the door. "You know, Granddad? It really does make me sad." He seems to think about saying more. I think about it, too. Something loving and comforting. Something that will finally bring us together. But the words in my brain don't make it down to my mouth, and before I know it the moment's gone. Chance shakes his head, swings his suit coat over his shoulder, and strolls down the walkway, leaving his cares behind him.

I take his damned mail machine into the kitchen, open the lid to the trash bin, and drop it inside with a clunk.

CHAPTER 4

When Chance turns his fancy foreign car around the corner, I feel my failure as a father stab at me all over again. I was so distant, so old-fashioned, and most of all, so gone; the boys were grown up before I realized what I'd missed. Guess it spilled right on down to the next generation. Like one of those giant water jugs ballplayers dump on their coaches these days after a big win. Makes a mess of everything.

Part of me wants to draw the blinds, close my eyes for a nap, and hope they never reopen. But then I remember the kid. And the list. I pull it out of my shirt pocket and read it through again. And I wonder what on God's green earth I'm doing, wasting time with my greedy grandson. The only thing I actually want to do right now is return this list to the little boy who owns it. Maybe help him check some of those wishes off, if I'm able.

So that's what I decide to do.

I make sure my bifocals are hanging around my neck, slip on my shoes and fedora, and head back into the world. I take a left turn at the corner of Fifth Street and climb the stone steps in front of St. Joseph's Church, moving somewhere around the pace of an arthritic turtle. My skin looks pretty reptilian these days, too. All scaly and dangly where it used to be smooth and firm. The change was so slow I didn't even know it was happening till one day I looked down and half my arm was hanging down like a towel on a clothesline. Surprised me so much I thought I had a disease, till I realized I was just old.

Inside the church, the faint smell of incense hits me like a fast-ball to the ribs. I close my eyes and there she is. Nineteen years old, the most beautiful bride in all the world, about to give some schmuck the best eighty years he could imagine. I try to keep it inside, but I just never know when it's all going to come bubbling out. You'd think it would happen more often when I'm at home and ready for it. Sometimes I even prepare for it—make sure I'm all alone and bring out a box of tissues. It never seems to come, times like that. But put me in line at the grocery or sitting, minding my own business in the third row behind home plate at the ballpark, and it'll blindside me every time. Before I know it I'm sobbing like a baby, missing my bride more than life itself.

"Murray, is that you?"

I wipe my eyes and clear my throat. You'd think a man could get more privacy than that. I swipe my nose with the back of my hand and after another sniffle I settle into the back pew, just like always. Father James sits down too, but a few pews in front of me, because he knows I like that.

"I didn't expect you for another couple hours."

"Well," I say. "I'll be here then, too. I'm not here for confession now. Got myself a little problem, see."

I tell him all about what Doc said about sad and alone, my trip to the hospital, and Jason. I hand over the list. Father James nods slowly, like he always does, and doesn't rush me to finish, even though I ramble. He's one of the few young folk who isn't in a big damn rush these days. Probably how he keeps his thick head of hair and long beard so black they match his priest getup.

"And you'd like to help him make his final wishes come true?" Father James says when I'm done.

"Sure thing. There's something about that kid that just got to me, Father."

"And what is that something?"

I think for a few moments, looking at the crucified Christ hanging up behind the altar. "It's not fair, that's what. That boy shouldn't have to deal with a father that treats him like that. Boy his age shouldn't have heart problems either. Why would God let me live a hundred healthy years and give that boy a bad ticker?"

"You know I don't have the answer to that, Murray."

Now that's one thing I'm not sure I like about Father James. He's always saying he doesn't know things. That it takes faith because there's no way we humans can understand what God wants or what He intended or what His plan is. Seems to me a man of God ought to know those things. I've told him that, too, but he just smiled and said some mumbo jumbo about humility.

"How do you think you could help this boy?" Father James asks now. "I don't have to tell you that you're not a young man, Murray, and some of these wishes are . . . difficult. Especially if he's so sick." He pats the list against his leg, like he thinks he might be able to shake them up a bit. "Do you really think you're the right person for this job?"

The good father's probably right. I'm too old and washed-up for this. Just a couple hours ago I was planning to end my life tomorrow. But the look on that boy's face as his father pulled him away—I just can't forget it. And going home to my Chef Boyardee isn't likely to help him any. If I do this right, maybe I can give Jason what I wasn't able to give my boys—a father figure who lets him know clear as day how much he cares.

"I can do it," I say. "I've got enough left in me."

Father James looks at me the same way Doc Keaton sometimes does. It's like he thinks I just told a joke at a funeral and he's not supposed to laugh but can't help himself.

"Well then," he says. "Maybe you should contact him."

The pew creaks and the sound echoes through the empty church. "Suppose I could. 'Course, I don't know his address. Or his telephone number."

"Follow me," Father says. "I might be able to help you out."

The good father knows about my age, so he moves at about the same pace I do. Like molasses dripping down the side of a mason jar, that's what. But I get myself up and follow him to the front of the church and through a doorway on the side. Can't say I've been in the back of a church. Not for a long time, anyhow. I was an altar boy as a kid, but that was a while back now. Back when most of us couldn't understand a lick of the service because it was in Latin. That never made much sense to me, but I kept my mouth shut about it. I knew if I didn't, my old man's belt would be waiting.

Father James leads me through hallways, farther than I knew the church went. Back to some offices. He waves to a woman working at a desk and I wonder what in the world a church needs someone working at a desk for.

"Here we go," Father says, and sits in a comfortable-looking chair. He flips through a Rolodex until he finds something he's looking for. Then he picks up the telephone and places a call. After a few moments, he talks as if he knows the person on the other end of the line. "Martha! It's Father James Gonzalez over at St. Joe's. . . . Great, thanks for asking, and you? I hear congratulations are in order."

They go on like that for a while, like they ought to. These days, some folk are all business. No time to even ask how someone's day has been before they get down to it. But not the good father. He and whoever he's talking to chat for a few minutes about a baby on the way, the hail that fell in the thunderstorm last week, and the newly remodeled rectory in the church. I let my mind wander a bit and take in the crucifix on the wall and the pictures Father James has on his desk. A young Father James with what must be his parents. A card of the Virgin Mary. And another card that looks like it came from a funeral, with the word *Peace* written on it and some scripture. When I hear Father say Jason's name, I start paying attention again.

"That's right," he says. "Cashman. C-A-S-H-M-A-N. Yep, like money . . . oh, whatever you have. A phone number, email address if he has one. You know kids these days . . . really? That'd be great. Thanks so much, Martha. I'll talk to you soon."

Father James hangs up and smiles at me. "I have some connections at the hospital. You'll be happy to know this Jason Cashman of yours has an email address. Cutting-edge kid, this one."

He turns to his computer and gives something a little shake—a mouse I once heard it called—and the screen lights right up. He punches some keys on the keyboard. That there's about the extent of my computer knowledge. Mouse. Keys. Keyboard. Never needed more than that. Everyone says computers are so important these days, but I don't see it. I got along just fine for a hundred years without one. Didn't starve or get a divorce or ever have a late payment on my mortgage.

"Okay then." Father hits a few more letters on the keyboard, then springs up from the chair and motions to it. "You can sit here and write the boy a message."

"A message? On the machine? How's that work?"

"Like I said, he has an email address."

"Email?"

"It's electronic. That's why it's called email. It uses the internet. You know about that, right?"

"Heard the word."

Father James laughs out loud. Some sense of humor he has. He motions to the chair and says, "Just type a message. I'll send it to the boy."

"A message? About what?"

"That's up to you. Type something in the 'subject' box and then say whatever you want to say."

I'm not sure what to write. That I want to help him with his list? That might seem a bit odd, coming from a stranger. But the chair looks mighty inviting, so I slowly lower myself down and look at the keyboard. Letters are all over the place, and it takes a while to find the right ones, but Jenny had a typewriter for a while, so it's nothing I haven't seen before. I push a few letters and start making some sentences.

> **Subject:** I met you today and we played a game on the television set. You won. I have something of yours that I should return to your possession.
>
> Dear Jason Cashman,
>
> My name is Murray McBride. You can call me Mr. McBride. I saw you at the hospital today. I have your list and would like to return it promptly.
>
> Sincerely,
> Mr. Murray McBride

"Okay," Father James says from over my shoulder. "That only took about twenty minutes." He chuckles like he said something funny and squints at the screen. "The subject is usually a bit shorter, but that's fine. Now we just send it." He pushes something on the mouse again and the computer makes a funny sound.

It feels weird to sit at a computer and write a letter to someone without any paper or pencil. Not quite natural. I push the chair back, but a pain shoots up my bad knee and I can't stifle a groan.

"Easy, Murray," Father says. "Just sit there as long as you need."

My knee might hurt something fierce, but I'm not about to sit here and have the good father pity me. "So what now?" I ask.

"Maybe he'll write back."

"How can he write back when I haven't sent him anything yet?"

"You did send him something. You sent him an email."

"Well how'd I do that? I don't even know his address."

"You know his email address, Murray. Remember? Do you have a computer at home?"

"Not exactly."

"Not exactly? How do you mean? Either you have a computer or you don't."

"Chance dropped off some kind of computer, but it's not really a computer. A mail machine of some sort."

"An email machine?" Father says. "That's great. It's a computer, but only used for email. You can use it to send messages to Jason."

"I already told you, I don't have his address."

"But you have his *email* address, Murray. Don't you understand? It's elec—Oh here! He's already responded."

He points at the computer screen, then leans over and pushes the mouse again. A little page gets bigger and I read it:

To: FatherJamesGonzalez@hotmail.com
From: jasoncashmanrules@aol.com
Subject: OMG!

OMG! dude that rocks didn't mean to leave it ass-dad wouldn't let me go back. return-sies please-ies? need it bad message my advocate. TTYL

"What in God's name is all that?" I ask.

"His response. You didn't tell me he was so young."

"Did too. I said he's a kid."

"Yes, well, anyway. It appears he'd like his list back."

I pull my bifocals up from my chest and set them on my nose. "Where's it say that?"

"Don't worry about it," Father James says. "I'll set up an email address for you and you can use your email machine at home to communicate with Jason. What kind of account do you want? Hotmail? Yahoo?"

"Excuse me?"

"Forget it. I'll just set something up for you. In the meantime, I'll make a few phone calls. You go on home and take that noon nap. I'll call you when I know something."

I'm flustered on the way home. Confused. But that's not all. Good things, too. When I think about meeting Jason and helping him with that list of his, I feel so happy I very nearly skip for the first time in a good nine decades.

CHAPTER 5

I haven't had a feeling like this in a good long while. Long enough it takes a spell to recognize it for what it is—anticipation. Boy-oh-boy, there were times when I was playing ball, I couldn't sleep the night before a big series. Couldn't think of anything else no matter how hard I tried. And I feel the same thing now. If I go home and wait for the good father to call, I'll end up sitting at the kitchen table staring at the telephone, waiting for it to ring. When it finally does, it'll likely give me a heart attack and I'll never get to return Jason's list.

I pull the list out of my shirt pocket again so I can stare at it, but another scrap of paper comes out and falls to the ground. Takes a while, but I get bent over far enough to pick it up. It's the information from Doc Keaton about that art class at the community college.

I figure it's something, anyway. Better than staring at the telephone and risking a heart attack right when I've finally decided I don't want one. The community college is a few blocks away and it's already been a big day, so I take the city bus instead of walking. Second time in one day.

I only ride for a minute. When it gets to the right stop the bus driver lets me off. Even helps me down the steps. He's a big Black man, probably more than three hundred pounds. But the ease in his stride makes me wonder if he used to be a ballplayer. A fella his age could have played in the Major Leagues, unlike in my day. The color line kept out any players who weren't just like us. At least until Jackie came around in '47. 'Course, my playing days were over by then.

But sometimes a couple of the fellas and I would drive down to Kansas City to see a Monarchs game and show them our support. Most people don't know it, but the teams wanted Black players to join us in the Major Leagues for many years before it finally happened. It was the owners that didn't want it.

The bus driver pats my hand like I'm a little baby and tells me to have a good day in a voice so loud I almost tell him to hush up, my ears work just fine.

I limp up to the community college entrance, thinking about how my world has shrunk in the last couple decades. I used to have train rides to cities all over the National League, nice hotels, beautiful stadiums. But now I rarely travel more than a few blocks from my house in Lemon Grove. There was a day I could have thrown a baseball from my house and hit St. Joseph's Church, Doc Keaton's office, and probably rolled it up to the grocery over in Skokie. Now, I rarely leave that circle, except for the occasional "modeling job," as they call it.

Truth is, I don't particularly enjoy these jobs, even when they are close to home. I know why they have me here, and it's not to be a good-looking fella next to a good-looking dame. Sometimes they need an old man, for whatever reason they might have. Demographics, one young man said to me as if I'd understand.

Still, I walk through the front doors of the local community college because I can't bear the thought of waiting for Father James's call. And because Doc Keaton seemed to think it might do me some good, and I have a lot of respect for Doc Keaton.

There's a secretary's desk at most of these buildings I come to, but since this is a community college, there's nothing and no one to guide me. Except the scrap of paper from Doc with the words *Lemon Grove C.C. Room 101, 4pm* written on it. Luckily, there's a room a few steps away with a little sign that says 101. A lot of me is worn out, but my eyes still work pretty decent. Long as I wear my bifocals.

But as soon as I step inside the room, I know I must've read the sign wrong. It's mostly dark with just a circle of five or six candles on a desk in front. About a dozen seats, filled with people of all ages, are wrapped around a chair set right in the middle. The smell is so strong I feel a little faint. I'm amazed candles can stink so bad, but then I see a stick of incense burning in a corner, and one just like it in each of the other three corners. I plug my nose and turn back toward the door, but a high, floating voice stops me.

"We welcome you, sir," it says, and it dances over to me along with a flowery dress and the woman swimming inside it. She has glasses thicker than mine and hair down past her waist, and even in the dim light I can tell her entire face is a mask of makeup. Jenny never did need to wear any of that. Looked perfectly beautiful without a dab of it. "You must be Murray," she says, and her breath smells just like the incense. I think maybe she's been using it like a stick of chewing gum.

"Yes, ma'am, but I'm not sure this is the right room."

'Course, I know it's the right room. How else would she know my name? But this sure isn't what I signed up for. The crazy lady loops her arm around mine and next thing I know I'm standing in the middle of the circle of chairs. Each person has a painting easel set up in front of them, so I can't see their faces unless they come out from behind to look at me. At least there's that. A bit of privacy. The chair next to me looks pretty inviting with the throbbing in my knee getting more intense, so I sit down. Guess I'm here, I might as well let them paint away.

There's a second chair I hadn't noticed because of the dark. In the middle, right next to mine. A nice-looking gentleman sits perfectly still with his hands folded on a desk in front of him. He smiles at me and I nod. Seems like a nice fella. After a hundred years a man can tell things like that right off the bat.

"Of course," the lady with the floating voice says, "we'll need you to disrobe before we begin."

"Disrobe? Like hell. What kind of class is this?"

I try to stand, but the incense is making me dizzy so I sit back down. The woman tries to calm me with some strange movements of her hands. "I'm sorry," she says. "I thought your agent would have made you aware." She taps her finger against her chin for a few seconds. "Perhaps, for today, you could keep your unspeakables on."

"Unspeakables?" I say. Guess she means my skivvies. "Now see here. I've got no intention of taking my clothes off. It's not proper, that's what."

"But sir, it's *art*," she says, as if that one word explains it all. After another few chin taps she comes right up to me and puts her hands on my shoulders, invading my personal space something fierce. "I understand. I'm sorry about the mix-up. Could you, perhaps, remove only your shirt, and we'll work on the face and upper body today?"

I'm not too sure what I think about taking my shirt off in front of all these people, but I'm also not in any hurry to get back home to an afternoon of nothing. Besides, it's so dark in here, it won't be much of a peepshow anyhow.

"I'll take off my shirt, but I'm leaving my undershirt on, see?"

She frowns a bit but doesn't disagree, so I start the long, slow process of unbuttoning. That makes the crazy woman giggle with excitement.

"Okay everyone, it's time to enter into our Zen states. Let the power of the universe flow through your body, through your hands and out your fingers. Chant with me now."

While they make some noises that sound like they come from another planet, I get my arms out of my shirt and set it in my lap. Just about the time I'm starting to feel pretty comfortable, the ceiling lights flash on and about blind me.

"Wonderful," the woman says. "A perfect balance of shadow and light."

The light shocks me a bit, that's for sure. But I don't want anyone to know that, so I act like I was expecting it and sit as tall as I can. 'Course, my shoulders have been rounded for a lot of years now and my head doesn't sit straight on my neck anymore. This acting natural thing isn't working too well.

"I remember my first time," says the man sitting next to me. I can't figure who he is, or why he's sitting there, fully clothed, with his hands folded on the desk. "I hated when she did that too," he says. "She told me to take my gloves off, then turned the lights on. I've never felt so naked in my life."

Can't say I understand what he's talking about right at first, but then it dawns on me. His hands. He must be here so the class can paint them. He does have some nice, strong-looking meat hooks, now that I look at them.

"That supposed to be a joke?" I ask.

"Yeah. Heavy on the *supposed to be*. Sorry about that." He nods his head toward me. "I'm Collins by the way. I'd shake your hand, but . . ." He flicks his head at the crazy lady.

"Okay everyone," she says just then. "Let's take a close look at our second model for today. Our . . . mature friend here. Look deeply. Notice the beautiful blemishes of a long life. The unique marks of experience."

Just like Chance, this here woman's talking in code. But I know the translation. The *beautiful blemishes of a long life* refers to all the liver spots on my face and arms. And the *unique marks of experience?* That's the wrinkles so deep lint gets stuck in them. It's how the skin sags off my jaw. She doesn't have to say it. I still hear it.

"But look beyond those things," she says. "Look deeper and you'll see the palest blue eyes you've ever seen. You can imagine his Scottish descent—"

"Irish," I say.

It's like she notices me for the first time since they started painting. "Um, what was that?"

"Irish. Name's McBride. My old man came over on a boat."

"Yes, of course. I'm afraid we need you to remain perfectly still, wasn't that explained to you? You see, when you talk, it moves the wrinkles around your mouth. The skin around your chin flaps a little bit and—"

"Yeah, yeah, I get it. I'm not a buffoon."

She continues on about all the different parts of my body that are falling apart. I should have walked out while I had the chance.

"See what I mean?" Collins says out of the side of his mouth. "I wouldn't admit this to just anyone, Mr. McBride, but that woman scares the hell out of me."

I see what the young man's doing. Trying to make me feel better. And it's a nice gesture, too. But it's not enough to stop me from hearing all the things that woman's saying about me.

Somewhere deep inside, I guess I was hoping they'd see something different. Maybe see a part of who I used to be. But it was stupid to think that could happen. Stupid that I'd even think it's possible. Stupid of Doc Keaton to suggest this.

I sit for an hour. Ignoring the pain in my knee and back. Ignoring the ache somewhere deep down in my chest. And ignoring the fact that all they see is some worn-out old man. Something without any value at all. Can't do what he used to do. Can't use his hands or his legs or even his mind very well anymore. Can't do anything but sit there and look old.

On the way out, I catch a glimpse of one of the student's paintings. The easel is cracked and leaning a little to the left. The canvas is faded and worn, like they couldn't afford new supplies for this here class.

But the getup looks brand new compared to the image of the old, broken-down man painted on it.

CHAPTER 6

It's late in the afternoon by the time I get back home, wishing I'd have skipped the art class. A lot of good that did me. If it wasn't for that boy Jason, I'd be right back where I started the day, ready to put it all to an end.

But I do have Jason. And that changes things. Changes just about everything, that's what.

I pull Chance's email machine out of the trash can and set it up on the kitchen table. It takes me about five seconds of staring at the keys to realize I haven't got a clue how to use the doggone contraption. That pit in my stomach comes back—the one that makes an appearance every time I run across something I've never seen before and don't know anything about. Used to happen once in a blue moon. These days, it's every time I leave the house. The fact that it's now happening *in* my house is the last straw. I admit to myself I need help with this thing, slam the machine with a fist, and hobble to my bedroom for a nap.

A ringing telephone wakes me up a couple hours later, just about when I should be walking back to the church for my daily confession. It's Father James, who tells me I should skip it this evening—now how's that for a priest? Says he's talked to someone at the hospital who has an idea how I can meet with Jason.

It's dark when Father James picks me up outside my house and drives me to the hospital in his big Lincoln Town Car. That might sound bad to some people, but the good father deserves to drive around in a decent car. I've seen plenty of parishioners with nicer. Not me, mind you. But some.

I ask Father James if he can do a confession right here in the car, since I have something to confess and at my age a guy never knows when he might keel over and die. He sports his sideways grin and then says the part about what sins have I come to confess. We always hop right over the "How long has it been since your last confession" part, because he always knows the answer— one day.

I confess my "dadgommit" and the good father grants forgiveness with a smile—only gives me one Hail Mary for it, which I think is probably because he wants to talk. I say three Hail Marys out loud just to prove a point and by that time, we're at the hospital.

Father James helps me out of the car, and I lean on his arm until we're through the main entrance and sitting across from some lady who introduces herself as Jason's "advocate," whatever that means. She asks what my interest is in Jason.

Being a hundred years old comes with a lot of . . . I can't think of the word . . . when I was young we called them horsefeathers. But there are some good things too. For example, "advocates" apparently think anyone older than eighty is perfectly harmless and worthy of complete trust.

"The boy made a list," I say. I dig in the front pocket of my button-down shirt, but can't get a grip on it. Father James helps me out—if it'd been anyone else I'd have slapped his hand away. But the good father, he means well.

I fiddle with the sticky part until it unfolds. The lady looks it over and her eyes get a little wet. Advocates must know their kids real well. She's careful not to say anything mean, but I get the gist of it. Tells me Jason's parents are divorced. The dad's working to make his next million; mom's a good lady but got cleaned out by the old man and is struggling to raise her son without help, except for one weekend a month. The mom thinks he needs more of a father figure so she has the kid on the waiting list for the Big Brother program.

Bingo, bango, bongo.

"But Mr. McBride," the woman says, and a little tear almost escapes before she swipes at it. "Jason's not . . . well, I'm not sure how to say it."

"Just go on and say it, I reckon."

"Okay. It's just that, when Jason's mother—Anna is her name—when she put Jason on the list for a Big Brother, she requested that we inform whoever that Big Brother might be about Jason's condition."

"The condition that put him in the heart ward?" I ask.

"Yes. You see, many mentors want to make a lasting impact on the lives of their Little Brothers. It's important to them. Do you understand?" When I stare at her for a moment, she says, "A *lasting* impact."

I look to Father James, who has a deep furrow in his brow, then back to the woman. I try to keep my voice calm, but inside I'm raging like a wild bull. "'Course I understand. But it's not right to disqualify me just because I'm old. I could live several years still. I can make a lasting impact on the boy."

"No, you don't understand." The woman shifts in her chair and touches her eye lightly with a finger. "It's not you. It's Jason. His heart . . . well, it's not going to last long. He's on the waiting list for a transplant, but . . ."

She doesn't say anything more. Doesn't have to either. But if she thinks I'm going to be scared away because Jason's sick, she's got another thing coming.

"Do you have a phone book?" I ask. "I'd like to get on the horn to Big Brothers right away."

The lady smiles, picks up her telephone from the desk, and punches some numbers. Five minutes later, Jason has the oldest Big Brother in the history of the program.

It's not the least bit funny, but I can't help but chuckle at the thought that my Little Brother and I might not have a year of life expectancy between the two of us.

Turns out having a heart condition doesn't get you your own advocate. Soon as the woman gets off the telephone, she says a quick thank-you and excuses herself. Actually, she kicks us out of her office, but she does it in such a polite way I don't even mind. Besides, I got what I came for.

"When you get home, you should email him," Father James says. "You'll have to call his parents to set up a time to meet, but he'd like it if you emailed him first."

"How do you know that?"

"Kids like that kind of thing. It's a new world, Murray."

The words I want to say turn into a grumble, thank the Good Lord.

We make our way to the Town Car and start back, me toward my house and Father James to God's House. The last thing I want to do is admit I don't know the first thing about these messages everyone's talking about. Father James would understand, sure, but that doesn't mean I want him to know. Still, if I don't ask, I won't be able to send a letter to Jason when I get home.

"Those email machines easy to use?" I ask. Maybe he'll get the point without me having to come right out and say it.

"Piece of cake," he says, and that's the end of it.

I shift a little bit to loosen up my knee. "Just plug it in and it starts right up?"

"Pretty much."

There's a little crinkle on the side of his lips, but it might as well be an out-and-out tooth-filled grin. "Well all right, fine. If you're going to be that way, I'll just say it."

"Say what?"

"You know damn well what. I haven't got the foggiest idea how to use that confounded machine. I can plug it in and I can find the right keys to push. Now who's going to teach me the rest?"

Now it is an out-and-out grin. "I suppose I could."

"You've got better things to do," I say, because I'll give away my '34 Topps baseball card before I let Father James see me struggling to learn how to use that email machine.

He pulls the Town Car onto a four-lane road and gets up to a speed I'd never contemplate. Must be pushing forty. Half the time he doesn't appear to be watching the road. He's too busy glancing sideways at me and trying to hold back that grin.

"There's a kid in my congregation, a teenager maybe fifteen, who belongs to an organization that does this exact thing," Father James says.

"What? Shows old-timers how to use email machines?"

"Among other things. They teach the elderly about technology of any kind. They'll do MP3s, PCs—"

"Okay, okay, you've made your point. But they can do email machines, right?"

"I'm completely certain, yes."

It's awful dark out. The streaking streetlights blind me every few seconds and by the time I get my sight back, there's another one. It's like watching a wave of fastballs fly by, too fast to see, much less hit.

"All right, then. When can he come over?"

"I'll give him a call as soon as I get back to the church. Have him come over as soon as he's available. Maybe even this evening.

Kids stay up so late, it seems." I grunt an okay and make a point of staring out the window. The good father seems to understand and changes the subject. "You know, you might be right."

"About what?" Doesn't seem to be much I'm right about these days, if I'm honest with myself.

"This kid. Who knows, he might be just what you need."

"What I need? You got it backward. I'm the one he needs. What would I need him for?"

The hum of the tires against the road fills the silence for a moment. "To bring you back to life," Father says, and when I look over, his grin is gone.

Sure enough, a kid comes knocking on my door a couple hours later—when I'm about to get into bed, actually. Wearing my pajamas, got my slippers on, even warmed up a glass of milk. But I suppose the timing is okay. About an hour ago I put the machine out on the table, eventually managed to turn it on, and have been staring at it ever since.

When I open the door, a kid with scrunched-up eyes behind inch-thick glasses and messy hair is standing on my stoop.

"Mr. McBride?" he says.

"That's right. Father James send you over?"

"Yep. I tried to text so you'd know I'd be coming, but you must have a landline or something."

"I have a telephone," I say, hoping that's the right answer.

The kid passes right under my arm and into my house. Even mumbles, "I always get the hardest ones." He sees the email machine on the table and pulls my chair right up to it. "Wow, this is ancient. Where did you get this thing?"

"I thought you knew about techno items," I say, because judging by his tone, he's never seen anything like my machine.

"I don't do retro," he says. But he pushes a button and the machine starts right up, which took me a good half hour to figure out. "So what do you need? Have you figured anything out yet?"

"Father James told me about a couple things before he dropped me off. Showed me where to put the words and all. But when I typed something, it didn't work."

"What'd you type?" the kid asks.

"I reckon it was *www.email.com*. The good father told me about the w-w-w part and I figured out the rest on my own."

The kid heaves a giant sigh and rubs his face hard. He attacks the keyboard, and the way his fingers dash all over it, you'd think it was connected to his hand. His mouth moves while he types, but no words come out.

"Do you think you'll be able to—"

"Shh." He holds his hand out like a stop sign.

Normally I'd scold a kid for doing such a thing, but there's something about his demeanor that stops me. Feels a bit like he's the teacher and I'm the student, which I guess isn't that far from the truth, even though he's a kid. I take my warmed milk from the table and limp into the front room. Seems like the kid doesn't need me around, so I sip my milk, enjoying how warm and smooth it is. A few minutes after I finish it, he pokes his head into the room.

"It's all set," he says. "Come on, I'll show you."

On the kitchen table, the screen of the email machine is full of things I've never seen before. I wonder how in the world a kid like this knows so much about computers. "You live in a techno world or something?" I ask.

He just stares at me like he doesn't understand, so I sit in the chair and the kid leans over my shoulder. He points to the various things on the screen.

"I made it as simple as possible," he says. "You really can't screw it up. Just click on this," and he points to something that says "Email." I move the mouse around but my hands shake more than they used to and it's hard to get the little arrow to go where I want. "Deep breaths," the kid says, and I wonder if he's mocking me. But there's no way he knows about my lungs. "Put yourself in their shoes," he says. "Try to be patient."

When I finally get to the right spot and click the mouse (I'm sure to say "click" and "mouse" when I do it, so he knows I know something) he seems like he's done.

"Just put the recipient's email address here," he says, "type your message here, and click on 'send' when you're done. If you have any questions, let Father James know and he can probably help you."

Before I can respond, he's leaving the kitchen. He yells a "good luck" and the door closes behind him. I stare at the screen, trying to remember the kid's instructions. I pull out the scrap of paper with Jason's email address on it and type it in, hoping it's the right place. Over the next half hour or so, I poke at the letters. Finally, I click on "send," just like my instructor told me, and hope for the best.

To: jasoncashmanrules@aol.com
From: MurrayMcBride@aol.com
Subject: I am the gentleman who has been assigned to be your big brother. It was my choice, though, they didn't assign you to me.

Dear Jason Cashman,

I emailed you previously from Father James's machine, but I have one of my own now. Would you

be so kind as to respond and let me know if this
works? I'm fairly new to techno things.

Sincerely,
Mr. Murray McBride.

To: MurrayMcBride@aol.com
From: jasoncashmanrules@aol.com
Subject: Re: I am the gentleman who has been
assigned to be your big brother. It was my choice,
though, they didn't assign you to me.

dude, we're bros! lol you don't have to use the priest
dude's email huh? Schweetness! people say i sound
older online but don't spaz i really am ten. how
old are you hospital lady said you're like an egyptian
pyramid or somethin' must be cool to be old do you
have a car later

To: jasoncashmanrules@aol.com
From: MurrayMcBride@aol.com
Subject: Re: I am the gentleman who has been
assigned to be your big brother. It was my choice,
though, they didn't assign you to me.

Dear Jason Cashman,

Thank you for your letter. Although some of it was
difficult to comprehend. I was taught that letters
should be formal. You might work on that. At least
use capital letters and punctuation with regularity.

To answer your questions (at least I think they
were questions), I'm currently celebrating my
100th birthday. I have a car, but haven't driven
for a long while.

You seem like a nice young man. I look forward to meeting you again soon.

Sincerely,
Mr. Murray McBride

To: MurrayMcBride@aol.com
From: jasoncashmanrules@aol.com
Subject: Re: I am the gentleman who has been assigned to be your big brother. It was my choice, though, they didn't assign you to me.

Duuuude! I can't believe you said "regularity." You're freaking hilarious. And "nice young man"? Gettin all syrupy on me? Creepy. Later! ps. I capitalized and punctuation-ed the crap out of this, didn't I? LOL. See you soon, big bro!

CHAPTER 7

I have a car. A tin can, we called them in my day. Mine's a 1967 Chevy that's sat in my garage gathering dust—right alongside the hanging wrenches and crowbars—ever since someone put a stop sign on the corner of 18th and College, where they'd never had a stop sign before. They can take away my license, but they can't force a man to sell something he owns. I tell Chance the reason I didn't sell it was because I couldn't get a good deal for it, but actually I had it in the back of my head that a situation like this might pop up someday. Well, not exactly like this. But you never can tell.

Just sliding the key into the ignition is its own form of nostalgia. It's been a lot of years since I've done that. I turn it forward, anticipating that engine roaring to life. But it whines and wheezes like an old-timer, and I know a little something about that. Finally, on the fourth try it kicks into life—after all, she's a Chevy.

I move the stick into reverse and try to turn around and look behind me, like I used to. But my neck must've stiffened up over the past couple decades because I can barely see out the passenger side window. This here's why they make rearview mirrors, I reckon, so I glance into that and it's a whole lot easier. I ease off the brake, make my way safely out of the garage and down the driveway, and hear a crunching sound the same time I feel a little jolt.

'Course, it doesn't worry me too bad—kids and dogs don't make crunching sounds. Probably nothing more than a cardboard box or a garbage can. I put the car back into park and work my way out the driver's side door.

Mailbox, it turns out. But I can't imagine what my mailbox would've been doing in my driveway, so I reckon I drove into the grass a bit. Might have to make sure I don't drive backward with the kid onboard.

After going drive-and-reverse a couple times, I get her straightened out and make it out of the driveway fine. Going forward, it all comes back right quick. The key is to drive slow. Kids these days don't know the definition of the word *limit*. If the limit is thirty, I'm well within my rights to drive the Chevy a consistent fifteen miles per hour if I please. But everyone's so impatient these days. Everything's right there right when they demand it and it's turning the human race into a bunch of brainless rats. I get three middle fingers before I drive a mile, which never would have happened in my day.

I pull out the directions the advocate lady gave me over the phone. Ten minutes later, I see the house. The gas pedal's a little loose so I end up speeding up to it at a good 20 miles an hour. The brakes must be a bit off too because when I tap on them the tires screech and I nearly hit my head on the windshield. Never have been too keen on seat belts. I manage to get the car pulled up where I want it, right next to a big gate. The front two wheels somehow got up on the sidewalk next to a little guardhouse, but that won't hurt anything.

Feels like I've pulled up to some kind of castle. The gate's wrought iron and a road beyond it makes a circle and then comes back out. A fountain in the middle is big enough for half a baseball team to swim in. There's a man in a uniform at the gate who scowls at me and looks down at his foot, which somehow got damn close to the front wheel. He motions for me to roll down my window. The crank's a little rusted, so it takes me a while, but I get it.

"Sir, can I ask what your business is here?" the security guard asks.

"Come to see Jason," I say. "To pick him up, actually. Got a surprise for him."

The uniformed lad looks at me sideways. "Is Mr. Cashman expecting you?"

I tell him he is, but he still says something into a walkie-talkie like he doesn't believe me, and waits for an answer before waving me through. I drive the rest of the way at a slower speed, so it takes a while to reach the door. Then after I park it in front it takes a while to get out of my car. Takes a while to walk to the door, too. I assume that's why no one answers when I knock—Mr. Cashman was expecting me sooner. Nothing when I ring the doorbell either. But my old knees can't stand out here all day, so I start ringing the bell over and over real quick-like until someone finally shows up.

It's a well-dressed man holding his pointer finger up at me like he's telling a three-year-old to be patient. He's looking down at his feet, talking to his shoes, and pressing something to his ear. Looks almost like a telephone, but there's no cord. Maybe it's a toy phone, although I don't know why a grown man would have it. When he finally looks up, I see the man who carried Jason out of the hospital. His father.

"Why don't you tell him what I said about it?" he says.

I try to answer, but realize I have no idea what he's talking about. "Excuse me," I say. "Can you repeat that?"

"Well Jesus, you think I have time for all this? I run a business, not a charity."

The man shakes his head and I realize something strange. He hasn't looked at me yet. Not at my eyes, anyway. He's looking all around me. I wonder if he's insane. Or maybe he's playing around, like a kid, pretending to have a telephone conversation. But I'm standing right in front of him. Can't he see me? "Just do it," he says. "And get back to me."

This is the strangest conversation I've ever had. I try to figure out what he's talking about, but maybe my mind is too slow. "Now see here," I say. "I'm not sure what you want me to do, but I'd appreciate it if you used a different tone of voice with me."

"I'll call you back," he says, and flips his toy phone shut. The man meets my eyes for the first time. He puts his hands on his hips and looks straight at me. "What do you want?"

My knees are killing me, but I shift my weight and soldier on. "I won't be spoken to in this manner. When someone comes to your home, it's not polite to berate them over and over, and for no reason at all. It's not gentlemanly."

"Berate you over and over?" the man says, incredulous. "I haven't even said five words to you. Who the hell are you and what are you doing at my house?"

I can't follow what he's talking about. He's been speaking to me rudely and inexplicably for the past full minute. Five words? The man's off his rocker. But I can't think of what to say about all that, so I figure it's water under the bridge. "Name's Murray McBride. I'm here for Jason."

The man looks confused for a moment, but then says, "Oh, right. The thing. He's inside."

He turns his back on me and strides down a hallway and into a room, where he slams the door and starts talking to himself again. But the front door's still open so I lift my bad leg—well, worse leg—up high over the step and find myself inside the most luxurious room I've seen in half a century.

A giant chandelier hangs directly over my head. Looks like it's made of crystal and would crush me if it fell. I shuffle out from under it and trip on the cobblestone floor. I stumble, but catch myself on a white marble fountain. Water falls out of a bucket tucked under the arm of a naked stone woman. I realize my hands are both wet and holding her breasts, but thankfully no one's here to see it. I remove my hands, stand up straight, and look more closely at the statue. Wonder if I need to confess this little episode to Father James.

I'm a bit confused about what to do next. If I have to search this entire house for that kid I'll be here all week. Thankfully, a whooping sound clues me in, and I follow it to a living room half the size of the Polo Grounds. Almost invisible in the folds of a leather sofa, the boy I remember as Jason is playing his computer game.

His oxygen tank is right next to him, but the mask is gone. Instead, a plastic tube runs inside his shirt and right up to his nose, where he's got a nasal cannula—least that's what the doctors called Jenny's—so he can breathe oxygen through his nose whenever he needs it.

"Hello there," I say. "Don't suppose you remember me."

The boy gives me about as much attention as his father did, except without the pointer finger commanding me to wait. "See here," I say, a little louder. "I said, I don't suppose you remember me."

Still no response, so I shuffle up to him and tap his shoulder nice and hard. It hurts the tip of my finger but it gets his attention. He jumps about half a foot off that couch. The kid hasn't heard a word I've said. Confounded machines.

He stares at me, first with wide eyes because he's still surprised, but then he smiles. "Hey, it's my new bro."

He squints like he's studying me and I realize I must be scowling. "Remember what I told you? A kid your age, you should be calling me 'mister' or 'sir.' In your computer letters, too."

He shrugs a little, like it's no skin off his nose. He seems healthier somehow, but still takes a nice, long pull through his nasal cannula. "Okay," he says. "Hey, it's Mr. Bro!"

I growl a little bit, but let it go. The kid's young. "We're not really brothers, of course. It's a program, see? Father James found out that you were on a wait list so he called the hospital and they told him . . ." The kid's obviously got no clue what I'm talking about, so I shake my head and cut to the chase. "Want to go see the baseball stadium?"

CHAPTER 8

The crack of a bat hitting a baseball is the most beautiful sound in the world. Second to Jenny saying "I love you," that is. 'Course, it has to be a wooden bat. A real bat. Kids these days playing with metal bats . . . makes me sick, to tell the truth of the matter. The ping of the ball about makes my ears bleed. It's sacrilegious, that's what. But as Jason and I approach the entrance of Lemon Grove Field, the echo of the wooden "crack" takes decades off my age. Granted, that's still elderly by most people's standards.

It's not yet noon, but the Class-A Cubs affiliate players are already out there taking hacks in the cage and shagging flies. Must be an afternoon game today. I've safely driven Jason to the place as far from the sickness and death of a hospital as I could think of. And as far from his uncaring father. A place both alive and peaceful. No better place in the world for that than a ballpark.

"Do you know why people go to the hospital?" Jason asks.

I assume the question's rhetorical, but as I nod to a security guard—who knows me by sight and opens the stadium gates for us—Jason answers his own question. "Because they're sick."

I nod, kind of lifting my chin high like I'm trying to say, *Now I understand*. But Jason continues. "I was in the hospital because I'm sick. I have a bad heart. And without a heart, you can't live. Did you know that?"

Do I know why people go to the hospital? Do I know you can't live without a heart? Is the kid setting me up for some sort of punch line? "Let's sit down there," I say, motioning to a couple stadium seats in the front row behind home plate. I take a few steps before I realize the kid's not with me. Still standing where he was, taking a couple deep breaths of oxygen from his mask. He probably should have kept the tube in, but I can understand not wanting to go out in public like that. Especially a kid, like him.

Once he's feeling better, he catches up to me. A lad named Javier Candela is in the cage, so I settle into a hard plastic seat to watch the phenom put on a show. Word is, the kid's going to make the jump all the way to the Big Leagues any day now.

"These guys are playing baseball," Jason says. "It's a game where you hit the ball as hard as you can and run the bases."

"And if you touch home plate, your team gets a run," I finish for him. He gives me a look of complete amazement. "I know quite a bit, actually," I say.

"But you're old."

"A hundred years is a long time. A person can learn a lot in that much time."

Jason squirms in his seat, like he's suddenly unable to find a comfortable position. Like his entire worldview has just been thrown out of whack. "You don't have to be embarrassed," he says.

"Embarrassed? What on God's green earth do I have to be embarrassed about?" Truth is getting old creates a lot of things to be embarrassed about, but the kid doesn't need to know all that.

"All-timers forget things," he says. "I know. So it's okay."

Javier lines a ball up the middle. I consider giving Jason a good talking-to, but think better of it. Seems like he probably gets plenty of that at home. "It's Alzheimer's," I say. "And not all old people have it. In fact, Doc Keaton says my mind is pretty sharp for my age."

Can't remember the last time I saw such skepticism as I see in the crease of Jason's brow. I have my work cut out for me if I'm going to convince my young friend that I'm not helpless and brainless. Teaching him a little respect for his elders wouldn't hurt either.

We watch Javier spray the ball around. Line drives, gappers, home runs. I see what all the hype is about. The kid has power to all fields. I dig into the inside pocket of my light jacket and pull out the Post-it note. "I think you might have dropped this at the hospital."

"My list!" Jason snatches it from my hand, stares at it for a moment, and wraps me in a hug.

"Okay, okay," I say. "Don't go getting schmaltzy on me." I pat his back a little awkwardly, then gently push him away. People these days are so . . . affectionate. We weren't like that in my day. A handshake and a quick second of eye contact is all it took to say all that needed saying. When Jason finally pulls away, there are tears in his eyes. He looks at the note like it's the polio vaccine.

"You should probably just memorize that if it means so much to you," I say.

"I have it memorized. Duh."

I don't understand what "duh" means, but I'm not about to tell my little friend that. "Then why did you need the list so bad?"

He clutches it to his chest. "I wrote this after the doctor told me about my heart. He said I'd die within six months if I didn't get a new heart. I got scared and it made me feel better when I made my list. So now I keep it in my pocket."

I'm not sure if the doctors should tell a kid his age about a prognosis like that. But I guess it makes sense. It's his life, after all. Poor kid. I want to ask when he was given the six months, but I reckon that's not my business. "Well, we should get started on that list, don't you think, duh?"

He gives me that look again, like I'm clueless. Maybe that's not how you use that word. But then he fingers the Post-it as if making sure it's real. "Can we start with number four? Mom needs a nice boyfriend bad."

"Let's just start with number one and see how it goes."

Jason doesn't miss a beat. Stands up and shakes his hips like the Beatles used to do when they set the world on fire. Kind of sways his butt, bites his lower lip, and clamps his eyes shut. It's been decades since I've seen anything so inappropriate, and this kid is only ten years old. To top it off, he starts singing in his high-pitched, prepubescent voice, "I'm gonna kiss a girl, yeah, I'm gonna kiss a girl. Right on the lips, so you better watch out, I'm gonna kiss a girl . . ."

"Jeepers creepers," I say, covering my eyes and ears at the same time. Just watching that has to be a sin. I realize I might have bitten off more than I can chew here. But after a celebration like that, I'm not sure how to back out.

"Mr. McBride," calls a voice from the field. Javier Candela stands just below us on the other side of the brick wall separating the field from the stands. He waves a hello through the net and talks with a thick Spanish accent. "What did you think of my hitting? I have a good swing?"

I've met the kid a couple times. They always make such a fuss whenever I come to a ballgame. I used to buy tickets up in the nosebleed section so no one would notice me, but these days I need a little assistance getting up there. Now they always put me right behind home plate. No charge. Once a Cub, always a Cub, they like to say.

"Pretty good," I say to Javier. "Stay behind that ball, though. Keep your weight back."

Truth is the kid's swing is perfect. If I'd had his swing, I'd have played another five years in the Big Leagues. But kids these days have enough ego as it is.

"Thank you, Mr. McBride. I will try."

There's a mechanical whir next to me and as Javier jogs toward his dugout I turn to see Jason taking a deep pull on his oxygen, his eyes doubled in size.

"He talked to you," Jason says.

"Yeah, well. He's just a ballplayer." Another player, someone I don't recognize, greets me as he walks by. I wave and nod. "Who's it going to be?" I say to Jason.

"Huh?" He can't quite get over the shock that I know what baseball is, and that a few of the players know me. Well, truth is all of them know me, but Jason doesn't need to know that.

"The lucky girl," I say, and when he gives me that confused look again, I shake my head. "Who are you going to kiss?"

"I don't know. Some girl."

This is worse than I thought. And the poor kid thinks I'm clueless? "Well, is there a dame at school who's really keen?"

"Huh?"

Jeez, this kid. "Is there a *girl*. At *school*. That you *like*."

"Oh, why didn't you just ask? Mia Harmon. I sat next to her in science. When I wasn't in the hospital, anyway. Sometimes I flicked applesauce into her hair at lunch."

The flicking applesauce comment reveals something: helping this kid kiss another fourth grader probably isn't the best idea. I'm not sure Mia Harmon's father would be very pleased to hear that a boy smooched his precious daughter. Especially a boy who can shake his hips like this kid.

"I'm sure Mia Harmon is great, but I think we should set our sights a little higher."

"Huh?"

That takes me to the end of my rope. If we're going to continue attempting to communicate, we need to get on the same page. "First of all, the word is *what*. Even better would be *pardon me* or *excuse me*. But enough with the grunting." He shrugs non-committally, but I decide not to push him on it for the time being. Maybe some of what I try to teach this kid will sink in. "Second, your sights. I think we should set them a little higher."

He seems deep in thought for a moment. "Pardon me, but, huh?"

At least he's trying. "Who is the most beautiful, stunning, knockout girl you've ever seen?"

"If you mean 'hot' then it's Sharon Stone, hands down."

"Great. Who's Sharon Stone? A girl in school?"

"Who's Sharon Stone? You have to be kidding me. You know about bad hearts and baseball, but you don't know Sharon Stone? She's the hottest movie star ever."

Why do I get the feeling we're not on the same wavelength here? "Okay, listen," I say. "Who's the most . . . hot . . . girl you've ever actually met?"

Jason opens his mouth, points down his throat, and pretends to vomit on the stadium seat. "Critical information here: Old people definitely should never say 'hot.' But it would probably be Mindy Applegate."

"Should I know who that is too?" I ask.

"Probably. She's only the captain of the cheerleading team for Lemon Grove High School. Her legs are super long and tan. One time she came to our school with some other cheerleaders to do some no-smoking thing and when she leaned down to tie her shoe, my friend Tommy saw down her shirt. He said she has the biggest—"

"Let's focus on her lips," I say. Holy moly. I couldn't have been like this when I was ten. "You have on your list that you want to kiss a girl on the *lips*. Would you like to kiss this Mindy Applegate's lips?"

"Well duh," he says, and I'm pretty sure I did misuse that word. "But that's, like, the most impossible thing in the world."

Has this kid even looked at the rest of his list?

I'm starting to think this experiment of mine isn't going to work out like I'd hoped. I guess I thought it would be easier. That we'd at least speak the same language. Has the world changed so much since I was young?

I'm about to change the subject, maybe spend the afternoon with Jason and then take him back and tell the lady at Big Brother that it isn't going to work after all. But then I see him gazing at his list. Just staring at it, clutching it like a lifeline. And unconsciously putting his oxygen mask against his pale cheeks. All at once, there's nothing I want more than to watch my little friend Jason plant a smooch on the cheerleading captain at Lemon Grove High School.

"You know," I say. "It might not be as impossible as you think." Suddenly, I have his undivided attention.

He laughs at my grunts as I stand from the seat, but when I start out of the stadium, he's right by my side, his rolling oxygen concentrator squeaking behind him. "Time for you and me to do a bit of reconnaissance," I say.

CHAPTER 9

"Where the hell are we? You said we're going to the high school."

I almost drive off the road. When did children start cussing in front of their elders? If I'd done that in my day someone would have taken me behind the shed and after the whooping, I wouldn't have been able to sit down for three days.

But that might not have been the best way to go about things either. I take a few moments to think through how to respond. "Hell isn't something to be taken lightly," I say. "So be careful what words you use. And I'm taking a short detour."

"Why?"

"Need to see someone right quick."

"Who?"

"My grandson. I want to see if he'll come along."

I ignore his grumbling and pull into Chance's driveway. It's fancy—ostentatious, Chance calls it proudly—but not as big as Jason's father's house. I'll keep that little tidbit to myself, though. If Chance knew there was someone within fifty miles who had more money than he did, he'd work himself to death trying to take the lead. I don't want to be responsible for that kind of thing.

Jason escapes from the Chevy, runs to the door with his oxygen right behind him, and rings the bell a half dozen times before I can catch up and pull his finger down. A few seconds later Chance opens the door, already furious. Not the way I wanted to start this little gathering. He scowls at Jason and then scowls at me. Doesn't take a genius to figure out he doesn't like kids. Then again, he's never met one like this here Jason.

"Hi, my name's Jason and your grandpa's my brother and I'm going to go kiss Mindy Applegate on the lips. Want to come?"

I would have phrased it differently, but it's too late for that now. One look at Chance's pulsing jaw and I know it's a good idea to have the kid scram for a bit. "Why don't you run inside for a minute?" I say to Jason. But Chance closes the door most of the way and blocks the remaining opening with his body.

"I don't think that's such a good idea, Granddad. Can't he just run around on the sidewalk or something?"

Jason doesn't seem to understand the rejection. He's still smiling and waiting for an answer to his invitation. "Run along for a few minutes," I say, patting his shoulder. "I'll be there in a bit. Stay close, now. Don't play in the road."

With Jason out of the way, Chance turns on me like I just threw a baseball through his window. "What's this all about? Bringing a kid to my house?"

"He's not poisonous."

"So you say. Who is he, anyway?"

"My Little Brother. You know, the program?"

"Don't you think you're a little old for that?"

I turn my back to Chance, partly because I don't want him to see how mad I am and partly to check on Jason. But the kid's nowhere to be found. Not on the sidewalk, not by the car, or in the car. I feel my heartbeat thump against my chest until he hobbles around the side of the house, chasing a cat of some sort. When the cat darts away, Jason starts spinning circles in the front lawn until he gets so dizzy he falls over. Makes me cringe when his oxygen topples over with him. I wonder if that thing could explode. It doesn't, thank the Good Lord.

"I wanted to say thank you for the computer machine," I say, still not looking at Chance. Saying things like this isn't easy for me. It's not in my nature, so to speak. "Turns out, I've been able to use it."

"Really? You figured it out?"

"Sure did," I say. He doesn't need to know the truth of the matter.

"Wait a second," Chance says. He steps outside for the first time and squints at the Chevy like he thinks he's seeing the Loch Ness Monster. "Is that your *car*? Please tell me you didn't drive here."

"Well the boy's not old enough."

"Granddad, you don't even have a license. Do you have any idea how much trouble you could get into? What happens if you hit someone? What happens if you *hurt* someone?"

"I'm careful," I say. "Keep her below the limit and don't drive backward anymore."

Chance heaves a big sigh, like he's dealing with a child. Guess that makes two children here, me and Jason. But I'd rather be grouped in with Jason right now than Chance. "Unbelievable," he mumbles. "So what do you need, Granddad? You just endangered everyone on the road to say thanks for the email machine? What'd the kid say about kissing someone?"

"The boy has a list. His five wishes. Things he wants to do before he dies. I'm helping him out."

"He's that sick?" Chance looks toward Jason with interest for the first time—didn't he notice the kid's hauling oxygen with him?—but I can't tell what's going through his head. The moment stretches so long I could almost sing "Take Me Out to the Ballgame." I want to say something nice, something loving. But nothing like that comes to mind.

"Like Jason said. I think you should come with. We're just doing recon today, but still."

Chance stares out at Jason, lying flat on his back in the grass. "I don't think so, Granddad. You know how I am with kids."

I want to explain the feeling I get when I'm with Jason. The new respect for life. The feeling of being young again. I haven't felt that way in years and Chance has probably never felt it in his life. But I don't know how to say any of that.

"I can't just drop everything, Granddad. I have work, you know?"

"You don't understand. This is important. Feeling young is what makes life worth living."

"No, having the money to do what you want is what makes life worth living. And before you say that sounds cynical, go ahead and give all your money away and live on the streets for a while. Then come talk to me about feeling young."

He gives me that look of his. The one that says he feels sorry for me, when we both know it's more than that. The truth is he's embarrassed to know me.

"Just forget it," I say.

"Alright, Granddad." Chance is closing the door before I even make to move toward the car. "Be careful out there."

CHAPTER 10

It's five o'clock in the afternoon. Preseason football practice is just wrapping up. Jason and I lean against the chain-link fence while groups of young lads walk along the other side with sweaty hair sticking up. Sleeveless shirts show their young arms carrying helmets and shoulder pads. Cleats crunch against the blacktop of the track.

I played football long ago. Back when a kid could play as many sports as he wanted. But practice was only an hour back then. Most of the boys had to be home with plenty of daylight left to help with the harvest. But these boys are just finishing up in time for supper.

In an open space across a parking lot, Mindy Applegate leads her squad in a cheer. *Be. Aggressive. Be-e Aggressive! B-E A-GG-R-E-SS-I-V-E, Aggressive!*

With the sleeve of my jacket, I wipe a bit of drool from Jason's open mouth. He slurps, swallows, and says, "She is so hot."

Together, we duck behind a car in the parking lot. We stand with our backs pressed against it like a couple of real spies. My knees are killing me but I'm worried that if I sit, Jason won't be able to help me get back up. But there are more important things to worry about right now.

"Wear this hat," I say. I take my fedora off and plop it down on Jason's head. He looks like a mobster's kid.

"Why?"

"We don't want Mindy Applegate to recognize you next time. It might throw off the whole plan."

"What plan? Do you even know what you're doing?"

"Trust me," I say. "And leave that here." I pull his rolling oxygen to my side and use it for support. "Here's the play," I say. "When the cheerleaders take a water break, approach the girl farthest away from Mindy Applegate. Ask her who Mindy's beau is."

"Huh—er, pardon me?"

"Her beau. You know, her boyfriend."

"Why do I care who her boyfriend is? It's not like she's going to go out with me."

I think for a moment, then decide "go out" means going steady. "We don't need her to go out with you," I say. "We just need to know if you're going to get pulverized for stealing a kiss."

"I'm not afraid to die in the name of love."

Up to now, the kid's had a hard time being serious about anything, so I assume he's cracking another joke. But this time, he's serious as a silo. I can't help but stare at his chest and wonder how a heart so full could be so weak. Then the cheerleaders break and walk toward their water bottles, all grouped together nearby. "Now's the time," I say before I start getting too sappy on him.

He steps around the car and tiptoe-runs into the park, to a giant oak tree halfway between us and the cheerleaders. I didn't tell him to be all secretive about it. He looks like a stalker out there. I get his attention with a short whistle and try to motion him to cut it out. But he doesn't get it. Instead, he lifts his hands into the shape of a pistol and does a terrible-looking somersault, squishing my fedora.

Now he's no longer behind the tree, and he's rubbing his neck because I think he rolled over a root. He realizes the cheerleaders are all looking at him so he goes straight to the girl on the outer part of the circle. She's sitting, relaxing back on her hands, but when she sees Jason, her back straightens like she's trying to decide on fight or flight.

I can't hear what's going on, but Jason bumps right into her (I think my fedora was blocking his view) and says something. The girl looks confused, but as soon as she answers, Jason takes off running back toward me. I turn my head away too quickly and almost lose my balance. I lean against the car and spend the next several seconds trying to stand up straight. Then I grab the oxygen and walk in the other direction so the cheerleaders don't see my face.

Jason catches up, all out of breath and hyped up on adrenaline. Kid's got moxie, I'll give him that. "She doesn't have a boyfriend," he says through thick, panting breaths. The running has really fatigued him, and I wonder if he has doctor's orders to avoid exercise. Something I should probably know. "But she likes Jarrod Miller, the quarterback of the football team."

It takes a while for the wheels in my head to start churning. Lots of rust and wear in there. But once I get them moving, I can still come up with a decent plan.

"Good work, soldier," I say. I take my hat back, punch the inside to fix the damage, and set it back on my head. Jason goes right for the oxygen and takes several long, deep breaths. "Let's give it a day, so we don't arouse any suspicions," I say. "But put on some ChapStick before bed tonight. Because tomorrow, young man, you're going to kiss Mindy Applegate on the lips."

CHAPTER 11

Back home, the answering machine is blinking. I push the button and open a can of ravioli. While I pour it into a pot, Brandon Chilson's voice fills the room.

"Murray. Hey it's Brandon. Why didn't you call me back last time? For the earmuffs spot? It's not cool to ignore your agent, you know. I'm on your side here.

"Anyway, just checking to see if Doctor Keaton convinced you to do the painting gig. And there's a shoot for a peanut butter company, of all things. They need an old man, and you're my go-to. The audition's on Wednesday at 4:00 p.m. sharp at the O'Connor Building, room 223. Be there, okay? You're exactly what they're looking for. It's easy money, Murray. Trust me."

I ignore the message, warm up my ravioli on the stove for three minutes and twenty seconds—the magic number—and think it's a good thing Chance isn't here. He gets quite a kick out of my modeling career. Calls it the Geriatric Yearbook Club.

I fill a glass with tap water and eat my dinner at the same round, wooden table Jenny and I used to sit at. Then I run the sink, scrub my dishes clean, and head into the living room.

This here's an old house, and it has an attic up above the living room. Haven't been up there for near a decade, but something's calling me tonight. I take an old broomstick from the corner and pull it free of cobwebs. Then I reach it toward the rope that hangs from a square in the ceiling. It takes a good dozen tries with the stick shaking left and right, then back to the left. But finally it catches and the rope falls down to where I can reach it.

I move out of the way, pull hard on that rope, and the square swings down, showing an opening to the attic. I pull the rope a bit more and the ladder that's built into the swinging door slides all the way down to the floor.

The climb up takes me a good ten minutes, and I'm sure Chance would give me an earful if he knew what I was up to. But I'm determined not to fall and break a hip. I won't give him any reason to throw me in a "home," or whatever he calls it. From what I hear, those places are about as far from a home as a right-hander is from a southpaw.

The attic is no bigger than a dugout, and full of cobwebs and dust. I pull a little chain in the middle of the ceiling and a bare bulb flicks on. There's not much up here. Mostly trophies and such. A few baseballs that are special to me, including my one-thousandth Major League hit. Lots of spiders. But none of that's what I'm looking for now.

There's a trunk near the back of the room, and that's what I'm interested in. It squeaks something fierce when I open it, but the card is right on top, sheathed in a plastic case. A 1934 Topps, and the best-looking baseball card I ever had. Most years, they'd have me grab a bat and stage a terrible picture. Tell me to stop halfway through my swing or some such thing. As if anyone would hit a baseball standing just outside the dugout.

But in '34, my last year in the Big Leagues, I missed picture day. Jenny and I'd gone out to dinner the night before. Pasta or some such thing. And I'd ended up with the biggest stomachache of my life. Spent that night and all the next day in the lavatory. Jenny felt so bad. Made me toast and chicken soup and nursed me back to health, but not in time for pictures. So they'd had to take an action shot during a game. Got me right when I made contact with the ball, at the point of extension. I try not to be one of those old-timers who brags all the time, but the picture on this here baseball card is the most athletic-looking I've ever been in my life. It's a picture of a young man in his prime. And it's the one card—the one piece of memorabilia of any kind—that I'll never part with. I'll take this one to the grave with me, and that's a promise. Have it buried right along with the rest of my bones. I've already told Father James not to let Chance get his grubby hands on it.

I stare at the baseball card for a long while, recalling those sunny day feelings I used to get at the ballpark. When my knees start to throb, I reluctantly return the card to the trunk. Inside, there's an old turntable I'd forgotten all about. I don't bother to wipe the dust off, or even look at what's inside. Simply lift it out, plug it in to an old wall socket, and turn it on. My knees really stiffen up from bending down to the plug, so I sit in a threadbare chair with plaid material that mice have been having at, and I listen.

It starts with a crackle. Then a voice, both deep and hallow, fills the attic.

Murray McBride steps to the plate. The thirty-seven-year-old veteran left-fielder is hitting .226 this season, and many think it'll be his last in a Cubbies uniform. Chicago will sure miss him when he's gone.

It's a game, I guess. I vaguely remember that an old friend recorded a few games on vinyl many years ago. Must be one of those.

There's something about the voice on the record. Something about the words and the way they're said, that takes me back. Makes me think of blue skies and green grass and the smell of leather and pine tar. I close my eyes and I'm thirty-seven again.

Bob Reynolds winds and fires. It's in there for strike one, a hard fastball on the inside corner.

I don't remember the at-bat. Don't remember the game. If I was thirty-seven it would have been 1934. My last season. I reach back into the trunk and pull out the '34 Topps baseball card. I cradle it in my hands, just to enjoy the feel of it.

Reynolds looks in for the sign . . . now he's got it. He kicks and fires again . . . swing and a miss by McBride, and he missed it by a foot. Old Murray McBride sure was fooled on that one.

Old Murray McBride. If only he could see me now.

That's the kind of thing people are talking about when they say McBride might be on his last leg. He's been a solid Major Leaguer for a long time, but this is a young man's game, as we all know. Reynolds shakes off his catcher, now he sees something he likes. I'd guess another curveball after seeing McBride's swing on the last one.

Make it a curveball. I dare you. I could really hit that ball, back when I was young. Wasn't a pitcher in the league I was afraid of, not even at thirty-seven. I can almost see the crowd, dressed up in their Sunday best for a day at the ballpark.

And here it comes from Reynolds . . . yes, it's another breaking ball, but McBride jumps all over this one, it's headed deep to left field. Greenburg going back, he's at the warning track . . . and he can't get it! It's off the wall and McBride is sprinting around second and headed for third—look at him run! Boy, he can still move. Here comes the throw to third . . . McBride slides and he is . . . safe! Murray McBride is safe at third with his fifth triple of the season and oh boy, maybe the old man's got a little left in the tank after all. Murray McBride, showing the world that he still has what it takes . . .

The announcer's voice continues, but seems to fade to the background. My thoughts are too loud. My memories too strong. I think of all the time I was away from Jenny. All the time I was away from the boys, traveling from city to city. Away from them day after day. Missing out on their schoolwork, their sports, their girlfriends . . . their lives, really. By the time I was done playing ball, the boys were grown and did exactly what we taught them to do—they went out into the world and made lives for themselves. Got married. Had families of their own. We always had a relationship. They were always cordial. They visited. They kept in touch. But they never looked at me the way they looked at Jenny. I've spent a lot of time and energy making sure I never acknowledge how much that hurt. Pretending it wasn't my fault.

I reach out for the record player and slam my hand against it. The arm breaks free and the announcer's voice cuts out.

I sit back in the chair and weep, clutching my baseball card for all I'm worth. Tears pour down my cheeks faster than any time in my life, save for Jenny's funeral. I squeeze my face tight, but it's no use.

I cry for my lost youth. I cry for Jenny and the boys. I cry for everything I missed out on. Like being the kind of man who can say the things he feels in his heart.

Like being the kind of father whose sons know they mean the world to him.

To: MurrayMcBride@aol.com
From: jasoncashmanrules@aol.com
Subject: Kissy-Kissy Smooch-Smooch Comin' My Way

To the esteemed Mr. Murray McBride,

Dude, seriously no idea what that means but I heard something like it in a rerun of Family Ties. I finally got to leave ass-dad's and I'm back at mom's and she said I have to tell you something about myself, and ask you to tell me something about you. She's weird like that. And she said I shouldn't put things like OMG and LOL because you won't know what they mean, which seems impossible. Are you even from earth?

Okay, fine. You know I'm ten. You've seen my list. Not much else to say about me. Oh, when I grow up I'm going to be a professional baseball player and a professional football player and maybe a professional basketball player if I want to. And I like Milk Duds and Cherry Coke, but mom doesn't let me have them much. She says it's because of my heart but I think that's bullcrap. Bullcrap is a weird word, but mom said I can't swear. Even the spell-check thinks bullcrap is weird. Spell-check changes like every word I write.

This has to be the most boringest email ever written. My mom is so dumb sometimes. But at least she's nice.

Later. Jason.

ps. Mom told me to write "sincerely" but I told her if she wants to write this email so bad she should just write it herself and that shut her up.

To: jasoncashmanrules@aol.com
From: MurrayMcBride@aol.com
Subject: Re: Kissy-Kissy Smooch-Smooch Comin' My Way

Dear Jason,

Thank you for your letter. Your mother sounds like a wonderful person. She's right to tell you not to cuss, and not to eat junk food. I'm sure she loves you very much. I'd tell you about myself, but after a hundred years, there's too much to tell in one letter.

I'm looking forward to seeing you tomorrow. Good
luck with the kiss.

Sincerely,
Mr. Murray McBride

To: MurrayMcBride@aol.com
From: jasoncashmanrules@aol.com
Subject: Re: Kissy-Kissy Smooch-Smooch Comin'
My Way

Dude, I can't believe you called it a "letter." Freaking
hilarious. Seriously.

CHAPTER 12

Jason's big day has arrived. I roll my Chevy up to a driveway that looks a lot different than his dad's. More normal, I guess. Cracked concrete and a few weeds here and there. A small ranch-style house that could use a new layer of dark blue paint. The white trim's not looking so hot either.

A pair of nice-looking young women sit in wicker chairs on the front porch, sipping something or other. Sarsaparilla maybe, since it's too early for a highball or anything like that. Least, it's too early for me. You never can tell about other people, but I reckon it's none of my business what they're drinking.

Jason's out the front door before I can even put the car in park. The kid's really gone all-out. He's wearing a pinstripe, three-piece suit with shoes that look like alligator skin. His hair is parted to the side and plastered down with a good half jar of gel. He takes a circular tin from his inside jacket pocket, removes a breath mint, and pops it in his mouth as he opens the car door and lifts his oxygen inside.

"Think you're going to a kitchen hop?" I say.

Jason's learning to ignore things I say if he doesn't understand. I wonder if he got that from me. "Mindy Applegate," he says, lifting his chin, "you are about to become mine."

One of the nice-looking ladies waves from her porch chair and Jason covers the side of his face with his hand. "Just drive," he says. "Seriously, just go." But I turn the keys and the car shuts off.

"That your mother?" I say.

"Yeah, but seriously dude, we can just go. She won't mind."

"See here," I say. "For the last time, my name isn't Dude. It's Mr. Murray McBride. I'll be just fine with Mr. McBride."

"Fine, but can't we just go?"

"Why? What's so bad about introducing me to your mother?"

He sighs and slumps in the seat. "She'll pat my head. It's like she thinks I'm a puppy."

"Well that doesn't sound so bad." He gives me a look like he's trying to make a flower wither. "Maybe she won't this time, since I'll be there."

"That's why she'll do it," Jason says. "If you weren't there, she'd kiss my forehead and squish her cheek against mine. It's gross. Not as bad as Tiegan's mom, but still bad."

"She's your mother," I say. And I open the door. When I finally make my way around the front of the car, I open his door too. He's slouched so low he's almost completely off the seat, but I lean against the door for support and wait him out.

"Geez!" he says. He heaves his oxygen cart into the back seat and pulls his moping body out.

When we get to the porch, his mother's eyebrows raise in a way that makes her eyes sparkle. Short brown hair and a cute little chin—turns out Jason's mother is a knockout.

"Hello," she says in a voice like a songbird. "You must be Murray McBride." She puts her drink down, stands, and offers her hand. I take it and kiss the soft skin on top. Then I think of Jenny. I'm sure she's having a good chuckle right about now, watching me flirt with a woman sixty years my junior. So's the woman next to Jason's mother, judging by the smile on her face. She stands to greet me, too, and her hair—with bright purple and blond streaks—is cut short and spiky. But she's got a nice smile, too, so I nod to her polite-like.

"Ma'am," I say to Jason's mother. "You've got a wonderful boy here. I'm grateful to have a chance to spend some time with him."

"Well!" she says, and I wonder if she's ever heard such things about Jason. I might have fudged a little bit, but every mother likes hearing nice things about her son. "I certainly hope a few of your manners rub off on him." She pats Jason's head and he squirms away. "And please, call me Anna. This is my neighbor, Della. So where are you boys off to today?" she asks. "You must have big plans for Jason to put his suit on. Usually it takes half an army to get him to dress up. But no matter how many times I asked, he wouldn't tell me where he was going. He said it was some big secret."

I know I should tell her. Mothers deserve to know what their sons are up to. But Jason's puppy-dog eyes catch my attention just before I speak, and I can't do it. "Yes, ma'am," I say. "Top secret man stuff."

Anna laughs a high, twinkling laugh. She pats Jason's head again. "Well, you two have fun. And I'd love to have you over for dinner sometime, Mr. McBride."

"Please, ma'am, call me Murray—"

"What?! Why does she get to call you that?"

"And I'd love to join your family for dinner."

"Great," Anna says. "I have to work tonight, so you can drop him off at his father's house."

"The jerk," the other woman says. Then she starts coughing loudly and clearing her throat. "Sorry! Oh my, what a cold I'm coming down with."

Anna continues like nothing happened. Seems she's used to the other woman's interjections. "I'll have Jason email you about dinner. He tells me you're quite the modern man with your computer skills."

"I never said that," Jason says. "He's clueless."

I can't help but stare at her. That smile's so warm and welcoming. I allow myself a quick glance and notice the smooth skin of her neck. Jenny wouldn't mind too much.

"That's right, ma'am. I'm a regular renaissance man."

I might have to confess that little fib to Father James. I wonder if a man of God understands about the spell of a woman. Jason pulls my hand and we say a quick goodbye to both women.

"Your mother's quite the lady," I say on the way to the car.

"Seriously? That's so gross."

"I don't mean it like that, understand? I'm not dizzy with a dame or anything. I just mean she's a . . . a real nice lady."

Just before we get to the car, a little boy sprints around a bush in front of the house next door, like he's been spying on us. Jason hustles the last few steps to the car, throws himself inside, and slams the door shut. The boy rushes by me and knocks on the window. "Hey J," he says in a high-pitched voice. "What are you doing? Why are you dressed up so much? Where are you going? Whose car is this? Does your mom know you're leaving with a stranger?"

"Shut up, Tiegan," Jason says from inside the car. "God. Girls are so annoying."

It takes me a minute to get near the car, but when I do I see that Jason's right. The little boy is a little girl. Not my fault for having it backward, though. She's wearing a baseball cap, see? A Chicago White Sox cap, unfortunately. With the bill curved so I can hardly see her face. And athletic shorts with blue socks pulled up over her knees. Even got a baseball jersey on. Says *Cougars* on the front, like she plays Little League. I knock on the window and after a loud groan, Jason rolls it down.

"This the way you treat your friends?" I ask him.

"No. She's not my friend."

"Who is she?"

"My name's Tiegan, sir," the girl says, and she puts her hand out for a shake. "Tiegan Rose Marie Atherton. First base girl and cleanup hitter." I'm a little taken aback by this kid; can't rightly say what it is about her actually. Her confidence maybe? Or her maturity. Jason here is a ten-year-old kid. Thinks like one, acts like one, looks like one, other than his size. But something about this girl seems beyond her years.

"It's a pleasure to meet you, Tiegan Rose Marie Atherton. My name's Murray McBride. I'm a friend of this here Jason."

"Neat," she says, bouncing more than a person ought to. "I'm a friend of this here Jason, too."

"Are not!" Jason yells, looking straight ahead through the windshield.

"Where you taking him?"

I hesitate a moment, then decide on the truth. "Going to kiss his first girl, that's what. It's a wish thing, see? You're welcome to join us, if it's okay with your folks."

"What, to like, watch? Thanks, but no thanks. It was nice to meet you, Mr. McBride. Bye, J!" And with that, she turns and bounces up to Jason's porch, where the woman next to Anna, the one with the colored hair, jumps to her feet and says something that sounds like, "Es-bee-kay" and gives Tiegan a big smooch on the cheek. She picks her up, twirls her around, and ends it with a bear hug. I would've thought the woman was her mother, except I've never seen a mother so excited to see her own child, unless they haven't been together for a good long time. Tiegan says that same thing back to the woman. "Es-bee-kay."

"I can't believe you invited her along," Jason says when I'm finally in the car. "She's a girl, don't you understand that? A girl."

I ignore him and drive to the parking lot of the high school football stadium. Feels almost like when I'd show up at Wrigley for a ballgame. The excitement and nerves, the anticipation for what's to come. The knowledge that anything could happen.

I pull into a spot close to the football stadium so as not to arouse suspicion. And there they are. A row of girls in blue-and-white skirts kicking and chanting and waving pompoms like it's nobody's business. When Jason sees Mindy Applegate in her cheerleader's outfit, his confidence vanishes and his face turns an odd shade of purple. Turns out I'm kind of glad little Tiegan didn't come along. Probably just make things harder for him.

"Breathe," I say, and I reach into the back and grab the oxygen mask. "Really fill your lungs." He fogs the mask up good. Gets a few deep breaths and starts to look better. "Do you remember the plan?"

He nods. No words. Then he pulls the Post-it note from his pocket and stares at it. His breathing slows and he closes his eyes.

"You can do it," I say. "Just remember, tell her you have a message from Jarrod Miller, and he'd like a response. When she asks what the message is, pucker your lips like you're Jarrod, looking for a kiss. With any luck, she'll give you a little peck. Then . . . well, then you turn and get yourself the hell out of there."

I'll definitely have to confess that cuss to Father James tomorrow—in front of a kid, no less. But he needs to know this could turn south if he doesn't stick to the plan. Jason folds his list and replaces it in his pocket. His face has turned ashen again but I think it's fear this time, not a lack of oxygen.

"I changed my mind," he says. "I don't want to do this anymore."

I study him close. Pale-white cheeks. Short, uneven breaths. For all I know, he could be an inch away from a heart attack, or whatever his condition might do to him. So I turn the keys and put the Chevy into drive.

"It's okay," I say. "There's no shame in turning back."

I inch the car forward, toward the exit of the parking lot. Before leaving Mindy Applegate behind for good, I steal one more glance at Jason. His eyes are closed, his face is in his hands, and one tiny tear is trickling down his cheek. I go to the nearest parking spot and put the Chevy right back into Park. I see what's going on here, and I won't be a part of it.

"Listen, son," I say, and he peeks at me through two fingers. "There are times in our lives when we're faced with something that scares us. I mean scares the bejesus out of us. We'd rather curl up into a hole and hide. Don't care what we miss out on. Don't care if we spend our whole lives in that hole, just as long as we don't have to face that scary thing. That about what you're feeling right now?"

He turns to look out the window—anywhere but at me. But I study him close and see the slightest nod.

"I understand," I say. "When I was going to kiss Jenny for the first time I nearly passed out and fell right over. Decided I couldn't do it, same as you. Decided if that's what kissing a girl felt like, I didn't want anything to do with it. So I didn't. But then you know what happened?"

A little shake of the head. An even littler voice. "No."

"Nothing, that's what. I did nothing. Then she decided I must not like her. When Ernie Wells asked her to go steady, she said yes. Wasn't until then that I realized she was worth coming out of my hole for. That I'd rather face that fear and have Jenny than live in that hole without her." I put my hand on his shoulder and squeeze, which is about as touchy-feely as I get. "You just have to decide. Is Mindy Applegate, is kissing a girl while you still can, worth climbing out of your hole for?"

Jason wipes his tears and stares hard at the dashboard. "What happened with that girl you liked and the guy, Ernie? Did you ever get the girl back?"

"Sure did."

"How?"

"I just realized life's not worth a pile of beans if you don't live it. So I started living it."

Jason swallows hard and touches the pocket where he put his list. He takes one more deep breath from his oxygen mask, and without a word, he leaves the car and strides toward the group of cheerleaders. He's not even waiting for them to take a break. Suddenly, I'm the one who can't breathe. If he gets himself slapped and loses all confidence, I don't know how I'll live with myself.

But it's too late now. Even though the girls are shouting and swinging their arms and kicking their legs, Jason strides right up to Mindy Applegate, narrowly avoiding a kick in the jaw. I see his mouth moving and Mindy stops her cheering and listens. I open the window to try to hear, but it's too muffled. Jason finishes talking and tilts his head up with his lips puckered out for a kiss. Now for the moment of truth.

Mindy's first response is not what I was hoping to see. As her fellow cheerleaders use the interruption as an excuse to take a break, Mindy leans away from Jason, as if the idea of kissing him is repulsive to her. All the while, Jason remains perfectly still, head tilted up in the sunlight, eyes closed, lips puckered . . . just waiting for his wish to come true.

After a few awkward moments, Mindy stops leaning away from him. She looks around, almost like she's making sure the coast is clear. Then, so quick I almost miss it, Mindy Applegate, captain of the cheerleading team for Lemon Grove High School and Jason Cashman's dream girl, leans forward and gives him the most fleeting of kisses, barely brushing his lips with hers.

Jason's body gives a jolt, as if he's been electrocuted. He stands frozen in place while Mindy casually walks away. He remains paralyzed, all by himself, for several long moments. Finally, he turns and sprints back toward the getaway car.

His face is lit up like the grand finale on the Fourth of July and he sports the biggest, ear-to-ear grin I've ever seen. Slap-happy is what he is. He's trying to run but can't stop himself from skipping every few steps. His arms are waving like the ten-year-old kid he is, and he seems to be giggling so hysterically he's about to cry. Behind him I hear the stunned voice of Mindy Applegate talking to her fellow cheerleaders. And since she's staring after Jason, she's facing the car enough that I can make out the words. "He said it was from Jarrod. Can you believe it? From Jarrod!"

I don't have a perfectly clean conscience about what's happened here. At some point, poor Mindy Applegate is going to realize the kiss wasn't a message from the hulky quarterback, and that some half-perverted kid played a joke on her. But one look at the utter glee on the face of this kid who might not live to ever have a girlfriend makes me forget Mindy. Whatever happens with her, we're sure not going to be around to see it.

"Shake a leg!" I yell out the window.

"Go, go, go!" Jason shouts when he gets in the car. And for the first time in nearly eighty years, I burn rubber and leave tracks like we're fleeing a crime scene.

CHAPTER 13

When it's time to drop Jason off, I ask if I can come in with him. I'd like to meet his father properly.

"He's busy," Jason says.

"Oh? Busy with what?"

His high from kissing Mindy Applegate crashes down, along with his smile. "I don't know. Adult stuff."

"Just for a minute," I say. "I won't be long."

"Whatever," he says, and leans the side of his head against the window as I pull the Chevy up to the gate and wave to the security guard. The gate slides open slowly and Jason tries again to talk me out of it. "He's probably not going to be able to talk to you," he says. "He's usually really busy."

The more he tries to change my mind, the more determined I am to do it. I park in the circular drive, then start the three-minute process of getting out of my car. Once inside, Jason yells, "I'm home," into the giant foyer. The only response is his echo off the chandelier. He shrugs an I-told-you-so, drags his oxygen into the TV room, and drops onto the couch, still in his three-piece suit. I give the fountain a wide berth and shuffle in behind him. "Want to play?" he asks.

"Not just now. Where can I find your father?"

"He works in his office all day," Jason says without taking his eyes off the screen.

"His office is here? At home?"

Without removing his eyes from the television, Jason points to a long hallway and I navigate my way down it. I find the room his father disappeared into last time I was here and put my ear against the door. There's a conversation, but it sounds one-sided. Probably a telephone call. I consider being polite and waiting until Jason's father hangs up, but then I think—he probably gets his way most of the time. If I want to make an impression, I'd better shake things up a bit.

So I walk in without knocking and declare in my loudest, most senile-sounding voice, "Oh, there you are! So happy I found you."

Jason's father stops mid-sentence. He's at his desk this time and sure enough, he holds the telephone to his ear. I don't think he's ever encountered a situation where someone would have the nerve to interrupt him and frankly, he seems at a complete loss.

Smoke from his cigarette swirls up and adds to the cloud floating above him. The carpet, the bookshelves, even the oak desk and leather chair reek of cigarette butts. After a few moments, he remembers himself and says into the phone, "I'll call you back."

If I weren't a hundred years old, I'm pretty sure he would punch me in the mouth. But I'm not deterred. Before he can yell at me, I offer a bony handshake and say, "My name's Murray McBride. I'm Jason's Big Brother."

He gives me a sideways glance for a split-second before saying, "I remember. The thing." He waves his hand, shooing something away. "I'm Benedict Cashman."

"I've just returned Jason home," I say. "The boy just got his first wish."

Part of me half-expects a handshake or a high five, maybe even a hug. After all, this is a doozy. His son's heart isn't going to last long—for all intents and purposes, he's dying, from what I gather. And he just checked off one of his five final wishes. But all I get is a blank stare.

"He kissed a girl," I say. "On the lips."

A deep line creases the space between Benedict's eyes. I wonder if he knows anything about the list. "He's ten years old."

"Yes, well, that does sound strange, I understand."

"Do you?"

This isn't how I envisioned the conversation going. But if only he had been there. If only he had seen the pure joy radiating from his son. How he skipped and danced—danced like the Andrews Sisters. How he giggled until he cried.

Benedict taps out a cigarette and stares at me over a puff of smoke. His eyes hold mine in complete silence, save for the hum coming from his array of computer machines. I think he's trying to intimidate me. To make me feel uncomfortable. But I've been around the block once or twice. I've stared down a ninety-mile-an-hour fastball making a beeline for my jaw. Nothing he can do will scare me.

"Jason has heart troubles," I say, pointing to his overflowing ash tray. "You think that's going to help things?"

He sucks in hard and blows smoke out his nose like a dragon. "I made 2.3 million dollars last year. And do you know why I worked so hard to make that money? Medical bills. You think insurance is going to pay? Not for what he needs. They call it experimental, so I pay for it. I do that. While you're taking him out, doing things you could get arrested for, I'm here providing for my family. Now who's the better man?"

It's not about who's the better man, I want to say. *It's about Jason.*

But I don't say any of that. Because if I stare really hard through the cigarette smoke, I can see that Benedict Cashman isn't a bad person. He's not a drug dealer. Doesn't hit his kid. He's just misguided. Got his priorities mixed up. Now I'm not saying he shouldn't do everything in his power to pay for his son's medications. But at what cost to their relationship?

'Course, that's a bit like the pot calling the kettle black, coming from me. Besides, considering what he's been through with his only child, I can't find it in me to scold him.

"My apologies," I say. "I'll show myself out."

I close the door behind me and go back to find Jason's character firing wildly at a giant spaceship at the top of the screen. I use the oxygen cart to lower myself next to him. My knees creak and groan in protest. "Show me the list," I say.

He reaches into his pocket with one hand while pressing buttons frantically with the other. His eyes never leave the screen. I take the list and see that next to *Kiss a girl (on the lips)* is a giant, red check mark. It's the most beautiful thing I've seen since Jenny bought herself a new sundress. My shaky finger moves down to the next one. *Hit a home run in a Major League baseball stadium.* This could be tricky.

"Are you a power hitter?" I ask.

"No."

"Hit a lot of doubles?"

"Not lately."

I hand the list back to him. He takes it and blindly shoves it back into his pocket. "Have you ever played a game of baseball in your life?"

"Nope."

"Oh, for crying out loud."

Why hadn't he just written *Travel back in time?* Our odds would be about the same. But here's the thing about loving someone—it makes you forget what "impossible" means. It was like that with Jenny for eighty years. Like that with both my kids, even if I didn't do a good job of letting them know it. To a certain degree, it's even like that with my grandson, Chance. And no one with half a heart could have seen Jason's reaction to kissing Mindy Applegate and not loved this boy.

So even though he's about as likely to walk on the moon as hit a home run in a major league baseball stadium, I start winding up those gears in my brain again.

I think it's high time to call on some old connections.

To: MurrayMcBride@aol.com
From: jasoncashmanrules@aol.com
Subject: My Treatment—LAME!!!

I got a treatment thing at the hospital today. Super super lame. Mom's gotta work and Dad doesn't like to be there because it's depressing and he's busy. Wanna come? J.

To: jasoncashmanrules@aol.com
From: MurrayMcBride@aol.com
Subject: Re: My Treatment—LAME!!!

Dear Jason,

I'd be honored to join you. However, I don't know the time or location, or if there's anything I'm supposed to do. Please share any information you might have on the matter.

Sincerely,
Mr. Murray McBride

To: MurrayMcBride@aol.com
From: jasoncashmanrules@aol.com
Subject: Re: My Treatment—LAME!!!

Dude, here's the "information I might have on the matter." So weird. Anyway, it's at one o'clock, like room 623 or whatever the one is right across from the girls' bathroom, I don't know, check with Mom.

CHAPTER 14

I call Jason's mother. She sounds just as bubbly and beautiful as
before, and she's gracious enough to confirm the time of Jason's
appointment as well as the room number. Apparently he goes to
the same room on the sixth floor of the hospital for some sort of
treatment twice a month. And according to Anna, he knows perfectly well the time and room number, so I'm not sure why he had
to act like he didn't. Laziness, far as I can tell. Maybe I'm cutting
this kid too much slack because of his condition, but I just can't
find it in me to hold anything against him.

Anna apologizes half a dozen times for not being able to stay
with him. Got called into work, she says, and if she starts turning
down hours, next thing she knows she'll be out of a job altogether.
But Tiegan's mother—Della, her name is, if I recall—will transport
the kids to and from, so I don't need to worry myself over that.

I don't know why Anna's job is so important. I think about
Benedict's mansion, his 2.3 million dollars, and I almost give Anna
a piece of my mind. But I catch myself in time. Figure I should
keep my nose out of other people's business. Besides, she probably
already knows everything I'd have to say. Be preaching to the choir.
And based on the first time I met her on the porch, I'd bet Della's
been doing enough preaching about it.

I'm getting the hang of this driving thing again. Enjoying it,
too. The freedom it gives me. Might have to start driving more
often. 'Course, the fact that I don't have a valid driver's license is
always in the back of my mind. I've been working up to higher
speeds so I don't stand out so much. Sometimes going too slow
can attract as much attention as going too fast. So I get her up near

twenty-five miles per hour in a thirty zone right at the same time a police car pulls out of a fast-food joint and slides in behind me.

My breathing changes right quick—all shallow and choppy. I try to take a deep breath, but the pill doesn't seem to be working quite as well today. Every few seconds I risk taking my eyes off the road to peek into the rearview. The officer is driving too close to the Chevy, pushing me to go faster. I tighten my grip on the wheel and push her up to twenty-eight, but the trees on the side of the road whip by so fast I go right to the brake and hit it too hard. I brace myself for the impact, certain the police car will rear-end me. Actually squeeze my eyes shut, although I know that's not the safest thing to do. Kind of like when a fastball's bearing down on my skull—can't help but close my eyes.

But I don't feel any crash and when I peek through my lids I see I'm at a stop sign. I was so worried about the officer I didn't realize I was nearing one. Good thing I slammed the brake, I guess. I still think the officer will pull me over any second, but instead he slides up next to my tin can, keeps right on going without even looking at me, and makes a right turn onto a four-lane.

My heart slowly returns to normal, I ease my grip off the wheel, and try to be a little extra careful the rest of the way to the hospital. Fortunately, the rest of the drive is uneventful, and I'm able to find a parking spot near the door.

When I get up to the sixth floor, I make my way to the room Jason's in and hear a couple voices through the door. I'd like to go in. Maybe sit next to him and plan out his home run. I even go right up to the door, close my eyes, and visualize walking in. But I can't make my feet cross the threshold of the room. Instead, I find a comfortable-looking bench nearby and have a seat. Takes about a half hour, but finally Jason comes out with Tiegan by his side, which seems unlikely after the way Jason treated her the first time I saw her. Makes me wonder if maybe Jason's claim that he doesn't like her is just an act. She's got pigtails dangling out of her ball cap today, looking just as cute as a button.

"Hey there, Champ," I say to Jason, but it sounds silly in a place like this. You don't call a kid in a hospital "Champ." Sounds fake.

He smiles at me, but it's a little sheepish. Like he's embarrassed I caught him with the girl. Tiegan Rose Marie Atherton, that's her name. Just goes to show I'm still sharp.

"Hi, Mr. McBride," Tiegan says. She extends her hand just like last time. I take it and don't want to let go. Her skin's so soft. So young. Just the feel of a young person can take me right back.

Of course, I don't let on that I'm thinking that. Might seem improper, even though it's innocent enough. My knee's doing its thing, so I sit back down on the bench. Jason and Tiegan sit on either side of me. Jason rolls his oxygen cart to his side. He puts the mask to his mouth and takes a deep breath while reading a piece of paper with some writing on it. I crane my neck to look over his list again, but it's not his list.

"What do you have there?" I ask.

He shrugs. "Tiegan's list."

"It's just a game, really," Tiegan says quickly. "It was just a way to pass the time until Jason's treatment was done. I don't really have wishes. I'm not sick or anything. But we thought it would be fun to see what mine would be."

"Yeah," Jason says. "And they're super lame. I'm talking ultra, psycho, crazy boring."

"I just don't need much," Tiegan says.

"Yeah, but seriously. Milk Duds for a year? A ride around the block in a convertible? And get this Murray dude—"

"It's Mr. McBride—"

"—to play every position in a baseball game. You need some help, woman. You should take a look at a real list, like mine."

"Don't call me 'woman,'" Tiegan says. She reaches across me, snatches Jason's list right from his pocket, and moves her finger down it. "These are impossible, J. Why didn't you just put 'Become God'?" He stares at her with a look of complete annoyance. "All right, fine," she says. "I'll do one like yours. Put me down for kissing a man. A beautiful man. But on the cheek is good enough."

Jason rolls his eyes. "You have got to be kidding me."

"I don't know why you always say that," Tiegan says. "It doesn't even mean anything anymore. You said it when I told you my favorite team is the White Sox. And you said it when I told you I got an A on that pop quiz in math last week. You even said it when I told you my great-grandma played in the All-American Girls Professional Baseball League."

"That's because it's not true. Everyone knows girls can't play baseball."

"Now hold on there, see?"

Up till now I've been enjoying this here conversation. Probably what it must have been like to be in the same room with me and Jenny. We could bicker with the best of them, back in our day. Makes me wonder just what Jason feels for this kid. "Tiegan's got it right," I say. "Girls played ball, and they played it slick. Some of those dames could really wallop that pill."

They both stare at me with wide, unwrinkled eyes for a moment before a light bulb of understanding goes off in Tiegan's head and she says, "That's what I've been trying to tell him."

My mind swarms with memories of a ballpark full of young women playing what was supposed to be a man's game. Jenny and

I in the stands, holding hands, watching the girls play ball better than anyone thought they could. We invited my boys and their families every time, but I don't remember them ever coming.

"It was after my playing days, of course," I say. "But I had a hard time going back to the yard I used to play in—old Wrigley. Couldn't walk through the gates without that burning desire to play again. So Jenny and I, we'd travel around the Midwest, sometimes watching the Negro League games, sometimes watching those dames play ball. Kenosha, South Bend, Racine—"

"That's where my great-grandma played!" Tiegan says. "Three seasons for the Racine Belles in Wisconsin and two more for the Rockford Peaches. That's where I get my long-ball power from." She stands up and fakes a swing, then puts her hand above her eyes like she's shading the sun, watching the ball fly. Kid's got a pretty good stroke, too.

"Who's your great-grandmother?" I ask.

"Well she's dead now, but she was none other than Lavonne 'Pepper' Paire, the woman who drove in the fourth-most runs in league history."

"Pepper Paire?" I say. "I remember her. Must have seen her play a dozen times."

"No way!" Tiegan says. "That's awesome!"

"Great ballplayer, as I remember. Except she was fifth in RBI, not fourth. Jenny and I were quite the fans of those girls."

"She was fourth," Tiegan says, and she's got a fire in her eyes as she says it. "She's only listed as fifth because she's after 'Lib' Mahon alphabetically. They both had exactly four hundred runs batted in."

"Well," I say, because I'm not sure how to respond to that. I'm not sure if what she says is true or not. Might have to look that one up when I get a chance.

A tall, white-coated man leans into the room Jason was in, his nose in a chart. When he finds it empty, he looks around, sees us sitting on the bench, and goes straight to Jason. "I hate to break up the party," he says while he scribbles a couple notes. "But I'll need to check your vitals before you go."

He puts a stethoscope against Jason's chest and scowls. I don't know much about medicine, but I've seen enough people pass through hospitals to know the look isn't good.

"What is it, doc?" I ask. "What's wrong?"

The doctor straightens up quickly, like I caught him cheating at a game of cards. "Just checking his vitals." He touches Jason's forehead, then his hands. Maybe I'm imagining it, but it looks like his shoulders tense. "How are you feeling today, Jason? Any dizziness? Feeling lightheaded at all?"

Jason shrugs and focuses on his list. "I'm okay. I'm pretty tough, you know? I'm not really a kid anymore."

"Don't I know it," the doctor says. His words are right, but the tone's all wrong. And his body language. Guess they don't teach how to lie in medical school.

"How often are you using the oxygen?" the doctor asks.

"Not much," Jason says. "Maybe a couple times an hour."

I start to speak up because that's not even close to the truth. His face starts to lose its color if he goes more than a couple minutes without taking a nice, long pull from that mask. But I'm not sure it's my place to speak up.

The doctor gives Jason instructions to take it easy and come back in if he's feeling dizzy. He looks around—probably looking for the parents.

"Are you his ride?" he asks me.

Tiegan chimes in, as comfortable talking to the doctor as she is talking with Jason. The kid's a bit of a marvel in my mind. "My mom's coming," she says. "She had to run to the post office, but she'll be back in a couple minutes." The doctor nods and leaves, his nose already into another chart.

"More than a couple times an hour," I say to Jason when the doctor's gone. He looks confused, so I say, "The oxygen. You use it a heck of a lot more than a couple times an hour, and you know it. Why'd you lie to the doctor?"

Jason looks around like he's shoplifting a candy bar. "Dude, I'm not going to wear that stupid nose thing around all the time. Are you kidding me?"

A group of doctors walks by all wearing white coats, like they should. Jason hides his face by scratching an eyebrow until they're past. Tiegan gives him a funny little smile. When she sees me watching, her cheeks turn pink.

"Jason and I are, like, best friends, Mr. McBride," she says. "We've known each other since before we were born because our moms are best friends, too. I've lived by him so long, we both remember when our dads lived with us."

Jason looks a bit uncomfortable about it all, but it's not hard to see the truth of the matter. "She's not my girlfriend," he says, and Tiegan nods hard.

"That's true. My boyfriend would have to be much better at baseball. Jason's, well . . ."

"At least I know how to make decent wishes," Jason says. "Kiss a beautiful man on the cheek? Are you serious?"

"Okay, fine," Tiegan says. "I'll make my last wish a big one. For my fifth and final wish . . . I wish to raise a million dollars for homeless people."

Jason writes it on the paper, but he's shaking his head like she still doesn't understand anything. Far as I'm concerned, it's the best wish out of the ten.

CHAPTER 15

The woman from Anna's porch—Della, with the purple and blond spiky hair—turns out to be Tiegan's mother after all, just like I'd suspected. She rushes out of the hospital elevator and wraps Tiegan in a hug with just as much excitement as she'd had on the porch. They both say the "Es-bee-kay" thing again and press their foreheads together for a moment.

In my day, we weren't so touchy-feely. It was a more stoic time with good, old-fashioned American values like work ethic and independence. But now I wonder if it wasn't a mistake. If maybe I should have listened to that part of me that wanted to grab up my sons, just like Tiegan's mother does, and squeeze them until they knew how much I cared. Can't help but admire these two for doing things their own way, despite what society says. They're making their own mind up about how they want to be. How they want to act.

Come to think of it, that sounds a lot like independence, too.

I say my goodbyes and watch them all leave, then make my way to the parking lot and find the car. This driving thing comes back a little more each time I do it. I get the Chevy up over twenty-eight for the first time, although I pull back as soon as the needle touches thirty, feeling a little bead of sweat on my brow. But driving feels natural. Like I've done it a thousand times. 'Course, I have done it a thousand times, but that was thousands of days ago.

I haven't had this kind of freedom for a long time, so instead of going home I take a short detour to the grocery. Got something I've been meaning to pick up.

The girl with the nose ring says an enthusiastic "Hey, there's my old friend" when I finally get the door open. They don't have the fancy automatic doors here. I don't say anything in return, but that's never bothered her in the past. I glance at her name tag because that seems like something I should know, if I'm going to go around telling people like Doc Keaton she's my friend.

Harmony.

Is that her name? Well no wonder she's got a nose ring. Name your kid something like that and you're asking for it. I bet half the tattooed and pierced population is named Harmony, or Temperance, or some such thing. But I don't meddle in other people's affairs. They can name their poor kid Lollapalooza, for all I care. I've seen stranger things in my day.

"Good thing you're here," Harmony says. "We're almost out of Chef Boyardee. Another couple hours and you might have been out of luck."

I try to smile and say something nice, but my knee's acting up so all I manage is a grunt. I'm not here for Chef Boyardee anyway. Got a good dozen cans sitting up in my cupboard. Still, I'm here. So when I go by the aisle I grab the last four cans of ravioli and drop them in my shopping cart.

The cart's got a sticky left rear wheel, which makes pushing it a lot tougher than it ought to be. You'd think with the prices I pay here I'd be able to get a decent shopping cart. Or an electric one I could ride in. But they only have one of those, and some blue-haired woman who couldn't be much more than eighty is driving it down the cereal aisle.

But if I want to complain, I'll have to go all the way back up front, and I'm not about to do that. Instead, I head over to the candy aisle and almost faint when I see all the different kinds. I tend to steer clear of this part of the store these days. Ever since I lost my sweet tooth. Grew out of it, I guess you could say. But back in my youth I remember having two choices—Tootsie Rolls and Charleston Chews. There's gotta be a hundred different ways to ruin your teeth in this aisle. 'Course, mine are fake these days, but that's not the point.

I see an employee start down the aisle—not Harmony, mind you—and I wave him down. "Milk Duds," I say, and he smiles and says something stupid like, "I'd be happy to help you with that, sir." I don't need him to be happy about anything, I just need him to show me where they keep the Milk Duds.

They stock so many kinds of candy, it takes two aisles to hold them all, and the Milk Duds are in the second one. I follow as fast as I can and Mr. Smiles over here points to a shelf full of what must be three dozen bags of the things. I drop every one of them into my cart, one by one, wondering if Harmony will ask about them.

She does.

"Got a sweet tooth, do you?" she says, sporting a bigger smile than you'd expect to see on someone with so many piercings. I notice a couple new ones—one in her eyebrow and another that doesn't seem to be attached to anything but looks almost like a shiny sticker on the tip of her chin. "You like it?" she asks, and I realize I've been staring. Well, what does she expect?

I grunt my answer, which for some reason makes her smile even bigger. Then I count out two twenty-dollar bills, two one-dollar bills, three quarters, and a penny. Harmony giggles while I do this. Glad I can provide so much amusement to young folk these days. I know it's not Harmony's fault, she's trying to be friendly. It's just that she's from another time. Or I am. But I can't help but feel my blood pressure tick up a bit.

I make my way to the car and drive almost thirty-five miles an hour on the way home, thinking the whole way that I'm going to get myself in an accident if I don't learn to better control this temper of mine.

To: MurrayMcBride@aol.com, LittleLeagueAllStar@hotmail.com
From: jasoncashmanrules@aol.com
Subject: Grubbin' like a fool

Yo Moo-RAY, and the annoying Tiegan Rose Marie Atherton,

We be grubbin' in mama's crib, yo. Party time is prime time, 7pm on the smacker. Esta Noche. Losers stay away, winners come to play.

Hit me back with an up or down.

J.

To: jasoncashmanrules@aol.com, LittleLeagueAllStar@hotmail.com
From: MurrayMcBride@aol.com
Subject: Re: Grubbin' like a fool

Hello Jason. Is Tiegan going to read this, too? I'm not sure how this works. If so, hello Tiegan.

Jason, I regret to inform you that I was unable to interpret your letter. Would it be possible to resend it, and use English words this time?

Sincerely,
Mr. Murray McBride

To: MurrayMcBride@aol.com, jasoncashmanrules@
aol.com
From: LittleLeagueAllStar@hotmail.com
Subject: Re: Grubbin' like a fool

Hi Jason. Hi Mr. McBride.

It was supposed to be a dinner invitation,
Mr. McBride. Don't feel bad about not being able
to understand. I had a bit of a hard time myself. But
dinner's at seven tonight at Jason's mom's house. My
mom says we'll be there.

And J, I know you don't think I'm annoying, so quit
saying that. Remember second grade? Behind your
house? You wanted to kiss me. Don't even try to
deny it.

—T.R.M.A.

To: MurrayMcBride@aol.com, LittleLeagueAllStar@
hotmail.com
From: jasoncashmanrules@aol.com
Subject: Re: Grubbin' like a fool

HUH!!! Second grade behind my house? Murray I
swear to God, dude, I don't have any idea what she's
talking about. Gross!

To: MurrayMcBride@aol.com, jasoncashmanrules@
aol.com
From: LittleLeagueAllStar@hotmail.com
Subject: Re: Grubbin' like a fool

Fine, don't admit it. But we both know the truth.

T.R.M.A.

CHAPTER 16

It's been a long time since I've dressed up for anything. Last time I wore a suit was seventeen months, three weeks, and four days ago at Jenny's funeral. It's black, depressing, and two sizes too big—I haven't been eating like I used to since Jenny passed. But it's also the only thing I have that's nice enough for a dinner. I might not be able to get togged to the bricks, but I'm not going to show up looking like a bum either. Got more respect for Anna than that, even though I've only met her the once.

She offered to pick me up, nice woman that she is. But I wasn't about to make her drive all the way over here, just to drive back to her own home. Told her I'd take the bus since I don't see as well at night, which is exactly what I'll do. I wrestle with the suit for a good half hour before I manage to get it all buttoned up, which leaves me out of breath.

Surprisingly out of breath.

I shuffle into the bathroom and open up the plastic container that holds my pills. Sure enough, the pill for today sits there, untouched.

For months now I've stared at those pills over my Bran Flakes, wondering if today is the day I should refuse to take it. Doc Keaton has told me what would happen. I'd make my way through the day, mostly normal with maybe a bit more trouble breathing than most days. But when you're as old as I am, small things like that aren't even noticeable. By about the time I warm up my Chef Boyardee for supper, I'd realize I'm short of breath. That'd be followed by a gurgling sound as fluid builds in my lungs. And sometime around bedtime, the fluid would overtake my lungs, my body wouldn't be able to get enough air, and I'd pass out. Die in my sleep, drowned in my own fluids.

I've thought long and hard about that pill. Morning after morning, it's the thought of not taking it that reminds me to take it. Strange that I'd forget now. But I can't be dying in the middle of dinner with some nice people, so I pop the pill quick and wash it down with a long drink of tap water. Just like that, I've got another twenty-four hours.

Then I pick up the telephone and call the Cubs' main offices. Leave a message with someone named Gerald Massey Jr., who is in charge of "Community Outreach," according to the message. I'm sure he'll call back soon. Anything to do with the Cubs, I get the VIP treatment. You'd think I was a Hall of Famer or something, but my career was average. Enough to stick in the Big Leagues, but I was never an All-Star. Never in MVP considerations. The only reason they're so good to me is because I'm so damn old. A living piece of history.

The doorbell rings, which happens none too often these days, and I hobble toward the door. I peer through the curtains, expecting Jason and his mom to have ignored my refusal for a ride. But it's not them. It's Chance. Dressed to the nines and looking at his watch, like he's already itching to get on home. Or maybe it's just a habit he's developed.

"Granddad!" he says when I open the door. "How are you?"

I grunt and move aside a little. He sweeps by and looks around the house. Not sure what he expected to change, but he creases his brow like it's an unpleasant surprise all the same. He goes right over to the couch where he sat last time—last several times, come to think of it—plops down and picks up my baseball mitt he wants to steal from me so bad.

"How are things?" he says.

I'm not one to beat around the bush. Way I see it, a man ought to say what's on his mind. "What are you here for?" I ask.

"Whoa. Granddad," he says, and puts his hands up in surrender. "I just wanted to check in on you, that's all. Maybe spend a little time with you."

I stare at him nice and hard, but he doesn't look away. Maybe it's true. Maybe he really has come to spend some time with his old grandfather. The thought makes me feel pretty happy, I have to admit that. With Jason's list being on my mind so much these days, my thoughts jump right to whether Chance would make a good boyfriend for Jason's mom. If he could change his ways a bit, that is.

Of course that could never happen. Chance is married, after all.

But here he is, paying his granddad a visit just to say hello. To check on him, because he cares. It's high time I tell him how much I care, too. Maybe not quite as aggressively as Tiegan's mother, but something. I decide to make my way to the couch and give him a hug, but before I can get my body to move, he speaks.

"Alright, you got me," he says, as if I've been accusing him in my mind the whole time. "The truth is, things aren't so hot on the home front. I needed a breather. To see some family. You know how it goes. You were married for, what, fifty years or something?"

"Eighty years, dadgommit!"

I know it's not very Christian to holler like that, but those last thirty years were some of our best. Never believe anyone who says old people don't know how to love each other just because their bodies are worn out and they bicker now and again. The way I see it, love's just getting going after fifty years.

"Oh, that's right," Chance says, but his voice is full of contempt. "You guys got married barely out of high school and had a storybook life without a single fight and nothing but complete happiness every second you had together."

"Don't you dare mock our marriage. It was a marriage like any other. Ups and downs, both. Only we loved each other enough to stick it out through the bad times."

"Oh, I get it now. I'm somehow inferior because of my divorces. Why don't you just say it, Granddad? You think you're better than me."

"I'm no better than anyone, don't you put words in my mouth. I'm just saying that back in my day—"

"But it's not your day anymore, don't you get that? Your day passed a long time ago. You're still hanging on, and we're all happy about that. Me, Janine, everyone. But make no mistake about it, 'your day,' as you call it, is history. The world has changed, and you've been left behind."

It's true. Dementia might be creeping its way into my mind now and again, but not so much that I can't understand the truth when I hear it. But that's not what hurts. What hurts is the disgust in Chance's voice when he says it.

We sit in silence for a good long while. There's no way I can give him that hug now. He stares at his shoes, and I wonder where his outburst came from. I wonder if he even knows. And I wonder what he's thinking, in his nice work clothes, afraid to go home to yet another woman he was supposed to love until the day he dies.

"Listen, Granddad. I'm sorry. I shouldn't talk to you like that. It's just, this job is driving me crazy, and Janine certainly doesn't understand . . ."

He keeps going on about his problems, but my thoughts have drifted away from him. I'm already at the dinner table with Jason and his beautiful mother. Already scheming more ways to make his five wishes come true—four now, actually. I'm proud of the fact that he's already gotten one wish, but a little hesitant, too. Maybe he'll fade away once his wishes are complete. Maybe the wishes are like his pill, and when the time comes that the wishes are gone, there'll be nothing left to sustain him. Nothing to give him his next twenty-four hours.

I force the thought from my mind.

"You drive here?" I ask Chance.

"Of course I drove here, how else would I have gotten here? You heard me, right? I'm sorry about what I said. It's just been a long day at work, you know? The stress of it gets to me after a while and Janine . . ."

I wave it off. He's family. Way I was raised, you forgive family. No matter what. Still, after the arguing, I can't get myself to consider the hug again. "I was wondering," I say. "Think you could give an old man a ride?"

CHAPTER 17

"You sure you should be doing this?" Chance asks. "You're not a young man anymore, remember? Maybe you should stay home and take care of yourself. Let someone else worry about this boy."

I can't think of anything to say that wouldn't lead to a fight, so I don't even respond. The rest of the ride to Jason's mom's house is uneventful. By "uneventful" I mean silent as St. Joseph's the second before Father James says the welcome. We all say things we shouldn't. Things we wish we could take back. Problem with my grandson and me is that we keep saying them, over and over. Might as well just keep our mouths shut for a change.

I want to do better with Chance than I did with my own boys. I want to tell him I love him and hold him tight in my arms. But that's just not the way I'm wired, so I don't do any more than wish on it.

"Appreciate the ride," I mumble as he pulls in front of the house.

"No sweat, Granddad."

And with that, he's off, back to his life. And I'm off, back to mine. I heave a big sigh and it feels pretty good, too, after just taking my pill not long ago. The air is thick with oxygen tonight.

Jason's mom is at the door waiting. Wearing an apron with the words *Kiss the Chef* right across a picture of that tower over in France. "Ma'am," I say when she opens the door for me. I take her apron's message literally, grab her hand and kiss it. She blushes a bit and says, "Please, Murray. Call me Anna."

"Yes, ma'am," I say.

I let her hand drop back to her side, but not before Jason pokes his head around her hip. The kid does his vomiting impression more than a boy ought to, far as I'm concerned. "Sorry," he says. "Just had to get that out. I'm feeling better now."

"Into the kitchen, young man," Anna says. "That table had better be set by the time we walk in there." He takes off like a gunshot. I'm amazed at how fast he moves, and he's not even wearing his oxygen. His heart must be having a good day. "And I don't want to hear that Tiegan did it all," Anna says.

The way she says it gets to me. It's a stern voice, sure. But anyone listening could tell you there's nothing but love behind it. Nothing but pure, beautiful loyalty. She could have told that boy to go to his room for the rest of his life and I would have heard the words behind it. A simple "I love you," that's what.

Jenny used to use that very same tone with me, now and again. I'd get back from a ballgame after going 0-for-4, and she'd say to me, "Murray, you'd better get yourself a nice glass of wine and meet me in the library. And you'd better snap to it." And I'd do it, too. That woman had some sort of power over me. I'd show up in the library, which only had but one bookshelf in it, and she'd be waiting to wrap me in a hug and talk my ear off about the flowers she put on her mother's gravestone or the second grader she met while volunteering down at the school who could read like a high schooler— anything to get my mind off the game and on to happier things.

"I'm sorry, Murray. Did I say something wrong?"

It's Anna, studying me with the same eyes full of empathy that Jenny had. She wipes my cheek clean before I realize I'm crying. "It's nothing," I say. "Man as old as me has a lot of memories, that's all."

"I don't doubt that for a moment," Anna says, and she takes my fedora and my coat and disappears into a bedroom. "You can head into the kitchen if you want," she says. "Dinner's almost ready. I'm just going to get some wineglasses out of storage."

"Thank you, ma'am," I say, even though she can't hear me from here.

Three people are in the kitchen when I get there. Jason, of course, Tiegan, and Tiegan's mother. "Ma'am," I say. "Name's Murray McBride, in case you don't remember."

"Of course, I remember," she says, and gives me that look I get a lot—the one that can't quite believe a man so old he looks like a mummy is able to walk and talk. I'm like a traveling sideshow sometimes. "It's wonderful to see you again."

Tiegan's the one setting the table. She's sporting a new cap, which doesn't bother me a bit. Never was a fan of the White Sox myself. I was a rookie when they threw the series in 1919 and I never forgave them. Joe Jackson and those other boys almost ruined our game for good.

This cap of Tiegan's has a dame in a skirt kicking high, about to pitch a baseball. I pull a yellow box of Milk Duds out of my suit pocket and slip it to her with a wink. Her smile is almost as beautiful as Jason's. She opens the box and pops a chocolate into her mouth, then leans up against her mother.

I can't help but watch the two of them together. Tiegan with her eyes closed, her head resting against her mother's chest. Her mother stroking Tiegan's hair and gazing at her like she's an angel. Haven't seen two people so obviously in love with each other since Jenny and me. Tiegan opens her eyes, looks at her mother, and says, "Es-bee-kay."

I'm not one to pry into other people's business, but that's the third time I've heard them say that word and my curiosity gets the better of me. "Excuse me," I say, "but I can't help but wonder what 'es-bee-kay' means. Don't believe I've ever heard the word. Is it foreign?"

Tiegan scratches at her eye and looks to the floor, but her mother says, "It's okay, sweetie. It's our story. You can tell him."

Tiegan still seems unsure. She stares at her mother for another long moment, but then shrugs. "It's letters, actually. S, B, and K."

"Letters, you say?"

"Yeah. When I was young, my dad lived with us. He wasn't a nice person. He used to hit my mom."

I can't help but look at Della, as if I'll see the bruises left over from years ago. I wonder if Tiegan's telling me the story because it's too painful for Della to tell. When she looks at me, I glance back to Tiegan right quick.

"She stayed with him because she was afraid for me," Tiegan says. "Afraid of what he might do to us if we left. But then one night he hit me—I don't remember it at all—but Mom decided right then that she'd leave.

"It was the middle of the night; my dad had been drinking until he fell asleep. And Mom whispered to me that we had to be strong. We had to be brave. And from now on, we'd be nothing but kind."

She stops talking like the story's over. I scratch the back of my head and think on it, but still don't know what their greeting means.

"S, B, K," Tiegan says. "Strong, brave, and kind. It's kind of our motto now, Mom says. And we say it to each other all the time."

"Hello and goodbye are meaningless," Della says, pulling Tiegan close to her again. "SBK is a constant reminder, every time we greet each other, every time we say goodbye, it's a reminder of how to live. It's so much more than a greeting."

I can't help but think of my own boys again. How little I showed them how much I cared. And here this woman is, showing her daughter over and over, every single day, never leaving a single doubt. I can't think of what to say to that, so I point to Tiegan's baseball hat.

"That a Kenosha Comets cap?"

She shakes her head hard, nestles into the crook of her mother's arm, and pops another Milk Dud into her mouth. "Rockford Peaches. League winners in 1945, '48, '49, and '50."

"She's always been intrigued with that league," Della says. "But recently it's taken on a life of its own."

"That's because Murray knew Great-Grandma Pepper," Tiegan says.

"What?" Della looks a bit confused, and I can't say I blame her. It was a long time ago. You just don't meet people who knew your grandmother. Don't run into them at the grocery or the post office.

"Can't rightly say I knew her," I say. "But I saw her play plenty. Met her once or twice."

"And you remember her?"

"Clear as a whistle."

"That's amazing." She strokes Tiegan's hair again while she speaks. "I always tell my baby, no one was more SBK than her great-grandma Pepper."

"It's why I'm not afraid of the ball, even if it's a pitch that's way inside," Tiegan says, and Della beams at her again. Suddenly I wish I could stick around to see what this kid ends up doing with her life. With such a loving mother teaching her things like strength, bravery, and kindness, I bet she could do just about anything she puts her mind to.

"Aw, man!" Jason says from his seat at a desk in the corner. Instead of helping set the table, he's been playing on the computer.

"Thought you were supposed to be helping your mother," I say, making my way over to him.

"Check this out," he says, which isn't an answer at all. But I lean over his shoulder and look at the screen.

"That the same game?"

"All-Powerful Gods and Bloodsucking Aliens, yeah." Without taking his eyes off the screen, he covers a second controller with his hand and slides it in front of me. "This game is so freaking cool."

"Your mother wants the table set," I say. "And Tiegan shouldn't have to do it. She's your guest." But I recognize the structure he's trying to build and have a hard time looking away.

"Put some stones next to mine," he says. "We'll build a castle with four turrets to shoot from."

I glance at the partially set table, but something about the game makes me curious. I push the only button I'm familiar with and a little roof appears over my character's head.

"Dude, use turbo to jump and spin. Castle rocks will appear." I try to decipher his words, but the kid hasn't got much patience. "Watch," he says, and slides a nob on his controller to the left. Sure enough, a big rock appears and I'm able to move my character toward it. I see the way Jason moves his controller and think I might actually be able to stack the rock on top of the structure he's started.

On the screen, my character stacks the rock, and I'm even able to replicate the move Jason made, which creates another stone. "Hey, hey! Look at that!"

A little something flips in my stomach. Pride, I think. Or maybe satisfaction. I might be able to really get into this game. But a beautiful voice interrupts. "I see Jason has already exerted his influence," Anna says, carrying three new-looking wineglasses.

I pull back quickly, so embarrassed I'm not even bothered by the pain that shoots from my knee to my hip. "He was just showing me his . . . game. Better get that table set now, Jason. Like I told you."

Jason rolls his eyes and Anna tries to hide her smile, but it's way too beautiful to be hidden. Like trying to hide a monarch butterfly fluttering through sunlight, that's what. Anna pulls out a chair for me and I settle down into it alongside Tiegan and her mother while Jason finishes setting the table. He brings a pile of dishes over and sets them on flowery placemats. But the kid must not be any good at simple math.

"Got one too many here, Jason," I say, and I point to a sixth placemat and plate. By my count, there's only five of us here.

Pretty sure I see Jason's cheeks flush a little bit at the exact same time the doorbell rings. We all look to the door like we expect it to open on its own because no one moves toward it. Then Anna wipes a bit of flour on her apron and puts her hands on her hips. "Jason?"

The one word says all that needs saying. Jason places the fancy wineglasses on the table as if nothing's out of the ordinary. "You should probably see who that is, Mom."

Anna gives him the most lovely scowl, but she can't let who-ever's out there just sit and wait, so she heads to the door, shaking her head. As soon as she's out of the room, Jason's giggles come bubbling right out of him. He pulls the list from his pocket and holds it up for me.

"Check it out," he says through an enormous grin. "Tonight, I'm taking down number four."

CHAPTER 18

Before I even lay eyes on the chap, I smell him. It's like the perfume section at JCPenney, but about ten times stronger. There are some voices in the entryway. Anna sounds sweet but more formal than usual and the other one is big, deep, and loud. Like he's talking to the entire household, even though it's just the two of them. Then Anna comes skirting back into the kitchen and I get the feeling she's running away from a charging bull. She looks right at me with big, round eyes. Like she's looking for a savior.

Following right on her heels is a tall, dark-haired man in a sport coat and a handful of flowers. He must've tried to give them to Anna at the doorway. Wish I could've seen that little interaction. When he gets to the kitchen, he stops like he hit a brick wall and stares at the four people in a room he surely expected to be empty.

"Well," Anna says, and she starts and stops a few more times. "Let's just eat, shall we?"

"Actually," Della says. "I just remembered, we have a roast in the oven at home and if we don't get back, it's going to burn."

Tiegan opens her mouth to speak, but her mother shushes her and corrals her toward the door. Anna's eyes are wide and pleading, but Della seems to be enjoying it just fine. After a quick "Goodbye" (Tiegan looks at me and says "SBK") and the squeak of the front door, they're gone and now it's just the four of us.

Not sure how Jason managed to get in touch with this young man, but judging by the scowl every time he looks at us, the chap apparently didn't get the message that there'd be an old-timer and a young kid around. If it had been me expecting a romantic date and I got this sprung on me, I'd probably look a lot like this fellow does now. Doesn't stop me from chuckling a bit, though.

We all stand twiddling our thumbs for a bit before a clock chimes and shakes Anna from her shock. "Murray, I'd like you to meet Derek . . . Lester, right?" she says, and she does an okay job keeping her voice pleasant. "Jason." You'd have to look a little deeper to find the love behind the look she gives him this time. "I believe you two have met, already. At the hospital."

Jason grins without a hint of embarrassment. Seems to me he should feel something more along the lines of shame and horror if he's responsible for this, not amusement. But he snatches a small computer device from the table, grabs my arm, and keeps his head down as he leads me toward the stairs. "Well, you two enjoy dinner. We'd love to join you, but you know, things to see and people to do."

"Hold it right there, young man," Anna says.

Jason stops, stares at the floor, and says, "Son of a . . ."

I take a look at this here situation and figure Anna could use as much help as she can get. She's not the type to be rude to a visitor, but she shouldn't have to endure dinner alone with this guy either. Not if it was never her intent. So I head right over to the lad and extend my hand to him.

"Name's Murray McBride. I'm a friend of the family."

The man looks at my hand, then at the flowers, and manages to shift what must be two dozen red roses into the crook of his arm to shake my hand. "Murray," he says with a nod, and I immediately know he's not right for Anna. A man ought to use "mister" or "sir" when addressing an elder. Someone who doesn't offer that kind of respect to a man he just met isn't going to show respect to his wife either. His handshake's a bit flimsy, too. In my day we had a term for a fella like this—wet rag.

"I'm Doctor Lester," he says, with plenty of emphasis on *Doctor*.

"That so? What kind of doctor?"

"Plastics," he says.

I can't quite get my brain around it. Far as I know, plastics are made in a laboratory. I knew some fellas who got in the ground floor on plastics and they did damn well for themselves, but they sure weren't doctors.

"Well," Anna says, flipping her hands up like she can't figure out what to do. "Let's eat, I guess."

We all sit at the dinner table and dig in. Derek (I'll be damned if I'm going to call him doctor) shifts his chair a bit too close to Anna, who scoots hers a bit farther away. Jason attacks his plateful of hamburger hot dish, but his eyes keep flicking up to get a good look at his mother and the new man. Derek sets his flowers on the table beside him and leans in toward Anna.

"So, you know I'm a doctor. Tell me about you."

"Me?" Anna says. "There's not much to tell, honestly."

"Oh, that's not what I hear. Tell me about Malaysia."

Anna's eyes bulge a bit and I wonder if she's choking on her hot dish. She sets her fork down hard and glares over at Jason, who's conveniently studying his dinner. "I'm sorry," Anna says. "I've actually never been out of the country."

Derek looks a bit confused, which suits his features just fine. "Then where did you study to become a Zen grandmaster?"

Across the table from his mother, Jason coughs loudly. He slurps his water, spilling a good bit on his shirt. "I'm afraid I don't know anything about Zen," Anna says. Her voice is sweet, but maybe a bit too sweet.

Derek, for his part, seems to be catching on to what's happening here. About time, too. "Let me guess," he says. "You were never a model in Paris either?"

"Ha!" Anna seems to get a genuine kick out of that one. "No. Definitely no Paris modeling in my past."

"And the eighteen months of studying the *Kama Sutra*?"

"Okay," Anna says, standing up so fast she bumps the table and sloshes water from every one of our dinner glasses. "You know what? You seem really nice, Dr. Lester—"

"Derek—"

"But I have to be honest with you. My son apparently took some liberties with my biography when he talked to you. I'm afraid I'm just not the person you were expecting. Thank you so much for the flowers, but I'm going to have to ask you to leave. Now."

Derek stands and glares at her and something in his eyes makes my insides jump. I stand up, too, although I'm sure any intimidation I once had disappeared decades ago. But my presence seems to give him a jolt, anyhow.

"I see. I didn't realize this was a child's game we were playing."

"I'm not a child," Jason says, daring to lift his face from his dinner for the first time since the conversation started. "I'm ten."

Derek doesn't seem to know what to say to that. Just shakes his head and storms out of the kitchen. A few seconds later, the front door slams hard and as far as I'm concerned, that's the end of Dr. Derek Lester.

It's pretty quiet in the kitchen now. Jason's gone back to his hot dish and is ignoring his mother's stare. "Well, he seemed nice," he says to his food.

The second hand of a clock ticks a few times while Anna tries to figure out how to respond to that. She puts one hand on her hip and the other against her forehead. "How, exactly, do you know about the *Kama Sutra*?"

A little shrug. "Kids at school."

"And what do you know about it?"

"I know it's super gross. Eli says it's all about how to kiss. Like, instructions and stuff. But adults sure like it. That dude got really interested after I said that part."

After a little hesitation, Anna bursts into laughter and messes Jason's hair. "I appreciate the attempt, little man. But how about from now on you contain your wishes to your own life?"

> **To:** jasoncashmanrules@aol.com, LittleLeague AllStar@hotmail.com
> **From:** MurrayMcBride@aol.com
> **Subject:** Batting Practice
>
> Dear Jason (and hello Tiegan),
>
> I've spoken with someone from the Cubs and they have agreed to let us use the field on the 21st of this month since they have no other events that day and the team is away. I figure we can make whatever adjustments are necessary. Maybe Jason can hit from second base.
>
> But if Jason is going to hit a home run, he should practice. How about 4pm on Monday? I'll pick you both up in the Chevy.
>
> Please RSVP at your earliest convenience.
>
> Sincerely,
> Mr. Murray McBride

> **To:** MurrayMcBride@aol.com, LittleLeagueAllStar@ hotmail.com
> **From:** jasoncashmanrules@aol.com
> **Subject:** Re: Batting Practice

Dude and dude-ette,

I can already drop bombs like Jose Canseco. Practice is for losers and wannabes. But I'll still give a little lesson on how to rake like Babe Ruth! HELLS YEAH! Prepare your minds to be blown!

J.
ps. Kama Sutra RULES!!!

To: MurrayMcBride@aol.com, jasoncashmanrules@aol.com
From: LittleLeagueAllStar@hotmail.com
Subject: Re: Batting Practice

In your dreams, J.

CHAPTER 19

I pull up to Anna's place, and Tiegan's right there, wearing her Rockford Peaches cap. She's got a glove, her Little League jersey, and some baseball pants on, pulled up high so her socks are showing. Jason stands next to her, a head shorter, in jeans and a T-shirt. He's leaning against his oxygen like it's a light post. As soon as I stop the Chevy, Jason races to the passenger-side door and hops in, then hauls his oxygen cart in by his feet and takes a deep breath from the mask.

"Aren't you going to give the lady the front seat?" I ask. But he just shrugs and Tiegan says, "It's fine," and opens the back door.

"Oh, for crying out loud," I say. Tiegan pops her head right in between us, smelling for all the world like a strawberry patch at harvest time.

"Hi, Mr. McBride. What's up?"

It's one of those kids' phrases, but I know it. She means *How are you*? At least that's what I think until Jason says something that sounds like *Yeah, sup*, and Tiegan takes it as an appropriate response. I pretend I didn't hear. I grab a box of Milk Duds from between the front seats and hand it to her. She tears right into it, sharing a little chocolate candy with Jason and me. My teeth stick together something fierce, and I have to chew a good long while before I can talk again.

"Got an old wood bat and a few beat-up baseballs in the trunk," I say. As I pull away, Tiegan rolls down the window and yells, "SBK," to her mother, who's blowing kisses from her doorstep. Strong, brave, and kind. I've been racking my old brain, trying to come up with anything better, but I just can't do it. Della really hit the nail on the head with that one.

I take it pretty easy on my Chevy—I've got kids with me now and besides, I still feel a little unnerved about seeing the police officer the other day. So we cruise along at about fifteen miles an hour.

"Mr. McBride," Tiegan says. "My mom says it's so cool you played for the Cubs. Did you ever play in a World Series?"

"Twice. Lost them both though. Philadelphia got us, and the Yankees. Got injured late in the season in '29, though. And in 1932, a young buck took my place. They traded him after the series and I got my spot back, but I never got a World Series at-bat."

"Still," Tiegan says. "My mom says it's 'beyond impressive.'"

"Yeah, it's pretty cool," Jason says. After a moment looking out the window he says, "I played for the Lightning Cheetahs."

Isn't that a laugher. The kid's one-upping me with his Little League team. "Thought you said you've never played."

"I haven't." His eyes shift to Tiegan, then quickly away. "I rode the bench," he says.

I try to stifle a grumble, but it's not easy. To think an American boy can't play in a baseball game because he's not a five-tool player—makes me sick to my stomach, that's what. Makes me a tad fonder for my little buddy, too, to tell the truth.

"Doesn't matter," he says. "I wouldn't be able to play in the field anyway." When I don't say anything for a while, he stares at his oxygen concentrator. "I can't take this thing with me on the field, and I can't be that far away from it."

Most of the time, the kid seems to be doing okay. Not great, of course, but okay. Then, every once in a while, he says something like that, and it hits home how serious his condition is. "Well, Mr. Lightning Cheetah," I say. "Any idea how far you can hit a baseball?"

"Probably a thousand feet. I'm so freaking strong."

Tiegan laughs and Jason gives her a dirty look but doesn't say anything. We drive by several ball fields, but each one is busy. At first, I'm encouraged. Lots of kids seem to be playing baseball. But after we pass the fourth field of kids in uniform, conducting drill after drill like soldiers in an army, my ulcer starts acting up.

Whatever happened to kids going out to the sandlot and playing ball all afternoon? These kids are in getups that probably cost two hundred bucks, getting yelled at by their coaches, and not even playing the game of baseball. It's no wonder Jason couldn't compete. These fields aren't full of kids, they're full of machines. I forget about finding an open baseball field and veer back toward my house. I know a place we can play.

"Who was the best player on your team last season?" I ask.

"Johnny Mazerouski," Jason says. "By far."

"I had a higher average," Tiegan says. "More RBIs too."

"Well," I say. I don't doubt Tiegan for one second, and that's the truth. "Johnny Mazerouski, get ready to eat your heart out."

"Excuse me, but huh?" Jason says. "That's so officially disgusting."

I pull into my driveway and start the process of getting out of my car. "I thought we were going to take batting practice," Jason says.

"We are. In Old Lady Willamette's garden."

Jason mumbles something about Nintendo, Sega-something, and other cryptic things while we pull the bats and balls out of the trunk. It took me the better part of a half hour to get the bag of baseballs into the trunk, but I'm not about to ask for help. I might have ninety years on these kids, but I don't want to be seen as a weakling any more than they do. Fortunately, Tiegan grabs the heavy bag before I have to admit I can't carry it.

Old Lady Willamette is actually quite a spring chicken. Eighty-four, if I remember correctly. But she acts old, so when a Girl

Scout came to my door trying to sell me overpriced cookies and said that "Old Lady Willamette" next door bought three boxes, I started calling her that too. Not to her face, of course. Old Lady Willamette is one nasty bird.

We pick our way through rows of asparagus and broccoli and continue to the unplanted section of the garden. If she sees us out here, there'll be hell to pay, but I can't think of anywhere else to go.

Jason swings the bat and wiggles his butt a little. Looks like a cartoon character, that's what. "Ladies first," I say.

"What? I'm the one who's going to hit a home run, not her."

"Now see here—"

"It's okay, Mr. McBride. J can go first. I like shagging flies anyway."

It's not right. The kid needs to learn how to treat a lady. But Tiegan's already running out near where the rows of corn start and Jason's standing with the bat on his shoulder, so I let it slide.

"You know how to hold a bat?" I ask.

Jason takes a quick hit of oxygen, then assumes a crouched stance and grips the bat like he's trying to choke it. He doesn't look all bad actually, except his hands are backward. I fix that problem, tell him to loosen his grip, and find a spot twenty feet away to pitch.

I haven't thrown a baseball in half a century, but I'm sure I can still fire it. I've never understood those old-timers you see throwing out the first pitch of a baseball game—they bounce it every time. How do you forget how to throw a baseball?

I wind up and cock my arm, then rotate and throw the first pitch to Jason. It goes about ten feet and plops into the tilled garden dirt. Meanwhile, a searing pain shoots through my shoulder and down to my elbow.

Come to think of it, I don't understand how all those old-timers who throw out the first pitch get it so far.

Jason looks a little confused. Like he knows something isn't quite right about what just happened, but isn't exactly sure what. I walk up to my pitched ball, pick it up, and stay right there.

"Let's try underhand first," I say.

Tiegan doesn't say a word about my throwing ability. I'm liking that kid more and more.

I pitch one underhanded and Jason swings. He probably would have come closer to hitting it if he'd left the bat on his shoulder.

"Just watch the ball, okay? See the ball, hit the ball. Don't think too much."

I pitch another one with the same result. I scratch my chin, bite my tongue, and pitch a third ball. He actually closes his eyes this time and swings like Reggie Jackson. His knee touches the ground, he grunts, and somehow—thank the Good Lord—he makes contact.

I hadn't really considered how much the kid has going against him. The bat hasn't been used since 1934. The ball is squishy and the seams are split. And we're playing in two inches of loose topsoil. When the ball hits the bat, it makes a small thud, and the ball sticks in the dirt near Jason's feet with about the same sound. We all stand in place and stare at it.

"Maybe Tiegan should try," Jason says. "I'll save my good ones for Wrigley."

Tiegan doesn't need to be told twice. She sprints in, pigtails bouncing behind her, and grabs the bat. Jason takes his oxygen cart and maneuvers it over rows of dirt toward where Tiegan had been standing.

Out of nowhere I'm hit by the realization that I never did this with my boys. Not once. Not that I can recall, anyhow. During the season I was always too busy. Gone half the time and at the ballpark most of the time I was in town. And I didn't get home from games until well after Jenny had put the boys to bed. In the offseason I had to work a job at the steel mill to pay the bills, and I had to exercise to keep in decent shape, too. There just wasn't time for playing ball with my sons.

By God, I wish I'd made the time now.

When Jason's finally out far enough, I hold the ball up for Tiegan.

"Now just keep your eye on the ball, see? Watch it hit the bat. It's okay if you miss. It's not easy."

"Okay, Mr. McBride," she says, and she seems happy as can be just having a bat in her hand. She turns her hat backward, spits on the ground, and says, "I'm Joanne Weaver."

She digs her toe into the dirt and I pitch one underhanded, just like I did for Jason. She wiggles the bat just a bit and slashes it toward the ball. The contact sounds like a thud because of the loose seams, but the ball shoots past me on a line before I can even flinch. Behind me, Jason jumps out of the way and runs several steps to his right where he stares at the ball, now wedged in the dirt near a row of onions.

"Sorry, Mr. McBride," Tiegan says.

Nothing to be sorry for, the way I see it. She could charge admission to watch that swing. I take a few steps back and toss her another one. She pulls this one to left field so it's nowhere near hitting me, and it sails four rows deep into the corn.

"Oh, shoot," she says, and takes off toward the cornfield to look for it.

Jason's squatting down like he's trying to hide. His face is lost in his glove. "This is so embarrassing," I hear him say.

Just then I see movement in the curtains of Old Lady Willamette's window. "Leave it!" I yell to Tiegan. "We have to skedaddle. Now!"

Tiegan and Jason hear the fear in my voice and take off toward the Chevy. I follow as fast as I'm able, trying to outrun a screechy old voice that says "McBride" and "vegetables" and something that sounds like "hell to pay." That woman can put the fear of the Good Lord in my bones. I've got more adrenaline pumping through my veins than after Jason kissed Mindy Applegate.

By the time I make it to the car, Jason and Tiegan are giggling hysterically as Old Lady Willamette yells and shakes her fist from her front step. Lucky for us, she's even less mobile than I am so I just keep the windows closed and drive off. Looks like Jason's just going to have to make due with the practice he got.

"Mr. McBride," Tiegan asks between giggles. "What's 'castrate' mean?"

CHAPTER 20

B enedict Cashman and I didn't get off on the right foot, that much I can tell you. If it was up to me, I'd have nothing to do with the man. He's a regular wet sock, as far as I'm concerned. Not that he's a terrible person, but the way I see it, it's best to just stay away from people you don't see eye to eye with. Once you get the hint that there're some irreconcilable differences, what's the point of hanging around each other?

'Course, that's what Chance used as an excuse for his second divorce. Irreconcilable differences. First divorce, too, actually. Probably where I first heard the term. But still, I'd rather not have to drive through the gate and up the circular driveway if I didn't have to.

But I do have to. The twenty-first is the day the Cubs are letting us use Wrigley, and it falls on a weekend. As luck would have it, it happens to be the one weekend a month that Jason spends with his father. More like it's the weekend he stays at his father's mansion. From what I've seen, they don't spend any time together. That kind of bothers me, to tell the truth, being that the kid has a heart defect and all. And he's over there way more than once a month, too, because sometimes Anna picks up an extra shift and can't afford to pay a babysitter every time.

But that's not really my business. All I know is I need permission for this trip I have planned. Either that or I have to go to Plan B. Now I have a Plan B to be sure. Just would rather not have to use it, as it could get a bit complicated.

See, Plan B involves things that could get me in a lot of trouble. Driving without a license would only be a small part of it. If I have to resort to Plan B, I figure I have a fifty-fifty shot at taking my last breath in prison. Bad things are likely to happen with Plan B. It'd be a whole lot easier this way. So I drop Jason and Tiegan off at their houses and make my way to Benedict Cashman's mansion.

The guard nods to me and lets me in without any questions this time. At least he seems friendly, but I don't expect the same from the master of the place. Sure enough, I'm forced to stand for a good minute or two waiting for him to answer the door. When he finally does, he doesn't look any happier than last time I was here.

"Mr. Cashman," I say. "Name's Murray McBride, Jason's Big Brother. We met last week briefly."

"You don't have to introduce yourself every time. I remember. You're the one who had my little boy kissing girls. What are you doing here?"

"Well, I'd like to take Jason up to the apple for a bit this weekend, see? But he's scheduled to be here."

"The apple? What, New York? Are you crazy?"

"Not New York, Chicago."

"But you said 'apple.'"

"Well, in my day, apple meant any—forget it. I'd like to take the boy to Chicago."

He looks finished with this conversation already, not that I can blame him. "For what?" he says.

"For a wish."

"A wish, huh? I suppose you couldn't find a strip club in Lemon Grove? Have to go to the 'apple' for that?"

I'm not sure how to answer that, but I don't appreciate it, I know that much. "He wants to hit a home run in a Major League stadium."

A belly laugh erupts out of him and he enjoys mocking me for a few moments. "And you're going to help him with that, are you? Have you even seen my son?"

"Yes, sir, I have. And he can do it. Least, we can figure a way to make it happen."

"I'll bet you can. But no, I'm not going to have some old pervert take my boy away the only weekend of the month I get him. When he's here, he's mine. Understand?"

I understand a lot more than he knows. I understand that his insecurity—or maybe just his desire for revenge against Anna—is driving him to hurt everyone around him. Even Jason. Does he think his son would rather sit on the couch watching TV or playing video games? But I've seen enough to know there's no give in Jason's father. Nothing I could say will sway him. He'll just gum the works even more, just to spite me. So I slap my fedora back on my head and tip my cap.

"I understand. Good day."

And with that, I move to Plan B.

CHAPTER 21

When Thursday rolls around, I wake to a telephone call from Anna. 'Course, I don't get to the phone the first time, but she calls back and I talk to her the second time. She invites me over for breakfast and when I politely decline, she asks if she and Jason can bring something over for me. Having some company sounds nice so I say yes before I realize I can't. That I have another commitment. I'm not real keen on telling Anna what it is, but she's persistent so I finally tell her about my art modeling job at the community college. She sounds a bit more interested than I'd expect and when I get to the stuffy art room, all dark and candle-lit again, I see why.

Anna, Jason, Tiegan, and Della are all there waiting for me.

"I hope it's okay," Anna says. She stands from the chair in front of her easel and hugs me. Guess I don't mind her hugs too much. "When Jason found out what you were doing, he just had to come." Something flashes across her face—a wave of fear, looks to me. "You don't . . . you don't get naked, do you? Oh my gosh, I should have thought of that."

"No, no." I pull at the sleeve of my flannel shirt. "Just the shirt. They convinced me to take my shirt off. In the name of art, you understand."

"Of course, of course. Oh, thank God. Not that you're not an attractive man, of course. I just don't know how Jason would handle it. He's not always, well, he's a little boy, you know?"

"I'm beginning to," I say.

Jason's already started plastering paint on the canvas stretched over his easel. Tiegan's next to him, frowning her disapproval. She's got her cap turned backward just like when she was hitting. A look of anticipation on her face.

"Mr. McBride!" comes a voice behind me. It's low and powerful, but somehow soft at the same time. "Great to see you. I was hoping you'd be back. It gets lonely up there all alone."

It's the Hands Man. I'm happy to see him, truth be told. But I've never been great at letting people know things like that. "I don't remember your name," I say, which is true, if not what I should have said.

"No worries. It's Collins. Collins Jackson. Just remember—two last names." He clasps my hand nice and firm.

"Eddie Collins, Reggie Jackson," I say.

"That'll work."

Well, this here's Mrs. Anna Cashman." It hits me right then that she probably doesn't go by that name anymore, considering the divorce and all.

"Anna Pierce," she says. "But just Anna. It's nice to meet you."

Jason's too busy smudging paint all over his canvas, but if he was here, even he might recognize the spark between these two. Anna's cheeks turn a little red and she's taken a sudden interest in her shoelaces. Collins hasn't been able to take his eyes off her since I introduced them. Della's been over talking to the crazy lady. They look like two peas in a pod with their colorful hair. But then the crazy lady pipes up and ruins the moment between Anna and Collins.

"Okay, artists. It's time to ejaculate every ounce of creativity from our souls."

Anna and Collins shift uncomfortably for a moment before Collins flicks his head to the front of the room. "Duty calls," he says. "I'll see you later?"

"Certainly."

Hands Man takes my elbow, which feels pretty good, to tell the truth. Like I can walk with confidence because if I stumble a bit, he'll be right there for me. For the last ten years Doc Keaton has been telling me to use a cane and I guess I see why, not that I'll ever admit it to him.

Collins escorts me to my chair and I sit as tall as I can. The crazy lady nods at me and I take my shirt off. Still got my undershirt though, so only my arms are showing. A loud snort comes from behind one of the easels, followed by smothered giggles and a loud "shush" from nearby. Collins sits in the next chair and folds his hands on the table in front of him.

"Again, I invite you to examine our subjects. On the left, look to the hands. Notice the lines, the pads, the old callouses from years of use."

I grunt a bit because I don't imagine Collins likes this woman scrutinizing his hands any more than I liked what she had to say about me last time. But he just winks and smiles.

"And to the right, we have our mature subject back again. Interesting, don't you think, that his shoulders seem straighter today. As I look closely, I see the mouth turned up ever so slightly, in contrast to last week. It's a fascinating look at how the human body is an ever-flowing river, an eagle gliding on the breeze, never stationary. What do you see? Anyone?"

"Hope," one student says.

"Anticipation," someone else says.

"Ancient history," Jason shouts, followed by another round of giggles.

"I invite you now to paint," the crazy woman says. "Be true to life, or paint what's in your soul. I leave these men in your capable hands."

Anna's brow is furrowed in focus. She sneaks glances toward the front of the room, but most of her attention is centered on the canvas in front of her. Della and Tiegan are both deep in concentration, but Jason's apparently done with his picture and is fiddling with some electronic device, probably playing that video game he likes so much. 'Course, I can't blame him. Between that game and learning all about the electronic letters, I'm becoming a regular techno man myself.

The hour goes a lot faster with my four friends in the room. Before I know it, the lights flick back off, the candles take over, and the crazy lady invites everyone to chant some stuff. When they're done, Collins walks with me to Tiegan's easel since she's throwing her hands around like she's starting the wave at a baseball stadium.

"What do you think, Mr. McBride? Do you like it?"

She holds up a pretty good depiction of me, but without most of the wrinkles and folds of skin hanging loose. Looks a lot like I did a good thirty years ago. "Well," I say. "That's a mighty nice picture you made there."

"It's beautiful," Della says, and kisses Tiegan's forehead.

"Dude, check this out," Jason says, and he holds up his picture.

"It's Mr. McBride," I say sternly, and his picture makes me snarl even more. It's a big pile of mud, near as I can tell.

"Get it?" he says. "Old as dirt?"

It should probably make me mad. But something about this kid—maybe the way his eyes light up the room. I know he doesn't mean anything bad by it. Just being a kid, that's what. A little boy, like Anna said. Usually, Anna would probably scold him for the stunt, but she's caught up talking to Collins again.

"What's yours like?" I ask Anna, when she starts studying her shoelaces again.

She holds the painting against her legs so no one can see, but Jason grabs it and flips it around. A pair of hands covers the canvas, clasped and strong and smooth. "I've never really been an artist," Anna says.

"It's beautiful," Collins says.

And anyone with half a brain could tell he's not talking about the painting.

To: jasoncashmanrules@aol.com
From: MurrayMcBride@aol.com
Subject: Your Wishes

Dear Jason,

First of all, a belated congratulations on fulfilling your first wish. Although it was a different sort of kiss than I had anticipated, I must say I'm proud of you. But since it happened different than I'd expected, I figure we ought to have a correspondence about your expectations for your upcoming wishes. Specifically, what do you mean by "Be a superhero"? Also, what kind of home run are you envisioning?

Thank you for your time.

Sincerely,
Mr. Murray McBride

To: MurrayMcBride@aol.com
From: jasoncashmanrules@aol.com
Subject: Re: Your Wishes

Mr. Murray Dude,

I "envision," if that really is a word, dropping a bomb. Straight-up laser shot over the scoreboard, or maybe onto Waveland Avenue (notice the punctuation? Studly). You know, crowd going crazy, maybe some fireworks. Basic stuff. As for a superhero, are you serious? You don't even know? Dude, superheroes jump from building to building, or scale the side of a skyscraper with their bare hands, or punch some bad guy right in the face and send him flying like twenty feet. But more than anything else, superheroes always save the damsel in distress. Always. That's, like, in every single superhero movie.

This is going to be so schweet.

J.

To: jasoncashmanrules@aol.com
From: MurrayMcBride@aol.com
Subject: Re: Your Wishes

Dear Jason,

First, and I've said this before, please address me as Mr. McBride. "Dude" is unnecessary and disrespectful. Second, I find myself questioning whether you know what a damsel in distress is.

Sincerely,
Mr. Murray McBride

To: MurrayMcBride@aol.com
From: jasoncashmanrules@aol.com
Subject: Re: Your Wishes

It's when the hot chick has most of her clothes ripped off and the bad guy is going to shoot her with a bazooka or chop her up with a lightsaber but he takes too long because he has to tell her the whole backstory and he says he's going to enjoy killing her and doesn't she wish she'd joined the dark side and they could be so good together if she'd just join him and she pretends like she might but actually she's buying time and then the superhero drops from the sky and kicks some serious butt. Duh.

CHAPTER 22

I've survived another art class. Went home and warmed up some ravioli while I emailed my young friend. I don't seem to want to do anything else but be with him, despite his crude language and his disrespect. When he's around, I could be sixty again, or thirty, or even a kid like him. It's not until I'm alone that I realize how old and worn down I am. So I'd rather not be alone.

After I sent him the letter clarifying his wishes, I stared at the screen for a long time. I couldn't help it—I sent another one, asking if it was okay with his mom if I came over. Just like a little boy might. As soon as he replied that it was, I started up the Chevy and skedaddled. Now I'm with him at Anna's house and the two of us are being kids again. Sitting on the couch, shoulder to shoulder, playing the video game with the God-awful name. It's not something I like to admit, but this here game is pretty entertaining. I especially like how he gets his whole body involved. He'll dip with his shoulders and dodge with his head, swinging the controller all over tarnation. Usually, anyhow. Today, he sits quiet. Focused on the game, I guess.

I'm having a hard time breathing, even though I remember taking my pill this morning. I guess it can't work forever. Modern medicine is more impressive than a Mickey Mantle home run, but it still has limits, I reckon. I set my controller down and use my hands to push my body up straight as I can. That usually makes it easier to breathe, but I can't seem to get quite enough oxygen this time. Enough to keep me going, but not enough to be comfortable. It's like there's a section of my lungs that doesn't want to work anymore. I try to take a deep breath—to really fill my lungs—but I can't quite get the air all the way in.

"Are you afraid to die?" Jason says.

That sure isn't what I was expecting. My character on the screen gets attacked by aliens and loses his brain. Although that's not too unusual. I try to figure out how to answer the question. Should probably tell him it's inevitable. Everyone will die someday. And when I die, I'll get to see Jenny and the boys again. Tell Jenny I've missed her so. Tell my boys I should have been a better father. Sounds pretty damn good to me. Nothing to be scared of.

"I am," Jason says. He seems extra focused on the video game, but his character isn't doing much.

"That's normal, seems to me. People can't understand it, see? We can't comprehend the end of time. Or infinity, for that matter. We're not meant to, I figure."

"Do you think it hurts?" he says.

Here I am thinking about the limitations of the human mind, and all he's thinking about is if it'll hurt. Well, you get to my age, and that's something you've considered a few times, too, I can tell you that much. But to talk about it with a ten-year-old boy . . . it just doesn't seem right. But I suppose he has a good reason. "I don't reckon it would be too bad."

"You mean you don't reckon it *will* be too bad." His eyes are sallow and his cheeks seem more gaunt than normal. Having a bad day, if I had to guess.

"Suppose so," I say.

"Why don't you think it'll hurt? It hurts just to get a cut or a scrape. I broke my arm when I fell off the monkey bars in second grade and that hurt so bad I couldn't breathe. Do you think dying hurts worse than a broken arm?"

He seems terrified by that thought, and I don't want to make it any worse. "I guess that probably depends on what you die from. Some things are worse than others, I figure."

"That's not what I mean."

"No?"

"No. You're talking about before you die. When you're sick or when you're almost going to die. I mean *when* you die. Like, the actual moment. The second it happens."

I put my controller down, but Jason refuses to look away from the television screen, so I pick it back up and start playing again. "I reckon it doesn't hurt. Not right then." I give a hard nod, like I'm sure of myself.

The building his character is working on falls over but Jason barely notices. "I bet it does. I bet it hurts worse than anything else in the whole world. That's why it's dying. If it didn't hurt, you wouldn't actually die."

"I think it'll be peaceful-like. Just like going to sleep, except you don't wake up, that's all."

Jason's eyes twitch, but he keeps staring at the screen. "I hope so." He heaves a giant sigh and looks at me for the first time. "I don't want it to hurt bad."

> **To:** jasoncashmanrules@aol.com, LittleLeague AllStar@hotmail.com
> **From:** MurrayMcBride@aol.com
> **Subject:** Plan B
>
> I've been a law-abiding citizen for a hundred years, see? Never had reason not to be, until now. But every once in a while something comes up that's even more important than following the law. Way I see it, this here's one of those times.

Jason's father doesn't want to let me take him into town this weekend. I plan to take him anyway.

Of course, only if you want to, Jason. If not, I understand. Probably better that way actually. But if you want to go, I'll take you. Figure we'll leave Friday night and stay in an apartment by the stadium, then go to Wrigley Field on Saturday. I'll take you home Saturday evening.

Tiegan, it's best if you don't come. You've got your whole life in front of you. No need to get in trouble with the law, and we just might. I can handle this on my own. Ask your mother to take you for a chocolate malt, or whatever kids do these days.

Jason, I just need to know if you'd like to do this. Please RSVP as soon as possible.

Sincerely,
Mr. Murray McBride

To: MurrayMcBride@aol.com, LittleLeagueAllStar@ hotmail.com
From: jasoncashmanrules@aol.com
Subject: Re: Plan B

This is so freakin' schweet! Think your car can outrun a cop? I hope we get to find out. And of course I want to do it, what a stupid question. You think I wanna go to ass-dad's house? LAME! Oh, sorry, they probably didn't say that "in your day." Gag me with a spoon or something then.

When you gonna pick me up? I'll pack my batting gloves and my best bubble gum.

Jason "Modern Day Hank Aaron" Cashman

To: MurrayMcBride@aol.com, jasoncashmanrules@
aol.com
From: LittleLeagueAllStar@hotmail.com
Subject: Re: Plan B

You're right, Mr. McBride. I shouldn't come. Besides,
I have a game at two o'clock against the Dynamite.
Thanks for understanding, and good luck, J. I know
you'll do great.

—T.R.M.A.

CHAPTER 23

The streets seem darker than normal. The Chevy's running a little louder. Every time I pass under a streetlight, I'm sure a police officer will see me in the driver's seat and know what I'm about to do. He'll arrest me as if I've already done it. Put me in the clink and I'll die a lonely old outlaw.

But that kid. He's all that matters now. I can't go back to before, when I had a date all picked out for my own death. And Jason can't go back to before either—hoping his heart will hold out until some unlucky schmuck kicks the can and gives him his. Who knows when that'll happen. Who knows if it'll happen.

No. Jason has to live. And he has to live now. While he can.

I pull into the parking lot of St. Joseph's. First time I've done this in a few decades. I've only ever walked to church. The doors are open, but the church is dark. Pitch dark. Then my eyes adjust a little and there's some light coming from a corner. I start toward it but have to stop after just a few pews. It's my knee again. Been acting up more than normal lately, but I guess that's part of the gig.

Halfway to the lights I realize what they are. Candles. A whole cluster of them, each one representing somebody's prayer. Somebody's wish. Only about six are lit, the rest sit there waiting for someone to say a prayer. Well I'm just the fella for it.

There's a matchbox sitting by a kneeler. I have to fiddle with the box for a bit, but eventually I get a match out and light it on my very first strike. I ignore the kneeler though. The Good Lord'll give me a pass on that, I reckon.

"For Jason's wishes," I say out loud to the candles. My voice echoes through the empty church. "And that the police don't catch us before he hits a home run."

"Now why would you have to worry about the police catching you?" says a voice behind me.

I turn around too fast and wince at the ache in my knee. There's Father James, a little smile on his face, but also looking genuinely confused. Can't say I blame him. A priest doesn't expect an old-timer like me to go afoul of the law.

"It's Jason, see? I need to take him to town for one of his wishes, but his father's set against it."

Father James's eyebrows sure do go high up on his forehead. "And?"

"Well. I mean to take him, anyhow."

"To kidnap him, you mean?"

"That seems a bit too harsh a word."

"I doubt the authorities would agree." He turns his back on me and walks to the nearest pew, where he sits and waits for me to join him. He has to wait a good, long while, but I make it there.

"And his mother?" Father says. "Have you asked her?"

"Best if she stays out of it, the way I see it. Last thing she needs is trouble. I'll leave a note so she doesn't worry."

"Murray, you can't do this. We have laws for a reason. They're important."

"You think it's more important to give a dying boy back to his father who cares nothing for him instead of making his innocent wishes come true before he dies? Because of the law? That's what you think?"

"Murray, I understand. Really, I do. But that's not the world we live in."

"I don't care about the world we live in. I don't have much time left in it anyhow." He sighs at that, but doesn't argue. The whole world knows that's true. "Look, Father, I've never told you this, but I'm not blessed with the faith you think I have. Truth is, I don't know much about God, for a fact. But I do know this. There is someone upstairs. And if he's worth a lick, he wants Jason's wishes to come true."

Father James looks at me real close-like. "You know this could turn out badly. A man your age, doing a thing like this. It's risky, Murray. Really risky."

"What's life without a little risk?" I say. "Besides, when was the last time I took a risk? Thirty years ago? Forty? I've been sitting around taking up space for too long. It's high time I do something with this life God gave me. He's kept me here for a reason, when everyone else I know is dead and buried. I think this is it. This is why the Good Lord has let me live so long."

Father James gives me another piercing stare. I think he's trying to see straight down into my soul. Then he shakes his head and looks up at the big crucifix in front.

"You know Murray, this is going to cost you a whole lot of Hail Marys."

CHAPTER 24

Back in the car now. The dark. The feeling of danger and risk. I know it has a name but can't quite put my finger on it. It's a feeling of something new. Butterflies in my old stomach. And then, finally, I place it. Youth. Just what Doc Keaton was talking about. Somehow, not knowing what will happen next—and knowing that some outcomes would be very bad—makes me feel young again.

Part of me wants to drive around in circles, enjoying the sensation all night. But I can't leave Jason out to dry like that and besides, it wouldn't work. That's the thing about youth. It's always moving. The best way to miss it is to sit around and watch it pass by. Or try to grab it on the way by. If you want to experience it, you have to live. You have to do.

So I do. I pull the Chevy around back of Anna's house and hit the lights. It's hard enough to see anything with headlights; without them, it's like I just walked into a cave fifty feet underground. I can't see two feet in front of the car, so I hit the brakes and cringe a bit when the wheels squeak. Should have worn my seat belt, too, but I'm still not in the habit. I turn the key and the rumble of the engine goes quiet.

I'm a good half-block away from the house, but I can't risk starting up the car again and turning on the lights. A dark car in the middle of the road is suspicious enough. But as long as no one looks out their window for the next few minutes, I reckon we'll be okay.

Something in the corner of my vision gets my attention right-quick. A streak of movement, although I'm too late to see what, exactly. Raccoon, maybe. But it looked big enough to be a deer, too. Both nocturnal animals, which reminds me it's almost midnight.

Never realized how squeaky the Chevy doors are until I need them to be quiet. But they screech and scream in the still night, so loud the streetlight down the road practically shakes. I move my leg a bit, trying to get the knots out, and head on up the road. I make it about two houses before I hear a sound like a tire losing air.

"Psssst."

I stop and listen, but if I did hear anything it was awful quiet, so I write it off as more proof that Doc Keaton was right when he recommended hearing aids. At the time, I told him those were for old fogies, but now I'm not so sure.

"Psssst."

There it is again. The noise. I look into the bushes in front of the nearest house, right next to Jason's. Nothing there, so I press on.

"Psssst. Psssst. Psssssssssssst!!! Dude, come *on!*"

Jason hobbles out from behind the very same bushes I'd been looking at. In one arm, he's got a suitcase as big as him and must weigh twice as much, the way he's struggling with it. In his other arm, cords dangle from a boxy object that can only be his video game machine. He's kicking the oxygen cart beside him with each step.

"Don't you know what *Pssst* means?" he says. "Is that some newfangled word they didn't have back in your day? I mean, seriously. You can't hear for sh—"

"Hey now," I say, interrupting him. "I would've understood just fine if you would have spoken up a bit. Making noises in the bushes . . . lucky no one's called the police on you."

It must be past his bedtime, the way he's behaving. Like a child having a temper tantrum. Guess I'm not doing much better, though.

"What-evs," he says. "Can you just help me get this stuff in the car before Mom hears?"

"What'd you go and pack so heavy for? We're only going to be gone for one night, see?"

"See what? You always say that. It doesn't make any sense."

"Look here," I say. But that isn't much different than *see*, now that I think of it. "You can take your things to the car. Take responsibility for your decisions. I have to go leave this here note for your mother."

Jason's voice gets very high and sounds nothing like mine. "*I have to go leave this here note for your mother. God!*"

He limps toward the Chevy, heaving his suitcase, kicking his oxygen cart, then shuffling forward a step. I start toward the house but after a few paces, I hear a clamor behind me—sounds an awful lot like a video game machine against blacktop if I had to wager a guess—and Jason has some choice words under his breath. Might have to have a little chat about his language soon.

I finally make it to Anna's house and start through the yard. My shoes are soaked with dew by the time I reach the back door. I don't want to wake her, so I wedge the note inside the screen door and hobble back toward the Chevy. It's not much, leaving a note telling a woman you stole her boy, but it makes clear to anybody who reads it that she had nothing to do with it, and that's the point. Besides, something tells me she'd be okay with what I'm doing here, lawful or not.

Jason's face is scrunched up in a look I recognize from my own boys, although only once or twice. Crabbiest face you've ever seen. Says something about his character that he keeps his mouth shut. I try to do the same, but can't do it.

"Didn't have to pack the kitchen sink," I say under my breath.

He shakes his head like it's the dumbest thing he's ever heard. "Why would *anyone* pack a kitchen sink? I mean seriously, how could you even get it in a suitcase?"

"It's an expression. Means you packed more than—"

"You couldn't even get it out of the kitchen! What, are you just supposed to pick it up?!"

There's a little shuffling in the back seat by Jason's suitcase, which seems just about impossible. I can't twist my head around very far these days, but in the rearview mirror, Tiegan Rose Marie Atherton's face is poking through a small hole between my little duffel bag and Jason's giant suitcase.

"Will you two be quiet? You're going to get us caught."

CHAPTER 25

Can't honestly say I was expecting that one. Tiegan in my back seat, I mean. I was pretty clear in my letter that she shouldn't come, and she sure seemed to agree with me on that point, if I remember correctly.

"What on God's green earth are you doing here?" I say.

"Schweet!" Jason says.

Tiegan just shrugs. "I obviously couldn't say I was coming with you, in case my mom checked my email. But did you really think I'd miss this?"

"I certainly did. What about your Little League game? What if we get caught? What if you go to jail?"

Tiegan waves it away with a flick of her wrist. "We're playing the Dynamite and they aren't any good. But Mr. McBride? We probably shouldn't sit here in the middle of the street, you know? We're not exactly inconspicuous."

Not sure what I think of a little girl using words I don't know, but I get the feeling every time I see her that she's more than meets the eye. A line-drive-hitting dictionary? Not your typical kid, that much even an old-timer like me can figure out.

I fiddle with the keys but it's dark as night out here. 'Course, it *is* night. The middle of the night. After a few seconds of scraping the key against the dashboard, Jason starts giggling. He's sure in a better mood since Tiegan arrived. I push the key harder, trying to find the ignition, but no dice. Jason's belly-laughing now and even Tiegan seems to be having a hard time holding it in. "I think it's a little to the left, Mr. McBride," Tiegan says, and sure enough, as soon as I move it left a bit I find the right spot.

I ignore Jason's bellowing laughs—so much for trying to keep a low profile—and start the car. A few moments later I pull the Chevy around the corner, just as a porch light flips on in the house we were sitting in front of. But they're too late. I weave my way through residential streets until Jason's neighborhood disappears from the rearview mirror.

Next stop, the Windy City.

CHAPTER 26

You'd think we were going to Disney World, the way Jason's acting. He wants to stop at every gas station to buy snacks and look for souvenirs, which actually works out pretty well for me considering I'm dealing with a one-hundred-year-old bladder. The first stop is on Glenview Road, before we even start to circle around Harms Woods. It's a nice new Shell station where he picks up a brightly colored drink of some sort and a hot dog—plain with no condiments at all—and two big Three Musketeers candy bars. The whole time Tiegan shakes her head at him from behind the display of overripe bananas, obviously disapproving of his midnight snack.

We make one more stop before we get to Old Orchard Road, but it turns out to be a waste of time because the convenience store and restrooms are closed. I roll right past the Interstate, which makes Jason choke on his drink.

"You missed the turn to Chicago," he says.

But I'll be damned if I'm going anywhere near a road where cars move so fast. It's twenty miles from my house to Wrigley Field, and usually takes about forty minutes. But not with me at the wheel. Not with kids in the car. More like an hour and a half for us, even though it's the middle of the night and there aren't many other cars around.

"I searched you on Yahoo last night, Mr. McBride," Tiegan says from the back seat as I pull onto Lemon Grove Boulevard and head south.

"Yahoo?"

"Yeah," she says. "It's a search website. On the internet."

"The internet?"

"Duh," Jason says. "The internet. Online. The World Wide Web." He stuffs the last of his hot dog into his mouth and talks around it while he opens a candy bar. "You can find anything."

"Like an encyclopedia?" I ask.

"A what?" Jason says.

"Pretty much," Tiegan says. "But, like, every encyclopedia ever written. And you can search for things. I learned last night that your best Major League season was in 1923. You batted .289 with sixteen home runs and sixty-three RBI."

"I did?" I know my statistics are around somewhere, but for the life of me I can't figure how this little girl found them on her computer last night.

The glare of the streetlamps is starting to make my eyes hurt, and they're drying out from keeping them open so wide. I slow down to a steady fifteen miles per hour.

"Ooh, gas station," Jason says as we pass a Chevron. "Turn around, I gotta pee."

"Again?" I say, but the truth is I could use the restroom again myself.

Turns out this station is rundown and has its bathrooms around back. I avoid the facilities on principle and Jason convinces me to buy him another bright orange drink called Gatorade and a T-shirt. Says *Kiss Me I'm Irish* or some such thing. Not sure if he's playing a joke on me or not.

When we finally get back in the car, I'm able to make some pretty decent time through Lincolnwood and North Park. I consult a scrap piece of paper with the address for the apartment the Cubs rented for the night, just for us. We're only about three miles from it, near as I can tell, when we hit a traffic jam.

A traffic jam long after midnight, if you can believe that. Road work or some such thing. Tiegan tells me I should go around it, but this town's changed a lot since I spent any time here and I don't want to get us lost. Graceland Cemetery is on the left, so I can't go that way. And I don't want to go right because I know that's the opposite direction from the apartment. Last thing I need is to be driving around in the middle of the night and end up in Elmwood Park.

So we sit, move a few feet forward, then sit some more. It goes on like that for a good long while. Finally, after about a half hour of it, Jason's head drops against the window and fatigue overtakes all the sugar he's eaten since we left home.

"Sure is a cute kid, isn't he?" Tiegan says, as if she's a full-grown adult.

"Sometimes." That one gets a laugh out of her. People these days always think I'm cracking jokes when I'm not. "How come you're so keen on him?"

Something crosses her face that I can't quite put a finger on, but it's intense, I know that much. Powerful. She's feeling something fierce in that head of hers, and I give her plenty of time, but she just shakes her head like she's trying to throw a thought right out of it.

"I've known him all my life. I just want to help him out, that's all. Anything wrong with that?"

"'Course there's nothing wrong with it. That's what I'm doing, too."

"And why are you doing it, Mr. McBride?" she asks. "Why are you so keen on him?"

I see what's going on here. She won't answer my question, then asks me the same thing? She's avoiding it. But if she won't tell me, I figure that's her right. "Guess I wanted to be surrounded by youth, like Doc Keaton said. If I'd known I was going to get messed up with this kid, I would've stayed home and ate my Chef Boyardee. That's what I would've done."

"No you wouldn't have," Tiegan says.

"Oh? And how do you know that?"

We come up to a construction worker holding a sign that says *Stop*. He gives me a look like he can't understand why I'd sit still on this road instead of turning to find another route. But I put the Chevy in park and wait.

"It's easy to see," Tiegan says. "You look at him like a belt-high fastball on a 3–1 count."

"How's that?"

"You know. Like there's nothing you'd rather see. Like it's the very best thing in the world."

How do you like that? A kid girl talking in baseball analogies. The kid's as rare as a triple play. The Chevy starts squealing something fierce and it takes me a moment to realize I've got my foot on the gas, which doesn't work so well when it's in Park. I ease my foot off and stifle a yawn. Next to me, the lights from the dashboard radio glow off Jason's cheek like a heavenly beam.

"What's the plan for tomorrow?" Tiegan asks.

"Supposed to be at the ballpark about four p.m. Figure we'll stay in the apartment during the day. Keep a low profile, see?"

I smother another yawn and she pulls on her pigtails. "You okay, Mr. McBride?"

"'Course I am," I say. "Just a little tired, that's all." Last time I stayed up past nine o'clock was a good year and a half ago. At that point, I was still crying so hard every night I couldn't possibly sleep. Although sometimes I was punching chairs and kicking tables instead of crying. Don't need to tell the girl that, of course.

"We should keep talking," Tiegan says. "That's what my mom says to do when she's tired of driving. Talking keeps her awake."

"Okay then," I say, but I can't think of what to talk about. After a few moments I say, "Your mother seems like a real nice person. She sure does love you."

"I know," Tiegan says. "Sometimes I get made fun of because of her, but I don't mind too much."

"You get made fun of? Who makes fun of you?" I know my blood pressure's rising because my breathing gets all quick and shallow. If I was a younger man, I'd go find whoever's making fun of Tiegan and Della and teach them a lesson or two.

"Just kids from school. And I get it, I guess. My mom's not like most people. Look at her hair, look at how much she hugs me and stuff. And SBK? It's weird."

"A person ought not to call her mother weird."

"Oh no, you don't understand. I don't mind. I love her exactly how she is. She's my mom. Other kids just don't understand. But someday they will."

I wonder if I should be embarrassed that a ten-year-old girl has more perspective and understanding than I do, but I decide if that ten-year-old is Tiegan Rose Marie Atherton, then I'm not embarrassed one lick.

Out on the road, the worker flips his sign to *Slow*, as if I'd consider any other speed. Then the construction eases up and we're alone on the road. We're close to the apartment and I feel sleep coming on right quick, but Tiegan's knees bounce like the car can barely contain her. Here she is, a kid taking a chance. Going on an adventure. Breaking the law, even. All for the sake of her friend and neighbor boy. Her gaze stays out the window. She doesn't look at me when her voice breaks the hum of the Chevy's engine.

"Mr. McBride?"

"Hmm?"

"I'm really glad you're here."

She catches my eye in the rearview and gives me a smile. Jason would be one lucky lad to know how much he means to her. I try to match the smile, but the Good Lord knows I could never look so innocent and beautiful.

"I'm glad you're here, too, kid," I say. "I'm glad you're here, too."

CHAPTER 27

When I wake up, the sun is streaming through thin curtains and birds are chirping through an open window. A breeze gives the room a little chill, but I'm in a bed, under some warm covers. I'm not sure how that could've happened, but then it comes back. Finding the address. Tiegan getting the keys from under the welcome mat. A nice big apartment with two bedrooms, a kitchen and a dining room, just two blocks from the stadium. I rub some crust out of my eyes and realize I slept through the night. First time that's happened in years.

Things hurt worst first thing in the morning. It's like death senses an opportunity—an old man lying down, eyes closed, breathing slowly. Like most of his job is already done for him and all he has to do is lower the final blow. Next thing you know, I'll be floating up to St. Peter's gate. Except I keep cheating death, one way or another. So each morning I wake up, feeling like death got a little closer than the last time, and I have to work a little more to get life back into my arms and legs, my eyelids and toes. Takes a while, too. Longer each morning, seems to me.

When I finally walk out of the bedroom, Tiegan is bustling all around. She has the kitchen looking and smelling like a breakfast diner. Looks like she raided the kitchenette because there're more blueberry muffins and waffles than I've seen in a good long time. But that's not all. She's got four containers of yogurt—each a different flavor, I see—a bowl of some bright-colored cereal, and six Styrofoam cups, three each of coffee and orange juice. The Cubs really went all-out in supplying this place. It's like a regular home.

"Good morning, Mr. McBride," Tiegan says in a voice entirely too chippy for the early hour. She's already sporting her cap and Little League uniform. She looks through the open door of the bedroom I just exited. Inside, a small form lies completely still under a pile of blankets. I hadn't even noticed. Probably just about tripped over him. "We might have to wake him up," Tiegan says. "Boys can be so lazy sometimes, can't they?"

I rub my face and look around the rest of the room. "Where'd you sleep?"

"Just over there," Tiegan says, pointing back into the room at a thin strip of floor near the base of the bed. A fluffy blanket is indented in the shape of a body, and there's a sheet and pillow down there, too. Apparently, we had a big old slumber party last night. "I guess I wanted to be close," she says. "New places can scare me. You should try a waffle. They're super good. You don't think I could do anything bad to his heart if I wake him up, do you?"

Before I can answer, a ringing sound fills the air and Tiegan runs to the kitchen counter. She picks up a telephone that looks like the one Benedict Cashman had to his ear and I realize it wasn't a toy after all. "You have a cordless telephone?" I say.

"It's my mom's," she says, staring at the screen. "She just got it. I left a note saying I was taking it and when I'd be home, but I'm sure she's worried. Should I answer it?"

I'm not sure what to tell her. Never been in this kind of situation before. If she answers it, she'll have to talk to her mother, who'll certainly ask where she is. She'll probably get in her car right quick and drive straight here. But if Tiegan doesn't answer, her mother will worry herself sick—note or no note. This here's a ten-year-old kid we're talking about.

Before I can figure what to tell her, the phone stops ringing and our decision has been made. "Maybe I'll call her later," she says. "So she won't worry, but also won't have time to get here before J hits his home run."

We stare at each other for a while, then Tiegan holds a button and the phone shuts off. Since I'm not sure what to do or say, I make my way to the table and take a seat. I'm two bites into a syrupy waffle—she's right, they are tasty—when I hear a whining voice, muffled by blankets and pillows.

"Leave me alone! I want to sleep!"

"You've slept all night. You can't hit a home run if you're unconscious. Of if you can't get rid of that hole in your swing, but that's another matter."

Quicker than a snap, Jason bolts upright, his hair flying in every conceivable direction. "It's morning? Are we in Chicago?"

"Follow me," Tiegan says, and she looks at me. "You too, Mr. McBride." She leads us out of the kitchen and up a little flight of stairs. At the top, it opens to a balcony directly below the El. A train comes by just then and rattles the fake teeth in my head. Jason puts his hands against his ears and cringes like he can't handle the pain.

"What the . . ." he says, when the rattling finally stops. I'm impressed by his restraint, to tell the truth. Not long ago, that would have ended with a cuss word. "What'd you bring us up here for? To blow out our eardrums?"

"No, crabby face. Look."

She goes to the corner of the balcony and cranes her head around the side of the building. When she leans back, her pigtails frame the biggest smile you can imagine. Jason and I lean around the building together and I see what all the fuss is about. The lights of Wrigley Field tower over everything. The grandstand, the lime-green grass, the flagpoles flapping in the breeze. It's all right there. For one brief, fleeting moment, I feel twenty-five again. Like I could take a ninety-mile-an-hour fastball, shoot it into the left-center field gap, and fly into second base with a hook-slide.

"I am so going to crush it," Jason says, which makes Tiegan giggle. She was in Old Lady Willamette's garden, too.

"Not without a good breakfast," I say, and we file back into the kitchen and the waiting waffles.

Jason takes my words seriously. He stuffs muffins and waffles into his mouth with so much zest I don't have the heart to tell him to chew with his mouth closed. Or to hold his fork properly. Or to use a napkin instead of his pajama sleeves. Geez, this kid. Eventually, he leans back in his chair and rests his hands on his bulging stomach. Takes a couple good pulls from his oxygen mask since he barely stopped shoveling food into his mouth long enough to breathe. A few seconds later, I almost jump out of my seat, startled at the loudest belch I've heard since my ball playing days.

Jason beams like it's his proudest moment, but then he sees my glare and says, "Excuse me," a little sheepishly. Just then, his eyes go vacant for a few moments. Empty-like. He presses the mask against his face and breathes heavily, but it doesn't seem to help. A deep crinkle forms in his brow, like he's confused at what's happening. I think maybe he's going to keel over right here.

Tiegan and I stare at him but neither of us knows what to do but wait. Another train rattles overhead, matching the chaos in my mind. But then whatever it is passes and Jason sits up straighter again, but still not as chipper as before. We all stare at each other over the sweet smell of waffles. "I forgot something in the car," he says.

He snags my car keys from the counter and waddles out the front door as if he hadn't almost died just now. I keep an eye on him out the window, but he does just fine. Unlocks the doors, opens the back one, then sticks his little rear end in the air while he digs around. He finally comes out with his video game machine in his arms and cords dangling down by his feet. As soon as he gets back inside, he hooks it up wordlessly. I watch in amazement. Got no idea how he knows which cord goes where, or what to push on the remote controller for the television. But somehow he gets the game up and running smooth as a brand-new Chevy.

We play for a good long time, with Tiegan watching every move. Jason has us playing against each other now, trying to build our "sustainable community" before the other, all while avoiding the aliens. Jason's fingers move so fast on his controller I can't tell what exactly he's doing, but before I know it he's got a nice-looking castle and his character is shooting at the alien spaceship. After a few minutes of it, the spaceship falls to the earth and Jason jumps up from his perch on the couch. He whoops and hollers and if I didn't know better, I'd say his heart is just fine. He stuffs an entire blueberry muffin into his mouth and tries to talk around it.

"You're getting better, really," he says. "I mean, you can't expect to be able to compete with the master. But you don't suck as bad."

"You could be a more gracious winner, you know," I say. "It's an important thing to know, to win with grace. And to lose with dignity, too."

"Dude, you use the weirdest words."

"You should listen to Mr. McBride," Tiegan says. "No one's going to want to play with you if you're a sore loser. Or if you're a jerk when you win."

"I'm not a jerk. I told him he doesn't suck as bad."

Tiegan shakes her head at him. I'm glad to have the girl along for the ride. She's got some sense, this one. "If you lose, you should shake hands and say good game," she says. "Maybe even congratulate your opponent on their win. And if you win, you should shake hands and say good game, and tell your opponent they played well."

Jason seems to study my hands on the controller. "But what if he didn't play well? I'm supposed to lie?"

"You're supposed to show a little respect," I say, although I don't intend my voice to be so sharp. "To be a mature person."

Jason looks like I just tried to teach him college-level philosophy. "But I'm not a mature person. I'm ten."

It's true, I suppose. Although I'm not sure it's any excuse. Jason restarts the game and stuffs another muffin in his mouth. "Hey, Tiegan," he says. "Don't you need to take a shower or something?"

Tiegan stands over him with her hands on her hips. "Excuse me?" she says.

"What, has this dude been teaching you how to talk?"

Tiegan doesn't move. Doesn't say a word. Just towers over him like she's his big sister, even though they're the same age. Wouldn't guess it by the size of him, though. After a few seconds getting more and more uncomfortable, Jason says in a small voice, "Can I have some time to talk to the old guy? Please."

"Of course," Tiegan says. As soon as the bathroom door shuts behind her, Jason looks straight at the television set in a way I recognize, and I wonder what he's going to ask me next.

CHAPTER 28

"Have you ever seen anyone die?"

I keep my eyes straight ahead. On the game. "Sure have."

"Who?"

"My two boys, to start with." I sniffle a bit and am still surprised all this time later that it can come on so quick, when it comes to Jenny and the boys. But I don't mind doing that in front of Jason. Not anymore.

"That must've really sucked."

"Worst days of my life," I say. "Those and when Jenny died. But none of them was unexpected. Unexpected always makes it worse. My boys were seventy-two and seventy-four when they died. Jenny was ninety-nine. Had some long, full lives. The unusual thing wasn't them dying, it was me living. And when the boys passed, I had Jenny, so we leaned on each other."

From the corner of my eye, Jason seems to be struggling with something. "But if you had died before . . . you, like, wouldn't be here with me now."

He's having a hard time with that idea, and I can't blame him. When a man's right in front of you, the thought of him not being there, and all the things that would be different if he wasn't . . . well, it's too much for a one-hundred-year-old mind, much less a ten-year-old one.

"How many?" Jason says.

"How many what?"

"People. How many people have you seen die?"

"Well. More than I can count on my fingers and toes by now. I'm old, see? Older than most."

"What's it like?"

"Watching someone die?"

A small nod. But no eye contact. I'd like to sugarcoat the best I can. Make the kid feel good. But somehow I feel like it's better to be honest about it.

"Someone dies—someone you love, now—it's like they take a little piece of you with them when they leave. Like you lose a little part of yourself the moment they stop breathing." I can't get myself to think of how much of myself I'll lose if I have to watch this here boy pass on. Don't want to either. After my boys and Jenny, I don't reckon there's enough left of me to witness an injustice like that.

"Is it really sad?" he asks. "When it happens, I mean?"

"Hurts like hell. Only different. Not physical, of course."

He's quiet for a long while now. Playing his video game but only partly paying attention. When he shoots down the alien spaceship, he whispers, "Yeah, baby. Better say your prayers." Normally he would have yelled it.

Out the window, a young family of four piles into a minivan and drives off to wherever they're off to. Vacation, maybe. Or visiting family. Maybe just the grocery. I can't understand why they get to do that. Why Jason can't have that kind of life. It seems so random. It's unfair, that's what.

"I want to plan my funeral," Jason says. "So it's not super lame."

"Don't you talk like that. You're not going to die."

"I could, you know. I'm supposed to. Soon."

"Who told you that?"

A small shrug. "Doctors."

Not sure they should be telling him that. Seems to me they should be filling him with hope. Unless there isn't any. "Well, they're just trying to make sure you enjoy every moment. Just in case."

"Yeah? Then they're stupid idiots. 'Cause it's not so easy to enjoy things when you think you might die."

I should scold him for saying such a thing about doctors, but I can't get myself to do it. If I read that doctor I saw in the hospital right, Jason might not have much of a chance. Maybe he should be planning his funeral. But I don't see how anyone could give up. Not on a kid like this.

Tiegan steps out of the bathroom with her hair already in pigtails, and a strong smell of strawberries fills the room.

On the television set, the alien spaceship is back, and both our characters start to shoot. But it doesn't seem to matter. The aliens drop a bomb on us and the game comes to a quick end. One of those times Jason mentioned the first time he told me about the game—*every once in a while they just blast you for no reason, even though you didn't do anything wrong.*

CHAPTER 29

Just about the time we're all packed up and ready to walk to the ballpark, a big thunderhead rolls in from the west. Lightning bolts flash in the sky and the clouds open up. It's a torrential downpour, that's what. The telephone on the wall rings and a gentlemen from the Cubs is on the other end. He says they have the tarp on the field and we can't use it like planned. He apologizes about a half-dozen times and assures me we can use the field tomorrow, even though the Cubs have a game that night. As long as we're done by five o'clock so the players can start batting practice on time, and as long as the field is in good enough condition after all the rain. I thank him and break the news to Jason and Tiegan.

Jason had started playing the video game and tosses his controller onto the couch. Then he punches the pillow next to him several times. None of us can stay cooped up in this apartment all day. Jason will just mope. Tiegan strikes me as the kind of girl that needs to be active. And I'm in town for the first time in more years than I can count.

"Maybe we should walk around the ballpark," I say. Tiegan squeals in delight, but Jason's still upset about the delay in trying for his home run. "Or we could ride the train," I say.

If you've ever seen one of those old cartoons with the cat getting electrocuted, you've got a pretty good idea of Jason's reaction. You'd think *Ride a train* would've been on his list, the way he jumps up. He's as excited as a rookie in his first at-bat.

It's been way too long for me to remember any routes, but I figure we'll just hop on, ride it to the end of the line, then ride

back. Fortunately, there's a station less than a block away from
the apartment.

We grab our raincoats, which all of us managed to remember
to pack, and find an umbrella in a closet. Just the feel of walking
the streets hits me hard. The smells from a corner bakery, the
rumble of the El shaking the ground every few minutes—even the
feel of the air on my skin is different. It's like we're a world away
from Lemon Grove.

At the El station, I try to find a ticket seller, but there doesn't
seem to be one. Just machines every few feet with confusing slots
and nonsense words. After a couple minutes of staring at one of
the machines, I realize there's a place to use a credit card, but I've
never had one of those. Just old fashioned greenbacks and coins.
There's a bank of turnstiles a ways beyond the ticket machine, and
people seem to be swiping something before they pass through.

"You two know how to use this thing?" I ask.

"Mom took me downtown once," Tiegan says, and she starts
reading the ticket machine. "We went to the Skydeck and the
aquarium. All the touristy stuff. I think we just . . . yeah, can I have
the money, Mr. McBride?"

I pull some cash from my jacket pocket. Don't really know
how much to give her so I just hold it all out. She slips a five-dollar
bill out and I replace the rest. A few minutes later, she hands us
each a ticket and we sweep through the turnstile. It's a bit tricky
getting Jason's oxygen up the concrete steps, but we take turns
lifting it a couple stairs at a time. Finally, we make it to the plat-
form and hop on the Red Line.

The rumble of the train, the screech against the tracks, even
the neighborhoods as we pass through Chicago, they all take me
back to my youth. Fifteen years I played baseball in this city. Fifteen years of riding the El and looking at that beautiful lake and

playing the game I loved in the Friendly Confines. What I wouldn't give to be a young man again, just for one glorious day.

There are all sorts on the train. Spiffy businessmen, with their suits and ties. Families, with parents who're overly friendly with us, all the while giving us sideways glances like they can't quite figure us out. And sadly, plenty of homeless folk, too, begging for money.

Tiegan's just as wrapped up in the ride as I am but Jason won't sit down. He grabs the nearest pole and climbs it, then when I tell him to quit doing that, he pokes his head under his seat to have a look around. I grab his oxygen cart so it doesn't roll away, since he's not paying it any attention. The kid just can't sit still. In desperation, I look to Tiegan, who rolls her eyes in a gesture that pretty much sums up my own feelings.

When we get to the end of the line, Jason spins through the exit turnstile like he's dancing in the rain. Doesn't listen a lick when I call him back either. Thankfully, Tiegan runs and catches him. Brings him back looking a little sheepish, but mostly still wide-eyed. Somehow, I ended up with his oxygen. I consider giving it back to him, but it's actually pretty nice to use as support. Jason doesn't seem to mind my having it, so I just keep it.

The rain's let up, but it's still coming down so we escape into one of those corner bakeries and I order a muffin and a coffee, black. Tiegan has an orange juice and an apple, and Jason has two cinnamon rolls and a tall glass of milk. He tried to order five cinnamon rolls, but I told him two was plenty. I peel a twenty-dollar bill out of my billfold and count what I've got left. Three more twenties is all. Enough for dinner tonight since it's a pretty special occasion and all, and gas on the way home. We'll have to figure on breakfast and lunch at the apartment.

Out of the blue, I think maybe I should have given Anna some way to get in touch with us. Tiegan has her mother's cordless telephone, of course, but if I'd given Anna a phone number or something, I'd feel better about things. I hope she's not worrying too much about Jason. In her absence, I figure I should try to be as fatherly as possible, so when I notice sugar coating his lips, I pull a handkerchief from my pocket and wipe at his face, but he swivels his head away.

"That's disgusting! You probably blew your nose all over that thing."

"It's my clean one," I say. "Think I'd use my nose handkerchief on your face?" But he doesn't seem to believe me. He wipes his mouth with his sleeve, which I guess is better than nothing. We finish our food and soon it's time to head on back.

My eyes are heavy on the train. I try to keep them open, seeing as how I'm responsible for these here kids, but my blinking's as slow as a hanging curveball, and next thing I know, Tiegan's tapping my shoulder because it's our stop. Guess I can't be completely certain who's responsible for who here. I startle when I realize I don't have Jason's oxygen, but he's got it. Right next to me, breathing deeply from the mask.

I suggest we head back and nap for a while before suppertime, but Jason isn't too fond of that idea. Even though he just had those cinnamon rolls at the bakery, he says he's so hungry he's about to faint. So we make our way down Waveland Avenue toward the ballpark, looking in the windows of restaurants as we walk. There are a whole lot of gin mills and clip joints that I don't want to take the little ones into. When I finally find a good family-friendly Mexican place, I reckon we've found a place to eat. Need to rest my legs soon anyhow.

But just inside the door, there's a newspaper lying on a counter, open to the local section. What I see in the lower right-hand corner of the page makes my old heart really start thumping. Right there, plain as day, are pictures of Jason and Tiegan under a head-line that says MISSING.

I know right off the bat that this is Jason's father's doing, which lights a little fire in my belly. He could have waited for us to return before he caused a stink, or even called Anna and talked to her about it—she and Tiegan's mom both know the kids are with me. Instead, he either went straight to the authorities or straight to the press. Either one seems unnecessary, at least in my mind.

Tiegan sees me staring at the newspaper and when she real-izes what I'm looking at, her eyes go wide. Jason's too, but for a different reason. He can barely get his words out through his laughter. "That. Is. Awesome!"

"I think we'd better get back to the apartment before anyone sees us," I say. "Order in tonight."

I give Jason his oxygen so I can take their hands and lead them back outside, then steer us toward our place. We're almost there when a voice stops us cold.

"Look at this," it says, and even though I turn to see a group of four boys, maybe twelve years old, it takes several moments to realize we're not about to go to jail. "It's Ted Williams," one of the boys says.

Another boy steps close to Tiegan—too close. "No it's not. It's David Ortiz."

Tiegan looks cute as a button in her baseball getup. These boys have no business picking on a harmless girl like this. They're bullies, that's what.

"In case you don't know," the first boy says, "girls can't play baseball."

"That's why they have softballs. If girls want to be able to hit, they have to use a bigger ball."

"Now see here," I say. "You shouldn't talk to her that way. Besides, this young lady could hit circles around any of you."

I'm pretty upset at these here lads. To think they'd go out of their way to pick on an innocent little girl like this. A girl who didn't do anything to them. It's disgusting, that's what. Makes me wonder what they're teaching kids in school these days. Jason's upset, too, I can tell. He's right by my side, punching his palm with his fist.

The boys have a good laugh, and I'm not sure if it's because of what Jason's doing or if they're laughing at what the old man said. I try to put my hand on Jason's and Tiegan's shoulders to steer them away from the boys, when one of the boys says, "That's right. Run on home with your little boyfriend."

I try to hold him back, but Jason pulls free. Next thing I know, he steps right up to the biggest of the four boys, who towers over him, twice his size. But Jason says, "You'll regret that, creep bag!" and punches the boy right in the crotch.

He must have hit him square, too, because the boy grunts and bends over double. My first thought is that this could turn ugly in a hurry, and I'm in no condition to do anything about it. Forty years ago, maybe, but not these days. Fortunately, the other three boys seem to think it's funnier than the "Who's on First?" routine. They lean on each other in laughter until the whole group of them falls to the sidewalk, holding their sides. The boy Jason hit drops to his knees, his hands clutched to his private parts. It just makes the boys laugh harder. They point and howl and cackle. Some friends. The kid on the ground, meantime, is looking a little white in the face. He takes a knee and puts his hand to his mouth like he might puke right here.

And Jason? He's sticking his chest out as far as it'll go, chin pointed high and his jaw sticking out. "Nobody messes with her when I'm around," he says, which brings on another round of laughter from the three friends. Just then, the boy Jason hit leans his face low to the ground and vomits all over the sidewalk. Jason leans over him and says, "That's what I thought." He takes Tiegan's hand, grabs his oxygen cart, and walks away.

It takes me a moment to catch up with them, but when I do Tiegan's staring at Jason like she's seeing him for the first time. Certainly wasn't something I expected out of him either, and that's a fact. Jason's got the same grin as after he kissed Mindy Applegate—so big his face can hardly hold it.

"I told you," he says to me.

"Told me what?"

"That's how it is in every movie. The superhero always saves the damsel in distress."

CHAPTER 30

After all the excitement of Jason granting his own superhero wish, we hurry back to the apartment and have Chicago-style pizza delivered from Giordano's. Sloppiest pizza I've ever had, but maybe the best tasting, too. Sure beats Chef Boyardee, anyhow. We turn on the television set, but it's mostly commercials for big pickup trucks and pills for old men to take if they want to "perform like when they were young." Jason plops down in a big chair and kicks his feet up on an ottoman like a conquering hero. But I go to the window and pull the curtain back a few inches, half-expecting the police to come any minute to knock down our door.

"Are you okay, Mr. McBride?" Tiegan asks. She even tugs on my sleeve a little, reminding me how young she really is.

"I made a mistake," I say. "Shouldn't have taken you kids like that. I thought I was doing something good, but maybe it was wrong, what I did."

Tiegan's gaze joins mine in staring out the window. "Mom always says 'intentions matter.' Like when I drop a plate and it breaks, but I was just trying to help clean up after supper." She shrugs. "Maybe you broke a plate. Sometimes that happens."

I do feel better, thanks to the kid. But it doesn't change the fact that there are two missing kids out there—and I have them holed up in an apartment in a city of millions of people, where anything could happen to them. I just can't figure it—did I do right or wrong? It used to be so clear. Doing what's right is more important than doing what's legal. But being cooped up in this apartment, knowing the police are looking for these kids, it's gotten a little foggy.

"I need a superhero name," Jason says, casually inspecting his fingernails on the recliner.

I sit by him and try not to dwell too much on our situation. What's done is done. I can either take them right home or stay another night and try to help Jason get his next wish. When I think of it that way, there's really no choice at all. "Okay, then," I say. "Have any ideas yet?"

"I like Ball-Puncher. What do you think?"

"Seems to me you ought to go with something more proper."

"Yeah. Probably. What about Zoth, Destroyer of Testicles?"

Not sure where he gets this stuff from. Television, most likely. "What about Strong Boy?"

"Excuse me? Are you serious? That has to be the worst super-hero name in the galaxy." He puts his feet on the floor and leans forward, like this here's a serious conversation. "Honestly, if I were to try to think up the dumbest, most stupidest superhero name ever, I could never in a zillion years think of one worse than Strong Boy."

"Okay, okay. No need to be so nasty about it. It was just an idea."

"No, here's an idea." He puts his hands together in the air, then spreads them like he's seeing the words in front of him. "The Fog Shadow."

"J?" Tiegan says. "Fog doesn't even have a shadow."

"That is so not the point. It's awesome. That's all that matters. Hence forth, and forevermore, I shall only respond when called by my true and rightful name—Fog Shadow."

Tiegan shakes her head and says, "I seriously can't take any more of this. I'm going to bed."

"What, not even a thank-you for saving your life?" Jason says.

Tiegan puts her hands together and leans her cheek against them, starts batting her eyelashes. "You're right," she says. "You're so very chivalrous. I am forever indebted for your show of strength and courage in the face of imminent danger."

"Schweet," Jason says, and Tiegan can't help but smile while she shakes her head.

"Good night, boys."

When she's gone to the bedroom, Jason keeps his feet kicked up on the sofa and switches them around like he's planning to stay there for a while. "What kind of superhero would you be?" he asks.

"I don't know much about all that."

"You don't want to save the world?"

"Save the world? Sure, I do. But I'm a realist."

"What's that?"

I start to tell him, it's the kind of person who sees things as they are, warts and all. Who doesn't buy into all the rainbows and butterflies some people talk about. Someone who sees that the world can be a hard, unforgiving place. But just before I say any of that, something stops me. Maybe it's the way the kid's leaning forward, like what I say will actually matter to him. Maybe it's the spark in his eye that looks like he wants me to believe in these things right along with him. Besides, a guy gets to be my age, he starts thinking about what he's done with his life. What people will say about him when he's gone. "Guess maybe I'd like to be a superhero. If I could, that is."

"Good point. You probably can't. I've never seen a superhero as crabby as you."

"Now see here, you shouldn't go around calling people crabby. It's not respectful."

Jason tries hard, I have to give him credit for that. But in the end, he bursts out in laughter. Takes me a while to realize he's laughing because he thinks my answer was a crabby one. And that's a bit strange, come to think of it. Truth is, I think the world's a pretty amazing place. Not sure when my words and tone stopped saying that. Guess it's easy to get frustrated with little things, and a hundred years'll give a fella a lot of things to get bitter about. But this here kid, he's a doozy. Got handed a death sentence and still runs around laughing and joking. Not taking things too seriously, that's what. The kid's got a passion for life.

"I got it," Jason says. "You can be a superhero who rolls around in a wheelchair passing out diapers to babies and old people. Super Dry Man!" He gets a good kick out of that one. I try not to scowl. "Okay, okay," he says. "Maybe a superhero is too much. You could be, like, a special agent. What kind of special agent do you want to be?"

"Can't say for sure. Just try to do good, I suppose."

Jason giggles again. "Murray McBride, Special Agent for Good."

Out of nowhere I hear the sound of the ocean—straight out of California, sounds like. But it's just one of those machines that makes noise to help folks sleep. Tiegan trying to drown out our voices, I suppose. Jason eyes the video game controller perched on the edge of the bed. "Fog Shadow challenges you to a game of All-Powerful Gods and Bloodsucking Aliens."

Don't know if I can handle the kid using his superhero name in the third person, but I grab up a controller anyhow and he starts the game. I've played enough to realize I don't have a chance to win but I don't say anything about it. The kid needs all the victories he can get.

"Did you know some people think you can come back?" he says. "After you die, I mean. They call it re-incarceration or something."

"Reincarnation," I say. "I've heard tell of it."

"Do you think it's true?"

To tell the truth of the matter, I'm not so sure what I think anymore. I'd never admit it to Father James, but when I try to picture where Jenny and my boys are, I just can't do it. Are they spirits somewhere in the sky? Or do they have their bodies back, walking around in heaven? None of it makes much sense to my old brain. "Can't rightly say, I reckon."

"*Can't rightly say, you reckon?* I don't even know what that means." He shakes his head but gets back on track quick. It would take something big to ruin his mood right now. "I think it's true. But I don't think you have to come back as a person. You can come back as anything. Anything you want. An elephant. A tree. Anything."

"And what would you come back as?"

"You mean what *will* I come back as." I don't answer, so he continues. "I'm not sure. For a while I wanted to be a bear, but right now I'm leaning toward a dog. A pitbull, so I can be in the fights. I'm going to be the champion dog fighter of the world."

The kid obviously has no idea about the brutality of a real dog fight, and I reckon this is no time to teach him about it. "Guess I'll be a flea then. Make you itch like nothing."

Jason gets a kick out of that one. "I'll be a rat."

"Then I'll be a snake."

More giggles. "I'll be a rhinoceros."

"Then I'll be a bird."

"A bird? Why the heck would you want to be a bird?"

"Why not?" I say. "I'd be able to follow you around, land on your shoulder, keep you company. I'll even find my bride and bring her along. She'll be a bird, too. And my boys. All of us."

Jason considers this for a bit. Gives it quite a lot more thought than I'd expect. "Alright," he says. "Fog Shadow will be a rhino and you be a bird. We can be best friends again. Let's promise."

I love how he says *again*. Like it's obvious we're best friends now, and that we'll want to be best friends again, when the time comes. Something tingly in my chest lets me know—as if I didn't already know it—that this kid means something special to me. That he's changing me somehow. Taking years and years off until I'm young like him all over again.

"I promise," I say.

"Cool. I promise, too."

But then, just as I think he's having the same level of heartfelt feelings as me, he stares off into space like he's really pondering something.

"Just think how big my poop will be," he says.

And together, we laugh like it's the funniest thing in the history of humor.

CHAPTER 31

Next morning when I open the curtains, there're still drops of water on the window, but they glow with rays of sunlight. Tiegan has breakfast all set up again. I see her telephone on the counter, same place as yesterday, and it looks like it's turned on. Every few minutes, it vibrates and beeps. Tiegan sees me looking at it and shrugs.

"I left my mom a note and you left J's mom a note, so they know we're with you." She stares at the telephone, and I wonder if she'll go to it. But she just looks at it. "I just want to know when she calls. We'll head back as soon as Jason's done with his home run, right?"

"The very minute," I say. "And you should call her before we go. Like the plan was yesterday. It'll be too late for anyone to stop us, and it'll make us both feel better. Here," I say, and I fish a pencil and notepad out of a drawer. "Write your home telephone number down and if you forget, I'll call it myself."

She scribbles two phone numbers down and hands me the paper. "The bottom number is my phone here, just in case we get separated somehow. Mom always says it's good to have a backup plan."

Jason stumbles into the kitchen, plops down into a chair, and eats even more waffles than yesterday. If a heart could be nourished by waffles, the kid would be healthy as a horse.

At noon, the call from the Cubs finally comes. The wall phone rings and we all gather around the receiver close as we can to hear the news. The field is still wet, the man from the Cubs says, but they're going to let us use it. Show up in two hours and be ready.

Nothing about Jason and Tiegan being on the evening news, which kept me up most of the night.

If I'm going to be out for a while, I reckon I'd better use the john. One of the more embarrassing parts of getting old, I reckon. Everyone knows about the wrinkles and the slouching and the slow movements, but the personal stuff becomes harder to keep personal. The kids notice when I head to the toilet again. Give me a sideways glance, but at least neither of them laughs.

When I get out, they're nowhere to be seen. It's quiet too, and for a moment I wonder if they're gone. Just up and left and didn't even let me know. But of course, that's not what happened. I hear whispering from the bedroom and reach out to open the door, but something about Jason's voice stops me.

"Fine, I admit it, I'm scared. Are you happy now?" An unnatural hissing sound tells me he's breathing through his mask.

Dying, that's what they're talking about. Must be the only thing on Jason's mind. How could it not be? Poor kid, to have that hanging over his head all the time. It's one thing for an old man to face that, quite another for a ten-year-old boy.

"Just relax," Tiegan says. "Keep your grip loose, keep your arms loose, let your lower body supply the power."

Ha! The kids aren't talking about death at all. Jason's afraid of not being able to hit a home run. It actually makes me smile, but instead of opening the door like I probably ought to, I angle my ear to the crack in the frame, the better to hear with.

"If it doesn't happen, it doesn't happen," Tiegan says in a low voice. "Just think, we get to go on the actual field. Isn't that amazing!" I don't hear a response, but I can picture the eye roll Jason gives her. So Tiegan tries a different track. "Mr. McBride could help. He did play for the Cubs, you know? The real Cubs."

"I know," Jason says, and if I didn't know better, I'd say there's something like awe in his voice. "It's unbelievable."

"Really? I mean, of course it is, but you didn't seem impressed before."

"How could I not be impressed? Who wouldn't be?"

"You should tell him."

"Tell him? Are you kidding?"

"Well, I'm sure he could at least give you some pointers on how to hit better."

"I know," Jason says, and for the first time in this here conversation, there's a long pause, like he doesn't know what to say next. "But then he'd know I'm not any good."

I'd know he's not any good? Does the kid think I had my eyes closed in Old Lady Willamette's garden?

"I hate not being good," he says. "I'm not good at anything. I'm not even good at staying alive."

There's a rustling of blankets and creaking of bedsprings. I resist the temptation to peek in, instead I just picture them. Jason on the edge of the bed, head down, talking to the floor. Tiegan inching closer to comfort him, but not so close to make him move away. "J, you have your whole life to become good at things."

"Thanks, Mom."

"I'm serious."

"Don't you guys pay any attention to what the doctors say? You're so blind. The truth is if I don't get a new heart, I'm going to die. And it's not going to be years from now."

No. We can't let the boy think that way. Tell him, Tiegan. Tell him he's going to live a long life. That he'll make it. He'll pull through. Tell him he's wrong.

But if she says anything like that, I can't hear it.

"It's supposed to be today, you know."

"Really? Already? What's the date?"

"August 22," Jason says.

August 22 . . . that date hits me hard for some reason. Stands out, although I can't pin down just why.

"And they gave you six months—"

"February 22. Remember? 'Guess what, Jason, you're going to die.'"

"That's not what they said."

"Is too. Pretty much, anyway."

The twenty-second, I got it now. That's the date I told Doc Keaton I wasn't going to take my pill. It's the day I was going to end my life. Who would've thought? The day I picked to end my life is the exact day the doctors told Jason that, without a new heart, he would be dead.

I shuffle away from the door before they expose my eavesdropping. Good thing, too. Before I even make it to the kitchen, they exit the bedroom, both looking a little long in the face. But Jason is decked out in his Little League uniform, complete with a cap, cleats, and batting gloves. Tiegan's wearing her jersey too, of course, so the two of them look like a pair of twins.

"Ready to go?" I ask, and hope like nothing they don't confront me about my spying. But they just nod and stand a little straighter at the prospect.

My knee's hurting something fierce so the thought of walking the two blocks to the ballpark doesn't sound too good. But neither does telling these two kids I'm not capable, so I suck it up and we head out into the beautiful summer day.

After about a block, my knee's acting up so bad I can hardly move. Each step shoots a pain up my leg so intense I can't even tell where it stops. Jason touches my elbow, but doesn't know what exactly to do about an old fogie grunting like a wounded pig. He pushes his oxygen cart toward me and I take it happily. Tiegan, bless her soul, takes my hand. "Maybe we should rest for a minute," she says.

Mercifully, a horn honks nearby and a red convertible slides up next to the curb in front of us. In the driver's seat is none other than Javier Candela, brand new to the Big Leagues and smiling ear to ear. "Mr. McBride? Is that you? My manager told me you're coming to our game today, yes?"

"That's right," I say. "If I can make it there, anyhow."

"Three of you," Javier says, and he motions to his car. "Three seats. Come sit, please."

Tiegan squeals a bit and I remember that riding in a convertible was one of her wishes. Around the block, if I recall. So I ask Javier if he wouldn't mind taking a cruise around the ballpark.

"Anything, Mr. McBride. Anything."

The kids hop in and I wrestle with the oxygen cart for a moment before Javier jumps out and handles it like it's a toothpick. He sets it in the trunk and a moment later, we're riding in the sunshine.

In the back seat, Jason leans out trying to touch other cars. Tiegan closes her eyes while the wind blows her pigtails behind her like birthday streamers. Just as we pull into the players' parking garage, I hear Jason say, "Wishes are so cool." Tiegan smiles so big she can't speak. When we walk into the stadium, it's like I'm coming home.

Now the Cubs don't owe me anything, see? All I did was play my favorite game, and they paid me to do it. So, as I see it, we're even. But they don't seem to view it that way, and in this case, that's a good thing. Javier introduces us to Gerald Massey Jr., from Community Outreach, then excuses himself, saying he's running late. Mr. Massey takes us on a tour of the clubhouse, the batting cages, and a small shrine they've put up, memorializing all the old ballplayers. Ernie Banks. Ferguson Jenkins. Ryne Sandberg. And right there with them is a faded black-and-white photograph of yours truly, along with the rest of the 1932 World Series team. Swept by the Yankees, but still a heck of a ball club. Tiegan and Jason gawk at it, like they didn't believe until just now that I actually played ball, once upon a time.

Our escort glances at his wristwatch and says, "Okay. Things should be ready. Shall we?"

He leads us through the dugout and onto the field. As soon as the sun hits my face and warms my cheeks, my eyes tear up. The smells of popcorn and hot dogs float on the stadium air, and the expanse of the yard has a feel of its own—the air takes on a lighter quality, as if I could float on its currents. Other than being in Jenny's arms, this is the most at home I've ever felt.

"Wow," Jason says, so I open my eyes.

I stare at the grass, unable to believe how the Cubs have come through. The field is pristine, like always, but beyond second base is where the magic is. The grounds crew has mowed small circles into the outfield grass, making it look like a miniature ball field. Standing at each imaginary position in the field is a member of the current Chicago Cubs lineup. Javier jogs out of the dugout behind us and I can't help but wonder if he was sent to pick us up.

A regulation-size plastic home plate is in the outfield grass, about twenty feet behind the real second base. When we get there, Javier holds out an aluminum bat. Jason takes a quick hit of oxygen, then pushes the cart toward me. He takes the bat and raps it against the sides of his shoes. He actually looks like a ballplayer, doing that.

"Ultra-light bat," Javier whispers to me as Jason takes some pretty ugly practice swings. "Specially designed to hit a ball far.

And the baseballs in the bucket are spun extra tight—juiced balls. Like for Home Run Derby before the All-Star Game." He sees Tiegan next to me, in uniform and too amazed to speak.

"After Jason, the girl will hit?"

"I think she'd like that," I say.

Tiegan just bounces like a blue jay, which is answer enough.

Everything is set up as perfectly as possible, but I still have my doubts. I saw Jason hit in Old Lady Willamette's garden, and even hitting from the outfield, it's still probably a 150-foot poke to the left field fence.

One of the Cubs coaches is ready to pitch—I think it's the one who throws batting practice to the team. Whoever he is, he puts strike after strike right in Jason's wheelhouse. After a few swings, the kid actually starts making contact. After about ten minutes, with the light bat, the tightly wrapped balls, and the adrenaline of being at Wrigley with the Cubs, he starts knocking the ball all around. He just has to get under it a bit and he might actually have a shot at this.

"Alright Jason," the coach says, holding up a ball. "This is the one. I can feel it."

The ball hits the bat with an unnatural ping and sails to left center field. It rises high into the air and has good distance. But it smacks against the wall and half the Cubs players fall over in exaggerated disappointment.

Not Jason. He's gripping his bat tighter than ever, ready for the next pitch. It's a blast to the opposite field this time. With a bit of practice, this kid could actually be good. He hits the next two pitches hard too, but on the ground. Then three swings and misses—he's trying too hard now. But then the stars align.

The pitch is low-and-in and Jason golfs it a bit. As soon as it leaves the bat, there's no doubt. The ball sails over the left field wall and slams into the seats three rows deep.

A home run in a Major League baseball stadium.

Fireworks shoot from somewhere near the top of the grandstand. Thousands of recorded voices cheer through the loudspeaker and a voice booms out, "Home run, Jason Cashman!"

Tiegan jumps up and down, pulling my sleeve with every leap into the air. She's more excited than I've ever seen her.

Jason hasn't moved. He's staring at the sky like he's wondering where the fireworks and the voices are coming from. "Run," the coach says, and Jason flips the bat high into the air in a move that would get him beaned in real baseball. After a few more seconds of staring at the spot his ball landed, he begins a perfectly paced home run trot. He steps on the corner of the spot in the grass mowed to look like first base and does a perfect Kirk Gibson fist pump. As he rounds second base, he lifts his hands high and continues his trot as if he's the only person in the world.

I get that same stab of pride in my gut as I watch. Jason's expression is different than after kissing Mindy Applegate, different than after he became a superhero with that cheap-shot punch. Different, but no less joyful. It's just that his joy seems to be mixed with serenity. Like there's nothing in the world he would change.

More than anything else, he looks healthy. This is how a ten-year-old boy should look. Glowing. Running. So wrapped up in the beauty and simplicity of being a kid, he believes in the deepest part of him that everything is as it should be. He carries the entire world in the palm of his hand. It feels like nothing could ever change this perfection.

But that's the thing about perfection. It doesn't last. It can't last. The world is too changing. Too harsh. Too real.

Jason stumbles as he rounds third. He grabs his chest and leans over, suddenly gasping for breath. Then his body, in apparent slow-motion, starts to fall to the ground as we all look on in horror.

CHAPTER 32

This is what happened:

First, my insides seized up. Stopped completely. A panic welled up inside my stomach, then burst up into my chest like a pipe bomb. By the time it hit my throat, it was acrid and burning. Maybe that's what happened to my voice—it burned away.

Then my muscles reacted, but not the way I wanted them to. They didn't spring to action, because there was no action that made any sense. There was nothing at all that made sense. Still, because of the pipe bomb in my insides, my muscles knew something big was happening. They were flooded with adrenaline. But there was nothing they could do, no action they could take. So they simply tensed up. Tighter than ever before.

And the owner of the body? The owner could do nothing, because of the tension in his muscles. Couldn't move. Couldn't think. The only option was to watch, and maybe it was the adrenaline, but the images seemed to slow down even more.

The seconds stretched long, like a fly ball that continues to gain elevation, rising into the sky, then drifting downward. Jason was in the air, on his way to the ground, for what felt like an eternity. So slowly I thought he might overcome gravity and float back to the way he was, smiling and running like a child.

But that's not what happened.

Instead, his legs crumbled and his arms dropped limply to his sides. He was unconscious before he hit the ground.

And hit the ground, he did. But not like a boy should when he stumbles. It wasn't his knee that hit first, or even his shoulder. No. It was his nose, which immediately started pouring blood.

Precious blood that his heart still seemed strong enough to pulse through his body, because the blood spurted out his nose in waves.

I tried to look away, but couldn't. I tried to move to help, but couldn't. I tried to yell, but couldn't.

Two Cubs players were the first to get to him. One waved to the dugout, calling a trainer. Javier knelt down and cradled Jason in his lap. Blood poured out of Jason's nose, onto his jersey and his pants and the pants and jersey of Javier Candela, until finally, mercifully, Javier thought to pinch Jason's nose and stop the flow.

Tiegan was the next to arrive. Her pigtails flew behind her like she was sprinting, but sprinting in slow motion. Her hands were on Jason's face, petting him like a puppy. In the back of my mind a scream barely registered, and I realized when I saw Tiegan's mouth open wide that it was coming from her. Her face twisted. She was no longer Jason's girl next door. She wasn't a tomboy with a perpetual smile. She was nothing but a voice. A scream. And it did nothing to help, because nothing could help.

The group of people around Jason grew. Someone must have taken the oxygen from me because it was next to Jason, the mask pressed to his face. I struggled to see if it was fogging with breath, but I was too far away.

Within minutes an ambulance drove right out onto the field. Paramedics jumped out. Huddled over Jason. Talked in quiet but urgent voices. They lifted Jason onto a stretcher, and I noticed how much grass had been colored red. They shoved the stretcher into the ambulance and Tiegan jumped in with them.

I hadn't moved. Time no longer registered in my old brain, but it must've been ten minutes since he'd fallen. Or maybe more. Twenty minutes? It had been years since I'd stood still for twenty minutes without agonizing pain in my knee, but I didn't feel a thing.

And that's the strangest thing about what happened here—I didn't feel a thing. Everything was empty. Everything was calm. The only thing going through my mind was Jason's voice, during the video game, repeating over and over and over:

Better say your prayers.

CHAPTER 33

Javier Candela helps me up. Grabs me under my arms, which is good because if he'd tried to pull me up, my shoulder would have come right out of its socket. Not sure how long I've been sitting on this here grass, but the ambulance is gone and the players are milling about, talking and pointing to the spot where Jason fell. The grounds crew is cleaning up the blood by hosing it down with enough water to drown an elephant.

I wish there was a way to save that blood.

"We'll get you a cab, Mr. McBride," Javier says. I don't realize until we're on the curb that he's led me out of the stadium and to the street. His uniform is covered with Jason's blood. My old knee should be throbbing, but it feels better than it has in decades. Or if it doesn't, I don't notice. Javier flags down a taxicab and I get in. "Children's Hospital," I say, and the cabbie turns the car toward the lake.

Next thing I know, I'm at another hospital, asking for another heart ward.

"Just need to know where I can find a boy named Jason Cashman," I say to a lady at a desk.

"How are you related?"

"I'm his brother."

The lady's fingers stop typing and she looks at me over her glasses. "I'm afraid I don't understand. The boy is your brother?"

I can tell this here's going to be a difficult conversation. I'm still not thinking quite right and the lady in front of me doesn't seem the helpful type. So I'm plenty thankful when Tiegan comes right on up to me and wraps her arms around me nice and hard.

"SBK," she says, then takes my hand and leads me away. And in this moment, I realize the power and the brilliance of the little greeting. I'm completely overwhelmed. Lost and scared. And somehow, those three letters make me feel a little better. A little stronger.

I expect Tiegan to take me to Jason's room, but instead we find some comfortable chairs nearby and she sits me down, like I'm the child and she's the adult.

"Where's Jason?" I ask.

She shakes her head. Looks like she's trying to say something, but can't. Then she pushes some hair out of her eyes and takes a deep breath. "I don't know," she says. "They won't tell me anything because I'm not a relative."

"They won't even tell you where he is?"

"In surgery. That's all they'll say. But when he's out, they said they need one of Jason's parents here. So I called my mom and she said to call his mom. I told her everything. How you picked us up and drove us here. How we stayed in the apartment. Mr. McBride, I'm so sorry. I didn't know what else to do."

"Don't you cry now," I say. "You did right. Anna needs to be here. She needs to know."

"I know, but . . ." Her voice fades and she pulls her hair back behind her head, wraps it up somehow and it stays. She looks different without pigtails. Older. "Jason's dad. He freaked out. He was the one that reported us missing."

From my seat, I can see the entrance of the hospital. A pair of police officers come in the front doors and go right up to the desk with the unhelpful lady. Can't hear what they're saying, but I don't need to.

"How's Anna?" I ask.

"She's coming. She sounded bad, Mr. McBride. Almost crazy."

To have to hear about something like this happening to her young kid, without her around? I'd be surprised if she wasn't crazy. Crazy with fear. Probably blaming herself. 'Course, she had nothing to do with it. I did.

"Mr. McBride? What's going to happen?"

Tiegan's such a good kid, so mature and grown up for a little girl of ten. It's easy to forget she still is a kid. But I remember now.

Before I can tell her it'll be okay, the police officer steps right up to my chair. "Sir, is your name Murray McBride?"

"That's right."

"You're going to have to come with me."

"Why's that? Where we going?"

"You're under arrest for the kidnapping of Jason Cashman and Tiegan Atherton."

I know I should argue. I should tell him Jason had his list and his father wasn't going to let him come. I should tell him I'm innocent.

But I'm not. I'm as far from innocent as I could be. So I stand slowly, leaning against the chair for support, and I allow the young police officer to wrap a pair of handcuffs around my old, bony wrists.

CHAPTER 34

The Cook County jail is a different kind of place than I've ever been, I'll tell you that much. Concrete floors, concrete walls, concrete ceiling. Guess it makes it hard to escape when you can't even put a dent in the wall. Makes me feel like they're about to take me to the hot squat, although I think they use injections these days.

Most of my getting here is lost to me because all I can think about is Jason. I don't even know if he'll live or die—heck I don't even know if he's alive right this second—and yet all I can do is sit in a Big House holding cell with a half-dozen other criminals.

And that's what I am—a criminal. There's no two ways about that. I'm no patsy. I stole a boy from his home and a girl from hers, as far as the law is concerned. Fact that they wanted to come had nothing to do with it. I'm expected to be the adult.

But guess what, I'd do it again if I had the chance. Don't know how I can make sense of that morally, but I don't much care either. Not right now, anyhow. The Good Lord will just have to understand, that's all. When I get to those pearly gates, he'll see right into me and know I didn't mean to do anything wrong. That I didn't know it would end up like this.

But that's the rub, isn't it: sometimes trying to do the right thing is the surest way to get yourself in a heap of trouble. Sometimes you break a plate. And if it's an old, worn-out plate whose time has come, that's one thing. But what if that plate is a fine piece of china? What do intentions matter then? I wish Tiegan was here to answer that question.

Three other fellas share the cell with me, but they keep their distance. Like they think they'll catch Old Age or something. One's a skinny Black man and the other two are overweight white boys who couldn't have forty years between them. They all sneak little sideways glances at me, probably wondering what an old-timer like me could've done to land in the clink. I try to keep my mind off Jason by coming up with stories they might be thinking about me—maybe I drugged my young girlfriend after she had another fella, or maybe I'm in for holding up a bank with a cane. But it doesn't work. Jason's all I can think of. Where he is. How his heart is holding out. Whether I'll see him again.

One big, long bench is all we have to sit on. Runs all along one of the two walls—the other two walls are bars. I'm sitting right on the end of the bench, so as to leave them all to themselves. Them and their imaginations. And they seem just fine with that. I'm like an alien species to them. But let me tell you this, the feeling's mutual.

I stretch my knee out as far as it'll go, but the pain's too much to get it much past forty-five degrees. I just leave it where it is, lean my head against the concrete wall, and try to ignore the throbbing, maybe get some shut-eye.

Just then a loud rattle startles me awake. My mouth feels like it's been sitting open for a while. Must've fallen off there for a bit. Sometimes fatigue wins the battle, no matter how much a fella has on his mind.

"Murray McBride," a man in a police uniform says. He says it again and is about to close the cell door by the time I'm able to stand up.

"I'm Murray McBride," I say.

"Follow me. You've posted bail."

"Bail? You mean I don't have to stay here?"

He raises his eyebrows as if to say, *You coming or not?* Then he leads me down a few hallways, longer than I can easily walk, to a barred window with a slot below it for things to go in and out. Papers and such. Standing right there waiting for me, a disappointed scowl on his face, is Chance.

"Granddad," he says, and I can't quite pin down his tone. It doesn't match his scowl. If I didn't know better, I'd say he was worried about me.

"Now don't go starting into a lecture, you hear? I'm a grown man, same as you. I can make my own decisions and I don't regret this one a bit, understand? Only regret what happened to Jason."

"I wasn't going to lecture you, Granddad. Actually, I'm glad you got arrested. It's probably for the best."

"Excuse me?" I say, because he's not making a lick of sense.

"Now you can be done," he says. He must see my jaw shake because he holds his hands out, palms up. "I know that kid's important to you, but you're not a young man, Granddad. You need to take care of yourself, not someone else. Especially not a kid who needs so much. It's going to wear you down. It has worn you down."

"I'll decide what I can handle, thank you very much. You just worry about whichever wife you have now."

I reckon that crossed a line. Knew it as soon as I said it. But that's the thing about words: once they leave your mouth, there's no taking them back. And sometimes, when a man's hurting, he lashes out and hurts others too. Like there's some part of us that can't handle hurting alone.

"Where'd we go wrong?" Chance asks. "We used to be close, remember? We used to really enjoy each other. When did that change?"

"When you started pining for my old baseball things," I say, and I regret that one right away, too. Something about being in this jail is bringing out the worst in me. Or maybe it's the realization that I can't show Chance I love him any more than I could my boys. Or maybe it's the constant thought that in trying to help Jason, I might have ended up killing him.

Chance is looking at me real close. Scrutinizing me, is what he's doing. Trying to figure something out, by the looks of it. "Are you serious?" he says. "Do you really think that? Why? What did I ever do to give you that impression?"

"I see the way you look at my mitt every time you come over. Like you can't wait to get your hands on it after I pass."

"Can't wait to get my hands on it?"

"Probably sell it before they even get me in the dirt."

"Hold on just a second! I would never sell that glove. You're right that I want it, but not so I can make money off it."

He seems pretty sincere, and pretty upset, too. Makes me wonder if I've misjudged things a bit. I won't lie—that scares the daylights out of me. Still, I force myself to ask, "Then why do you want it so bad?"

Chance leans forward, actually touches my arm. "Don't you remember?" I don't know what he's talking about, so I just wait until he explains it to me. "When I was a kid, Dad had just opened that hardware store," he says. "He was gone all the time, always working. But you, you were there for me. You were around. You played catch with me. You let me use your own glove."

There are tears in his eyes, and that's something I've never seen before. I don't doubt for a second he's telling the truth, but I don't have any recollection of it. I try hard to remember, and every second that goes by without a memory of it scares me more and more. My mind, it's always been so sharp. Sure, I've forgotten a fair few things over the years, but never something like this. If I can't remember playing catch with my own grandson, what's next? Will my boys fade? Is it possible I could wake up someday and Jenny would be gone?

I stumble against the concrete wall and Chance lunges forward to catch me. My shoulder hits and it's like a ninety-mile-an-hour fastball got me square. Chance stops me from falling, thank the Good Lord. He squeezes my arms tight, like he's afraid I'll tumble over if he lets me go. I'm not sure who starts it, but next thing I know his chest is pushed right up against mine, our arms are wrapped around each other, and I'm hugging my grandson for the first time in way too many years. My shoulder feels wet from all his tears. Pretty sure I'm giving his shirt a good wash, too.

"I used to brag to all my friends," he says through tight sobs. "My granddad played for the Cubs. I was so proud to be your grandson. All I wanted was for you to be proud of me, too."

I slap his back hard. So hard I wonder if it hurts him, until I remember how old I am. He grabs up the back of my shirt and squeezes it like he's trying to wring water out. I push him back and look straight into his eyes.

"I've been wrong about you, see? You're a good kid. I'm the reason we drifted apart. I got old and crabby, that's what. But I don't feel so old anymore, Chance. Not since meeting that boy Jason. Can you understand that?"

Chance smiles at me for the first time since I can remember. "I'm trying, Granddad. And I'll keep trying."

He pulls me into another hug, and I can't help but keep on searching my memory, trying like nothing to remember playing catch with my grandson.

"Sign here," says the man behind the desk, and he gives me a clipboard. I don't even bother to read it. If he's letting me leave this jail, I'll sign anything. I need to get to Jason as soon as I can.

"Can you point me in the direction of a cab? Need to get to the hospital."

"I'll take you, Granddad," Chance says. But the officer interrupts.

"Can't do that," he says. He takes the clipboard from me and points to the form I just signed. "You've got a restraining order against you. If you're found within five hundred feet of Jason Cashman, you'll be sent back to jail. And this time you won't get out so quick."

"A restraining order?" I try to understand what that means. "I can't even go to the hospital? Five hundred feet?"

"That's right. And I wouldn't recommend trying to get around it. Judges don't like that." He tucks the clipboard under his arm. "You're free to go."

"Just not to the hospital."

"Not if Jason Cashman is there."

He looks down at some papers, which lets me know he's done talking to me. Chance puts his hand on my shoulder and I cover it with my own hand.

"Can I use your telephone?" I ask.

He fishes his new telephone out of his coat while I pat my pockets for little Tiegan's number. When I find it, I punch in the digits, and she picks up right quick. "Please be Mr. McBride," she says into the phone.

"Jason. How's Jason?"

"Here, his mom's right here. You should talk to her."

"Anna?"

"Murray. Thank God you called. Where are you?"

"Jail. But I'm getting out now. How's Jason?"

There's a good long silence. I wonder if she knew I was in jail. "I'm so sorry about that," she says. "Jason's . . . well, he's hanging in there. He's out of surgery and he's stable. But, well, he needs a new heart."

"Already knew that, didn't we?"

"Yes. Of course we did. But, well, it's become more urgent. Much more. The doctors aren't sure how much longer he can last without a new one. They're not talking about months anymore. More like days."

I consider what it is, exactly, that she's saying. But I stop doing that right quick. Never felt so much fear in my life. "They tell me I can't come see him. Some kind of restrictive order?"

There's a heavy sigh on the other end and a crackling of some sort. "I'm sorry, Murray. I'm working on that. I've spoken with my lawyer, and I'll talk to Benedict as soon as I can. We'll try to get it figured out. I know Jason will want to see you."

I swallow hard, look around the room, but Chance is the only one watching me. "I want to see him, too. Tell him I'm sorry."

"Sorry? Oh Murray, you have nothing to be sorry for. You've . . ."

But she isn't able to talk anymore. I should be there with her. A wonderful woman like that, she doesn't deserve to go through something like this all alone.

"What am I supposed to do now?" I say.

"I don't know, Murray. Maybe it's best if you go home until I can figure things out."

"Go home? But Jason's there."

"And you can't see him. What good is that? Jason will be up and running around again in no time, I'm sure of it."

Over the telephone her voice sounds pretty convincing, but I'm sure her face would give her away. "What about Tiegan?"

"Tiegan will stay here. Della's here too. She says Tiegan can stay. Not that she has much choice. Tiegan hasn't left Jason's side since we got here. But with the restraining order, there's not much you can do. You should get back to your normal routine. I don't want this to affect your health, too. Jason's resting most of the time anyway. I think it might be best. Until things calm down with Benedict."

I don't have much to say to that. How can I explain that I can't go back to my old routine? That I was a horsehair away from not taking my pill and ending this whole ride before I met that kid? But Anna's right about one thing—there's nothing I can do.

So Chance drives me back to the apartment, where the Chevy's collecting dust. It'll probably take me three hours to get home, considering the traffic and the way I drive. No point in wasting time or I'll have to drive in the dark again. Chance pulls his car up next to mine to escort me back. So I start up the Chevy and point her toward home.

Funny thing is, the closer I get to my own house, the farther I feel from home.

CHAPTER 35

The drive home can be summed up in one measly word: Empty. Empty car. Empty plans. Empty soul. Last time I felt like my insides had been dumped out with nothing left over was the day Jenny died. And that's the thing about loving someone: somehow or another, it always ends bad.

Maybe it's a breakup. Chance knows all about that. A man and woman drift apart, as he says. Irreconcilable differences. Or maybe one of them breaks their marriage vows, and that's the end. Kaput.

Then there are the rare relationships, the ones like Jenny and I had, where we made a life together. We loved each other through good times and bad, in sickness and in health, just like the Good Lord says to do. But even that can't last forever. Sooner or later, death takes what it has coming. I can tell you from experience, that's a bad end too. The beginning was great. Middle too. But it always ends bad.

About the only way I can figure for it not to end bad is to be the one to die. And, so far anyway, I haven't had the pleasure of experiencing that side of it. Not that I haven't considered it. 'Course, the thing I've considered ending hasn't been a great love. Just a worn-out life.

I get home just before dark and go right to bed. Try not to give my mind any more time to be awake then I have to. In the morning, I head straight for the cupboard. Bran Flakes, crushed pill, and a battle to the finish. Back to the way things were. Back to the same-old-same-old. Back to wondering why it's worth getting up in the morning.

Except I've never been a quitter, and I can't quit on Jason now. Sure, he's down in that hospital, and I'm up here in Lemon Grove and not allowed to see him. But I have to believe he's doing everything he can to hang on. So I'll do the same. For him. Because his wishes aren't done. Not just yet, anyhow. Still has to get Anna a nice boyfriend and become a magician.

I want to talk to him so bad it hurts, right in my chest. Haven't felt this helpless in ages. About the only thing I can think to do is write him a computer message, so I fire up the old email machine, click on his address and punch at the keys.

To: jasoncashmanrules@aol.com
From: MurrayMcBride@aol.com
Subject: I Miss My Friend

Dear Jason,

I'm sorry about what happened at the ballpark. I know it was my fault. I know I'm the one responsible. I just wish I could tell you that in person. I shouldn't have put you in that situation. It wasn't right, that's what. It wasn't right and I'm sorry.

I also want to say that your home run was truly incredible. I don't think I've ever been so proud in all my one hundred years of living. Thank you for that.

Last of all, and this isn't easy for a crabby old codger like me to say, but I miss you something fierce. To tell the truth of the matter, I do believe I love you, son.

Sincerely,
Mr. Murray McBride

Before I have a chance to change my mind, I click on the SEND button and the message is gone. Maybe it was too personal, or too mushy, or something. But it was also the truth. It was the feelings I have deep down inside me, whether an old man like me is supposed to feel them or not. In short, it was everything I should have told my own sons, but never did.

I think about Jason's remaining wishes again. Not sure how I'm going to make either of them happen, but I do know that if Jason won't quit on me, then I won't quit on him either.

And that means staying alive until Anna can get me permission to see him. But if I stay in this old house for very long, staying alive's going to start losing its appeal, see? I need somewhere to go, something to do. And it just so happens there's an art class with Hands Man and that crazy woman this morning at the community college. I wasn't planning on ever going back there, but since I'm stuck in town and all . . .

Hands Man is there when I arrive. Collins is his name, if I remember right. 'Course, he's already there. I'm a good twenty minutes late. The room's already lit up and I see the empty chair up front meant for me. Crazy Lady escorts me up there like I'm a child and I dutifully get into my undershirt and sit.

"Collins," I say nice and loud, because I don't much care what that lady has to say about it.

"Mr. McBride," he responds nice and polite-like, if quite a bit quieter than me.

"What do you suppose they'll say I look like today?" I ask.

"Shh," Crazy Lady says. "Silence please, remember? The wrinkles near your mouth—"

"Yeah, yeah, they droop and sag or whatever."

She purses her lips like she might scold me, but instead says, "Since he brought it up, what do you see in our subject today?"

"Fatigue," one lad says.

"It looks like it's taking a lot more effort to sit there," a girl says.

"Very good," Crazy Lady says. "This is truly a unique opportunity. Imagine what he might look like . . . in a few years."

Doesn't take a genius to figure out she's saying I'm so old, so broken, I could die any second. The blood would stop running through my veins. My body would turn cold, skin would start to decompose. It would smell.

"Let your visions inform your artistry," the lady says, and I think she's done talking, thank the Good Lord.

"I'd've said I look like piss and vinegar," I say to Collins. "Least that's how I'm feeling."

Collins chuckles but holds his hands still. Very professional. Crazy Lady clears her throat, but she can go on clearing her throat all hour. Heck, she can toss me right out of the room if it suits her fancy. I've had about enough of her.

It's hard to focus on anything other than Jason and next thing I know, the room's emptying out and the session's over. Collins stands next to me with his hand out and I take it. He helps me up and out of the room.

"You remember that kid?" I say. "The one with the beautiful mom, Anna?"

"Who could forget? Is the kid okay? I noticed his oxygen tank, obviously."

I try to talk, can't, then try again. "Kid's sick, that's what. Sick real bad."

Collins seems to consider this. His face scrunches up so it's not as handsome as usual. Then he puts a big hand on my back. "Are you doing okay, Mr. McBride? Anything I can do to help?" I say no thank you, but he writes his telephone number on a piece of paper and hands it to me.

"Be sure to call me if there's anything you need, okay? You have a phone, don't you?"

"That's right."

"Well, call me, okay? If you need anything. Anything at all."

Now that there is how a young man ought to act. He's the kind of lad that will treat a woman right. That much I can tell just from the way he is with me. And that makes me think long and hard about wish number four.

"Speaking of that beautiful mom . . ."

"Yes?" he says with obvious interest.

"Well, that boy's in the hospital and I can't see him."

Truth is, I just want to get Collins back in the same room with Anna. Give wish number four a chance. But now that I think of it, I can kill two birds with one stone.

"Give me a ride to my house?" I say. "There's something there I need you to take him."

On the way home, sitting next to Collins in a nice new foreign car of some sort, I realize what I'm about to do. What I'm about to trust him with. Makes me think I need to get to know this lad a little better. I trust my instincts, and that's the truth. They led me to Jenny, and to baseball, I'd even argue they somehow led me to Jason. And with the restrictive order and all, Collins's my only option, anyhow. But a little assurance never hurt anyone.

"Tell me about yourself," I say.

He doesn't seem taken aback at all. Just smiles a bit and keeps his eyes on the road. "What do you want to know? Biographical information or my deepest, darkest secret?"

"Either one."

"Well, my name's not actually Collins Jackson."

"No?"

"Nope. Other way around. Jackson Collins. But I spent a few years in Colombia, and it seemed like everyone switched it around for some reason. Maybe it's the whole noun-before-the-adjective thing in Spanish, I don't know. But I got so used to being called Collins Jackson, now I introduce myself that way."

"Where you from?" I ask.

"A small town in Minnesota called Sparkling Pond. Beautiful place, right on the Mississippi River, in the bluffs. I get back there as often as I can."

"Any brothers or sisters?"

"A sister. Aspen. She's still at home. She and her husband are part owners of a restaurant with Claire Lyons, who's kind of a local legend out there."

"Get along with your parents?" I ask, because that's an important one in my book.

"They're gone, I'm afraid." The wind whistles through a crack in the window, making me think maybe the car isn't as new as I'd thought. "I was in Colombia when it happened. My mom was in an accident; no way I could have gotten back. But my dad was sick for a little while. Unfortunately, I wasn't able to get home in time to see him either."

"What were you doing in Colombia?"

Collins answers each question quickly. If my prying bothers him, he sure doesn't let on. "Peace Corps," he says. "I mostly dug wells in very remote areas. One day I got back to Bogotá and called home. Aspen told me our dad had died and she was getting married." He stares out the window longer than a fella should when he's driving. "I think I helped a lot of people, but I missed out on a lot when I was away."

We pull up to the house before I can get to know as much as I'd like about the fella, but I guess I heard enough. It'll be up to Anna whether she likes him or not.

"This is a nice place," Collins says when we step into the living room. It's no fancier than it's ever been, but he seems to like it.

"Mind helping me with that?" I say, pointing to the broomstick I use to reach the rope on the ceiling.

Collins is able to get the rope on his first try, then he pulls open the swinging door and sets the ladder up just right. He follows me from rung to rung and doesn't once tell me to get a move on.

"Wow," Collins says when we're in the attic. You'd think he's never seen a bunch of old stuff before. He's leaning in close, looking at various things like he's in a museum. 'Course, some of the things are about as old as I am.

"This here's why we're in the attic," I say, moving toward the trunk. I ignore the recordings from my playing days and pick up the '34 Topps card. I hand it to Collins, who stares at it for a long moment, then jumps back like it's poisonous.

"Is that you? This is . . . this is amazing."

Most of the things up here, I'd say he's crazy for calling them amazing. But the '34 Topps card, well, it has a special place in my heart. "Wasn't my best year, statistically," I say, because I was taught to be modest.

"But you played for the Cubs," he says, more than a tinge of awe in his voice. "The Big League club? The Chicago Cubs?"

"That's the team," I say. "I want you to give that card to Jason. Anna's boy. That is, if you would. He's at the Children's Hospital in Chicago, see. And I . . ." I'm not sure how much to tell Collins.

Not sure what he'd think if he knew I was a kidnapper and jail-bird. "I'm not able to go see him just now, much as I'd like to."

Collins takes the card but doesn't answer for a good long while. Finally, he looks from the card to me, still with that twinge of awe in his eyes. "I'd be honored, Mr. McBride," he says.

CHAPTER 36

Jason doesn't return my email. Not that night, not the next morning. I check my machine every five minutes, all day long. It's killing me, not knowing what's going on. How he's doing. Wait and wait and wait, that's all I can do. Nothing can drive a man crazy faster than waiting on something that means a lot to him. To have no control over something so important lets a fella know right where he stands in the grand scheme of things. Somewhere pretty damn close to nowhere.

Maybe that's why I feel so lost.

Finally, just when I feel like I could pop, the telephone rings and Anna's voice is on the other end. She's quiet, subdued, and doesn't have much to say. Just wanted to update me because she thought I might be going crazy—she really is quite a lady. But when I hang up, I realize I haven't learned anything. I guess there's nothing to learn.

Jason's alive. He's not doing well. He needs a new heart. The only new detail I learned is that he's third on the list of transplant recipients. Unfortunately, it usually takes about four months for a heart to become available. And there's no way Benedict can speed that up with money—and it sounds like he's tried. The only way Jason could jump spots is if a heart becomes available locally, like if someone dies real close to him, geographically. Anna says they'll sometimes make an exception, in cases like that.

I wander into St. Joseph's, thinking I might have to break down and get that cane Doc Keaton's always pushing on me. Not sure how much more I can take from this knee. I find the nearest pew and sit my old body down in it. The smell of incense calms me. This is the real stuff, the pungent stuff that can just about knock a fella on his rear end. Not the fruity kind down at that art class that just makes you dizzy.

Father James is nowhere to be seen. No people, actually. No sounds, even. It's as quiet in here as I've ever heard it. No hum from the radiator; no rustle of the congregation, not even the light crackle from the pack of prayer candles. Maybe that's why Father James's footsteps, when they finally come, are so loud.

"Murray," he says, and sits down a few feet from me. Several seconds go by with both of us staring up at the altar, the crucified Christ. "I heard," he says.

But he doesn't say any more so I'm not sure what he's heard. Something I haven't? That Jason died in the last few minutes? That there's been some development in his condition? Or just that things didn't go as planned. "Fact is, I love that kid, Father."

He slides closer, pats my knee. And for some reason, I don't mind his leg against mine. "That's great, Murray. Really great."

"Great? How can you say it's great when he's going to die. How can anything about that be great?"

I expect him to say *The Lord works in mysterious ways* or some such thing. But he doesn't. "Without love, our lives would be nothing," he says. "The world would be nothing. Without love, we might as well not even exist."

"Well," I say, because his young brain works faster than mine and I can't think how to respond to something like that. Finally, I tell the simple truth. "Love hurts sometimes, Father. Hurts like hell, and I'm not sorry to say that word. Hurts like hell and I don't know if I can take it anymore."

"What other option do you have? To curl up and insulate yourself from the world and everyone in it?" He gives me a mean- ingful look. "To forget to take your pill? You'll have plenty of time to be dead, Murray. But this is the only time you have to live. Don't throw that gift away."

He pats my leg again and stands to leave. But suddenly, I don't want to be alone. "I don't know what to do," I say. "I don't know how to . . . not feel so lost." He doesn't answer right away, so I fight back the tightening in my throat and wipe at my eyes. "Just tell me. What should I do?"

Father James looks into the vastness of the church for a good, long while. The stone pillars, the paintings of the Stations of the Cross, and the rows of pews padded with red felt, so empty and old. "At my first church, there was a young couple who used to be in my congregation," he says, his voice wispy and strange. "They were vibrant. Happy. The all-American family. They used to come every Sunday and sit right in the front pew, where they would sing and pray. The whole church watched them—they were like that. You couldn't take your eyes off them. Something about them was . . . more alive than the rest of us. It was like God had given them something. An energy, I guess, that most people don't get.

"The woman became pregnant and they had a little boy, and everyone could tell, the first time they saw him, that the boy had the same energy. The same life. But tragedy struck that family. That boy. And like a lot of families that experience tragedy, it changed the couple.

"The woman, though devastated, was eventually able to find meaning in her life. She was able to remain true to herself, and to the spirit that made her so special. The man, well, he became lost. Lost in the grief. Lost in the pain. Lost in the guilt, though he had done nothing wrong. He remained lost, unable to find his way to the other side."

If the good father thinks telling me a story about a boy who died is helpful, he's got another thing coming. Still, his words have meaning, even if my old brain has a hard time figuring them out.

"We're never as lost as it seems, Murray," Father says. "There's always a path to take. But we have to want to take it."

He walks to the front of the church, genuflects near the altar, and continues to the side door. Just before he disappears, he turns back.

"Find yourself, Murray. And you'll find your path."

Find myself, and I'll find my path.

It sounds like gibberish, if you ask me. Something the crazy lady in art class would say, not Father James. But I let the words rattle around in my old brain, trying not to feel the emptiness inside. Trying not to feel so alone. So lost.

The only time I don't feel lost is when I drive by Jason's house, so I do that. Been doing that a lot, actually. Been home from Chicago for two and a half days and I've made six trips around his block. There's the spot by the maple tree I saw him dressed to the nines, ready for his kiss. Around back, there's the spot I parked the Chevy when I picked him up late at night. All the places are still here. Now all I need is the kid.

And that's when I realize what's going on. I'm slowly dying here while Jason's slowly dying in the hospital. The kid's become my navigational beacon. My compass. And I like to think maybe I've become his.

No wonder I feel so lost.

It hits me like a home plate collision, Father James's words. I have to find myself, to figure out who I am and who I want to be. And there's no doubt in my mind who I want to be. I want to be Jason's friend.

I turn the Chevy around and head straight for Benedict Cashman's mansion.

The guard at the gate waves me in like we're old pals now, but Benedict makes me wait, like always. When he finally opens the door, I launch right in. "Now see here," I say. "I only want what's best for Jason and what you're doing with the restrictive order is just not right, that's what. I demand to be able to see that boy."

Think I might have shocked him a little—it's not every day a hundred-year-old man shows up on your doorstep hollering at you. But it only lasts a second and then he's back on the offensive.

"You kidnapped my son," he says. "And you think I'm going to let you anywhere near him again? Ever? You're as insane as you are ancient."

"What do you have against me?" I ask. "Why do you want to stop my happiness? Why do you want to stop your own son from being happy?"

"You kidnapped him!"

"I tried to make his wishes come true! Because you were too busy to be bothered!" My voice cracks and I feel the crazed look on my face. "Too busy till he was laying flat on a hospital bed. Now what kind of a father is that?"

I could have smacked him in the jaw and I don't think it would have hit him any harder. I don't understand how he couldn't have thought that exact thing a million times. But maybe he's been so wrapped up in his business world he hasn't noticed what kind of a father he's become. Maybe he's rationalized his actions, his lack of involvement in Jason's life, by making money to pay for medical bills and figuring that was enough.

I know a thing or two about that. And as I lecture him on what he's missing out on, I'm talking to my thirty-year-old self every bit as much as him.

"There's more to being a father than making money, see? There's Little League games and crushes on girls. Superhero dreams and learning magic tricks. Birthdays and Halloweens and Christmases. That's the good stuff, but you haven't been around for any of it. You haven't seen what a great kid you have because you won't let yourself see. But I've seen. Believe you me, I've seen plenty. And I understand you better than you think."

"What do you understand?"

"That sometimes it's easier to hide away behind a tough exterior than it is to face the fact that you have a son—an amazing little boy—who just might die before you or I get to see him again. But whether you admit it to yourself or not, here's the truth—your boy could die any minute waiting for a heart, and you're not even there. I think that's despicable."

The blast that knocks me off my feet feels like a bomb—or at least how the lads who came home from the war described it. On my feet one moment, and then BAM! Next thing I know I'm staring up from the ground, trying to figure out how I got on my butt and waiting for my body to figure out what hurts most.

Benedict Cashman stands over me, but he looks nothing like the man who shoved me just now. His eyes are wide with fear—and I like to think it's not just fear of a lawsuit. I like to think that maybe, deep down inside, he flat-out cares. If this is what it took to bring that side of him out to where the world can see it, I'd be willing to have him push me down a hundred times over.

That said, I can't seem to move my left leg at all, and the adrenaline must be wearing off because a pain like I've never felt shoots through my knee and spreads through my entire body, like it has tentacles that can reach every inch of me. I keep it all in, but the effort makes it impossible to move. I see Benedict's hand reaching out, hoping to help me to my feet. But I can't take it.

"I'm sorry," he mumbles. And once my senses start to return a bit I realize he's repeating it. He pulls me to my feet, which sends another wave of pain through me, but especially my leg. There might actually be something seriously wrong with my knee. He brushes some gravel from my shirt and bends down to wipe my pant leg clean, but when he gets close to my knee I start hollering something fierce. "I'm sorry," he says again. "I just . . . there's no excuse. I apologize."

I reckon I'm within my rights to cuss him out good. To threaten to sue him, and maybe even to go through with it. But there are more important things to think about. And now, thanks to Benedict's short temper, I've got the upper hand.

"Jason," I say simply. "I need to see Jason."

"Of course, of course. I'll call the police immediately and have the restraining order lifted. Of course you can see him, of course. Please, I'm sorry about this. No hard feelings?"

I try to stand up tall. To put out my chest and set my shoulders back. But I'm not sure I actually move at all. "I don't know what happened between you and Anna. Don't rightly care either. But you have a son. A wonderful little boy. And he needs you, see? Doesn't matter what happened, a time like this, a boy needs his father." I stare at him hard. He's not the same man he was just minutes ago. Something about shoving an old codger to the ground shook something free inside him. "You should be with him," I say. Then I turn my back and walk away, hoping like nothing that my leg holds out.

CHAPTER 37

The agony of my knee has spread to my entire leg, even up my back. I try to sprint from Benedict's mansion and into my car, but instead my walk is frustratingly slow.

This here's a level of pain I can't say I've ever had to deal with before. Physical pain, that is. The other kind, the kind that makes it feel like your chest might collapse in on itself and your heart might explode like a hand grenade, well, that kind I'm more familiar with.

And now, out of the blue, it strikes again. Because I loved and lost a woman who made my heart skip a beat, who made my dreams come true, who was my soulmate for longer than most people live. The pain that comes with that kind of loss is as unpredictable as it is powerful. So even though I'm able to see Jason again and try to make the rest of his wishes come true, I'm paralyzed by the memory of my beautiful bride. It hurts all over again. Like she just left me yesterday. If I didn't know it before, I sure know it now—this kind of pain will never leave me.

But it's fleeting—at least this time. I manage to get myself into the Chevy and make my way home because I can't leave without packing a few things. I don't reckon I'll be coming home again for a while. Maybe not ever. Not if Jason's as sick as I'm afraid he is—there's still been no answer to my email, far as I can tell. If that boy dies, I suppose I'll lie down and die right next to him. No need to come back to the house in that case.

I'll have to say a proper goodbye to this house. Quick, sure. But proper. After all, it's the place Jenny and I lived when we got married. Brought our boys home as newborns to this house. Raised them. Sent them off. And still, it was Jenny and me, just the two of us in our own little house. A little slice of heaven. It'd only be right to say a proper goodbye. Maybe walk through every room and let the memories wash over me once more.

When I come through the front door, much slower than usual and still struggling with the pain centered just above my knee, the light on the answering machine is flashing. So I limp over and push the play button.

"Murray, it's Brandon. I hear you've been doing the art class. Great to hear it. Sounds like you need to study up on their rules about sitting still and not talking, but we can discuss that later. I've got your check for you. Listen. Murray. The old-man-look is huge right now. I'm talking rake-in-the-cash ginormous, capiche? You've got to ride the wave—"

I smash the button to erase the message and take satisfaction in the beep. I have just enough time to say out loud, "You just want to make money for yourself, you selfish—" before I'm cut off by the next message. I can barely make out the voice through her crying.

"Murray? Murray, it's Anna, are you there? Murray, pick up. Murray, I need you. I need you here. Jason needs you. He's . . . he's not doing well, Murray, not well at all. I heard you convinced Ben to lift the restraining order. If you get this, please come. Right away. We don't have much time."

Of all the things I should be thinking, the very last is to wonder how she knew about what happened with me and Benedict. There was a time when news like that would take days to make the rounds. Weeks sometimes, if the people were a long ways apart. And here, Anna knew about what happened with Benedict before I even returned home from his mansion. The speed of the world amazes me.

Someone once told me computers are run on nothing but zeros and ones. That somehow a code made up of only those two numbers has created all of the digital insanity of the world today. Sometimes I imagine a line of zeros and ones—a big, long string of them—just floating through the sky. Then another identical line, and another next to that one, until all the air space is covered with lines of zeros and ones. It's a swarm, like mosquitoes, so thick it blocks out the sun. So heavy we can't even breathe anymore. It chokes me now, the swarm of zeros and ones. Fills my lungs right up through my nostrils, packs down my throat so tight I can't get any air at all.

The message machine beeps, waking me from my visions of zeros and ones, and I realize with a jerk that it's not the zeros and ones choking me at all. That there's something else. Something just as all-consuming, just as powerful, that's making it impossible to breathe.

If you get this, please come. We don't have much time.

I take off out of the entryway faster than I've moved in years. Can't feel my knee at all. And I don't even think twice about saying a proper goodbye to the old house.

There's a voice I heard behind Anna's words. If the voice is right, I have a different goodbye to say.

CHAPTER 38

I never made it very far past the front desk my first time in this hospital, but this time they escort me through like I'm some sort of celebrity. A nice lady in a pantsuit leads me straight to an elevator and up to Jason's room.

"Here it is," she says, and goes to push the door open.

"Not just yet," I say, and I'm barely able to grab her hand before she starts to push the door. There are voices inside and one of them, clear as a bell, is Anna's. I should go in there; I know I should. And I want to. Hell, I need to. Almost as bad as I need not to. "I just need a minute. I appreciate your help."

I can't quite interpret the look she gives me as she walks away, but at least she walks away. When I'm sure she's gone, I lean my head against the doorframe and close my eyes. Last time I was in a hospital room—and I mean inside the actual room—Jenny lost her life. I laid with her those last few hours, agonizing over the question they asked me over and over: *Do you want to let her go?*

That's how they asked it. Thought it was tactful, I reckon. Better than *Do you want to pull the plug?* or *Should we let her die now?* It was just a matter of words, I knew that. But when they asked it that way—*Do you want to let her go now?*—how could I answer anything other than *No! I'm not ready! I'll never be able to let her go, she's my wife!*

So that's what I answered, over and over. Until a doctor with a calm, gentle voice told me it was time. That she wasn't coming back. She wasn't going to get better. She'd lived a good, long life and part of a good, long life, inevitably, is death.

So I agreed to let her go.

THE FIVE WISHES OF MR. MURRAY McBRIDE

It took a long while for me to be okay with that. Eventually, I came to understand that the doctor had been right. That it had taken courage for him to do that. But when she took her last breath, with my forehead pressed against hers and my arms wrapped around her frail shoulders, all I could feel was guilt. Guilt and loss.

They had to lift me off the bed, hours later. They had to pry each of my fingers loose from both her hands. They had to bring in a social worker to tell me it was okay. To escort me out of the room. At the doorway I turned back. She lay there so still. The love of my life. So peaceful. So beautiful, even in death. I wanted so much to break free of the social worker and lay with her again. To stay with her. To never leave that bed until I took my last breath too, and then I'd never have to let her go. But the social worker pressed a gentle hand against my back and slowly, slowly, I left Jenny behind.

I haven't set foot in a hospital room since.

But Anna's voice is inside, and now I hear Tiegan's laughter as well, although it sounds more strained than I recall. I close my eyes and ask Jenny for strength. Then I take a deep breath and push the door open.

First thing I see is Jason and he's sitting up, and if he's sitting up, he can't be in as bad a shape as I'd feared. But I quickly realize he's in one of those beds that folds up, he has more tubes and monitors on him than a boy ought to, and his eyes are closed. I walk closer and see, clutched in his hands like he'll never let it go, my '34 Topps card.

Hands Man came through after all.

I look away before I start to cry right here and now. Tiegan's got her normal pigtails back, but no baseball uniform now. Still got her cap, of course, and looks ready to go knock the ball around the park, but she also looks more like a little girl. Reminds me a lot of the All-American Girls Professional Baseball players, which shouldn't be a shocker at all, I guess. And in a pair of big soft chairs in the corner, Della sits next to Anna, who is staring at her boy from a small distance.

When I step into the room, they all look my way. Della gives me a sweet smile and Anna rises from the chair, more slowly than suits her, and wraps me in a hug. "Thank you for coming," she says. "He's been asking for you."

She tells me Jason's been asleep for a good long time. They never know for sure when he'll wake up—or even if he'll wake up, if they're honest—but if he sticks to the schedule he's been on recently, he should wake up soon. Della insists I take the chair next to Anna, so we ease into the soft fabric and I hold her hand tightly while we stare at Jason's closed eyelids.

Several minutes later, Collins arrives with three steaming cups of coffee and a hot chocolate. He offers me his coffee, but I say no thank you. Caffeine doesn't agree with my digestive system these days. I offer Collins my seat, but thankfully he insists I stay, and finds two folding chairs from a nearby room for Della and himself.

With every minute that goes by, I get more scared. Start to worry something fierce that Jason won't wake up at all. Every breath he takes fogs up the oxygen mask covering his face. I almost smile at the thought of Fog Shadow fogging up his oxygen, but I don't because it makes him look like the villain in one of his superhero movies, not the hero. I've been in the room for near an hour when I hear Jason's voice from the bed.

"Finally. The old dude arrives." We all hop up and rush to his bedside, where Tiegan has been the whole time. He holds the oxygen mask near his mouth, I guess so he can put it back right quick if he feels the need. I lean over and give him a pat on the shoulder. Feels good, too, despite the throbbing in my knee.

We're all here. Jason's awake. It almost feels normal. Should feel normal, if the world was a just world. But it's not, and something about Jason's joking feels forced. Something about my shoulder pat feels desperate. Something about the silence in the room now feels unnatural.

"Guys," Jason says. "I've been waiting for days to smoke Murray Dude in All-Powerful Gods and Bloodsucking Aliens. Spare him the embarrassment and go get some lunch or something."

"It's Mr. McBride," I say, but I can't muster anything behind it. Not that it matters. If he hasn't learned by now, he never will.

"Of course," Anna says, and everyone begins to shuffle out. Tiegan doesn't leave at first, instead she studies Jason close. She leans over him and puts her hand on his cheek, gazing at him. I'm amazed that Jason lays there, either unable or unwilling to move away. They stare at each other, and I think for a moment they might kiss. If maybe Tiegan will decide Jason is her beautiful man and kiss him on the cheek. But after a few seconds Tiegan turns away. Her mother and Collins follow, and the door closes behind them.

I drag my chair to Jason's bedside and try not to think about Jenny. But that doesn't work a lick, so instead I ask her again for strength. Because I can tell now that this poor boy isn't well. He's not well at all. If the monitors and tubes and oxygen mask didn't convince me, the sallow skin and ragged breathing sure would.

Up until now, I've figured he'll pull through fine. I've heard all about his heart problems, but to tell the truth, he seemed okay to me. Kissed a girl—and skipped across the field in celebration. Punched a boy much bigger than him and put him on the ground. Even hit a ball over the Wrigley Field fence. How could a boy have that much heart and still die?

But now I see it. It's because there are two hearts in each of us. The one that shows what we're made of. How much we love and how well we live. Jason's got more of that heart than anyone I've ever met, along with maybe Tiegan. But there's also the physical heart. The one that only has one job—to push blood through our bodies and keep us alive.

And it's that one, the physical heart, that's quickly killing Jason.

CHAPTER 39

"Why does God make everyone die?"

We're playing the video game, just like Jason said. But I never thought for a second it was about the game. Still, this question takes me by surprise. Even at my age, it's something I've wondered. How can I explain it to a ten-year-old kid if I don't even understand it myself?

"I suppose everyone just has their time. Maybe they've finished what they were meant to do in this world, so Jesus calls them up to be with him."

"But I've heard that kids in Africa starve to death," he says. Didn't even skip a beat. I can tell he's been thinking on this for a while. "And kids in the Middle East can get blown up by a bomb," he continues. "Some of them are really little. What if they hadn't done what they were meant to do yet? What if it's too early?"

This here's a tough one, so I try to think on what Father James has said. "Well, I guess there's evil in the world. When those bad things happen, that's the devil at work."

"Yeah, but God's supposed to be stronger than the devil. So why does he let it happen?"

He's not letting me off the hook here. Not giving me an inch. And you know what? He shouldn't. A kid in his position should be able to get some answers. I reckon he deserves it. So I keep trying.

"I guess he gives people free will," I say. "And that has consequences."

"No!" Jason throws his controller hard. It smacks against the wall and breaks into three pieces. He's heard enough. Enough of the same answers that don't really answer anything at all. "That's bullshit!" he screams. "You hear me, Murray? It's bullshit! If God's strong enough to stop it, he should stop it! He should let me live!"

"Easy now. Just calm down."

"No! I won't calm down! I don't want to die! Why do I have to die?"

He stands from his bed and pulls some cords out. I stand too and it's a good thing because he doesn't have the strength and he collapses into me. I catch him but fall back against the bed while he keeps yelling, keeps searching for answers.

"You get to be a hundred years old, and I'm going to die at ten! Why can't I live to be a hundred, too? It's bullshit, Murray!"

He presses his face against my chest and sobs. His wails are muffled, and he gasps for breath every few seconds. A doctor bursts into the room but stops short when he sees me wrapping Jason in a hug. "I know," I say. "I know." I stroke his hair until he calms down. His breathing is still labored, but his sobs start to slow.

"It's bullshit," I say. "Nothing but a bunch of bullshit."

CHAPTER 40

It's impossible to watch a boy give in to fear and anger like that and not be moved. Impossible to see that and not do everything, and I mean everything, in a man's power to help. For the doctors, that means keeping him alive until a heart becomes available. For Anna, it means staying with him and praying something fierce. But for me, it means something more.

A lot more.

When the doctor and I get Jason settled back into his bed, it's a matter of seconds before he's asleep. Apparently the excitement and effort knocked him out good.

"He's been doing a lot of that," the doctor says. "Sleeping, that is. It's the best thing for him now."

"Where is he on the heart list?" I ask.

"Second, last I checked."

"So he moved up one. Do you think that means he'll make it?"

The doctor looks at me like it's not a question I should ask. "Anything's possible. We have to stay positive."

"That's not good enough." I stand as straight as I can and say, "I have a heart of a fifty-year-old, Doc Keaton tells me. I want to donate it."

The doctor lifts his chin and stares down at me from the space between his glasses and his cheeks. "Make sure you've made it clear that you want to be an organ donor when you die. When the time comes, your heart, if it's healthy enough, will be given to someone in need."

I stomp my foot and nearly fall over from the shot of pain that flashes down my shin. "You don't understand," I say. "I don't want to donate my heart to a random person after I die. I want to donate my heart to this boy. Today."

There's a loud beeping from the monitor by Jason's bed. The doctor looks at it briefly but doesn't react. "I'm afraid it just doesn't work that way."

"Then how can we make it work that way?" My voice cracks a bit because Jason deserves a life. He's right about that. It's not fair, the hand he's been dealt. And if I can give him more, I'm ready to do it.

"Listen," the doctor says. He tries to be sneaky, but I see him glance at his wristwatch. "Even if there were a situation where we could allow you to choose who to donate your heart to, there are two problems. First, you can't donate a heart when you're still alive. You have to have died."

Something attached to his belt starts beeping and he holds up his hand, as if I were the one talking. He pushes a couple buttons on a small device, grimaces, and snaps it back onto his belt. "Listen," he says. "It's a nice thought. A nice gesture, you know? But I'm sorry. It's just not possible."

He's gone before I even raise my hand up to stop him. Swept off into the next emergency in that fast-paced world he lives in. Jason's no closer to getting a heart, and I'm no closer to giving him mine. But I didn't get to be a hundred years old by being an idiot. If that doctor won't help me, I'm perfectly capable of taking matters into my own hands. Anna told me the way around the heart list— the availability of a heart locally. It doesn't get much more local than this.

It's getting late in the day and I haven't taken my pill yet. Normally, I would have taken it, without thinking, along with breakfast. But with all that has happened, and with Jason in the hospital, I'm off my routine. My head's already spinning a little bit. My chest feels like it's full of liquid tar. If Dr. Keaton knows what he's talking about, my body's going to start shutting down for the long, deep sleep before pretty soon. A few hours from now, with no intervention, I'll be a goner.

And Jason can have my heart.

There's a pen and a pad of paper on a tin table with wheels, right next to Jason's untouched biscuit and half tub of applesauce. I go to it and write a quick note. My knee throbs as much as ever, but it's the blurring vision that gives me a pretty good idea that Doc Keaton is right. As soon as I finish the note, I wonder if I'd have the strength to do it again. Fortunately, I don't need to. I tuck the note into the shirt pocket on my chest and make my way to the chair Anna sat in. I close my eyes and focus on keeping my composure even as breathing becomes steadily more difficult.

After a while, Anna, Collins, Della, and Tiegan return with food from the cafeteria, but I only notice them through narrow slits in my eyelids, and then I close them again. They talk in hushed voices, assuming I'm asleep. I can sense them moving around Jason's bed. I focus my thoughts on Jenny. I hope to be seeing her soon.

She'll be in her wedding gown, I've always known that. Not sure how, but I just do. I'll see her at the gates of heaven and hope they let me in. And if they do, she'll step forward, arms outstretched, her green eyes gleaming, and a little curl of her red hair loose over her cheek. When I hug her, I'll squeeze her tight. So tight. And she'll feel as warm and as loving as ever. She'll be my bride, and I'll be her beau.

And my boys. My boys will see the love I'm capable of. They'll understand that all the love I have for Jason, I have for them as well. Always have, even if I didn't know how to show it.

A cough comes out of nowhere and racks my entire body. It's sharp, full of mucus, and unlike anything I've felt before. It reminds me once again that I'm an old man. But I'm not useless. At least, not all of me. Jason can have the part of me that works, and I'll happily ride off into the sunset.

Father James says suicide is a sin. But this isn't suicide. Not in my book. In my book it's a sacrifice.

It takes longer than I would have thought, but eventually my breathing becomes uncomfortable, and then finally, as the sunlight fades behind the window blinds, it becomes very painful. But it's nothing worse than I've felt before. Probably because I know what I'm doing here is right. Jason can live, and I can go to Jenny and the boys.

I would have thought that sacrificing myself like this would be scary. Actually, I feel quite peaceful.

CHAPTER 41

I wake up in heaven. At least, I think it's heaven. It's surely not hell anyway, and I consider that both a good thing and a mistake. But I've read enough of the Old Testament to know that if I was in hell, my skin would be on fire, my soul would be in agony, and the retching odor of sulfur would be filling my lungs.

But what I smell is more . . . sterile. And Jenny's nowhere to be seen. It takes a while and I'm pretty foggy, but eventually I figure out I'm still in the hospital. Which makes it highly unlikely that I'm actually in heaven, or even dead.

I blink my eyes and see a cluster of faces above me. Five in all, making a little circle. There's Tiegan, Della, Anna, and Collins, which is a bit of a surprise. Still not used to him being around. And there's the doctor I had spoken with—the one who told me I couldn't donate organs while I was still alive.

"Mr. McBride," the doctor says. "It's good to have you back." He backs away but returns a moment later, holding something up in front of my face like a lawyer showing a defendant a damning piece of evidence.

"*When I die, please give my heart to the boy in this room,*" he says. Reads, actually, since it's straight from my note. "Did you really think that was going to work? You do realize you're in a hospital, right? We don't just let people die here."

I'm able to sit up a bit. The thing about my condition is that it has to do with my ability to breathe. So if I don't take my pills and I'm unable to breathe, I'll die rather quickly. But if my lungs work, I actually feel pretty good. So I guess this case is somewhat like a child who throws a temper tantrum and holds his breath until he passes out. Once unconscious, he starts to breathe again, wakes up a few moments later, and is no worse for the wear. Once they got my lungs working again, there was really nothing else wrong with me, and I, too, feel surprisingly no worse for the wear. All things considered, that is.

To my right, Jason lies in his bed, unconscious and breathing with the help of a machine, which is new. Nasal cannulas disappear into his nostrils—exactly what he didn't want. It doesn't look like he has moved since I last saw him.

I scratch my eyes, rub them for a moment, and notice Anna standing over me. Her cheeks have lines down them and her makeup is running down her face like a Halloween costume. She tries to say something, but nothing comes out. Then she slaps my face hard.

"You thought one death wasn't enough? You had to go and make it two?" I'm in such a state of shock I can't respond. "Do you have any idea how scared we were? We thought you were dead. And you did it on purpose!"

"For Jason," I say.

Collins pulls Anna away from my bed until I can only hear her crying. The doctor reappears over me and glances at Anna and Collins, then studies me like I'm a *Grey's Anatomy* textbook. "For the sake of argument, let's overlook the ethical issues involved with what you just did. This kid—"

"Jason," I say, trying to put Anna's accusations out of my mind. "He's a good kid and we should call him by his name."

The doctor squeezes the bridge of his nose. He looks over at Jason, who's sleeping, thank the Good Lord. He doesn't need to witness all this. "Fine. Jason is, how old? Ten?"

"Ten years old. Much too young to die."

"And, unfortunately, much too young to receive the heart of a full-grown, adult male," the doctor says. He puts his hand on my shoulder, as if trying to be supportive. I suppose, in fairness, he probably is trying. "Listen. I'm sorry to have to be the bearer of bad news. But there is just no way for you to donate your heart to a ten-year—to Jason. Medically, physiologically, it just won't work."

The beeps of Jason's heart monitor speed up, increasing in pitch as well as pace. It sounds like an emergency to me, but the doctor just glances at the monitor, then turns away, as if it isn't a big deal.

Anna comes back to my bed, tears now flowing from her eyes. I flinch, expecting another slap. But instead she buries her head in my chest and sobs.

"I'm so sorry, Murray," she says. "I don't know what got into me. I can't explain . . . there's no excuse . . . I'm just so . . . everything's just so hard."

"Shh," I say, stroking her hair and breathing in the scent of jasmine. "You've nothing to be sorry about. Nothing at all."

"What are you guys talking about over there?"

Everyone who's able turns immediately to Jason's bed, next to mine. I try to sit up, but I'm still too worn out from almost dying.

"I was just telling them what a loser you are," Tiegan says. I hadn't even noticed she was still in the room. "How you couldn't even run around the bases without tripping."

I'm shocked by her words. Tiegan—the sweetest girl I know—making fun of her friend as he lies dying in bed? But Jason cracks a smile and I realize the normalcy is exactly what he needs.

"Yeah," he says. "But the Gibson fist pump was schweet."

The room erupts in laughter. Not because what he said was so funny, but simply because he's able to say it. Della pulls Tiegan into a hug, like she's congratulating her for saying just the right thing. Anna leans her head onto Collins's shoulder and Collins gently kisses her forehead. On his bed, Jason gasps at his mother, looks straight over to me, and holds up four fingers. Then he wiggles them like he's calling for a changeup. Wish number four has come true.

It's amazing, that's what. The kid made a list of five impossible things, and together we've made four of them happen. It should make me want to sing for joy. Shout from the rooftops.

But it doesn't. Instead, it just makes me feel sad, like we're approaching the end. When we still had several wishes to go, there was a lot to look forward to. But now, with four wishes down and Jason staring death in the face, how much could possibly be left? It's like we've made it to the World Series. The highest point.

But this here's the problem with the highest point—there's only one way to go from there. And if Jason's going to survive, it'll take nothing short of his fifth and final wish—real magic.

CHAPTER 42

When the doctor suggests we go into a different room to talk, I know things are about to go from bad to worse. What I don't know is how. Can I get in trouble for trying to kill myself and donate my heart to Jason? Could I end up back in jail for this?

He asks Tiegan to keep Jason company and leads the adults into the hallway. We take a right out of the room and run straight into the bewildered and slightly embarrassed face of Benedict Cashman.

"Anna," he says. His eyes dart at me and fear flashes over his features. He nods, but doesn't look like he wants anything to do with me. "I'm just . . . well . . . is, ah . . . Jason in there?"

"He is," Anna says, her voice cool. She takes Collins's hand in what looks like a gesture of defiance. Della leans forward on her toes like she's about to pounce, but she holds herself back.

"Can I see him?"

"He *is* your son," Anna says, and I'm sure there are a lot of words she swallows. Like *Why are you just getting here now?* and maybe even *Jason doesn't want to see you.* But she doesn't say any of that, and Benedict cowers past her. It shocks me good when he puts a hand very gently on my forearm. "I just didn't want to give him hope if there wasn't any, can you understand that? I didn't mean to be a bad father. But hope . . ." He squeezes his lips tight, like if he closes them tight enough, his eyes will hold the tears back, too. "Hope just makes it harder." His shoulders sink and his head droops as he walks past us and into Jason's room. Anna lets out a deep breath and Collins wraps his arm around her. The doctor leads us into an office room across the hallway and shuts the door behind me. I let Collins have the chair next to Anna and lower myself very slowly next to him, with Della on my other side. Moving around has gotten harder and harder over the years, but now every movement is excruciating. Every motion infused with extreme pain.

The doctor doesn't sit, which isn't good. Whenever a manager had to tell a player he was traded, he'd have the lad sit, but the manager always stood.

"Some tests have come back," the doctor says, and he doesn't have to say the results aren't good. The angle of his eyebrows, the delicate tone of voice, everything is speaking loud and clear. Question is, how bad is it? "Based on what we're seeing, I don't know how Jason's alive right now. I do know he can't last much longer. Not without a new heart. We're helping him keep his SAT levels up for now, but there's only so much we can do."

Anna doesn't even flinch. I wonder if she didn't hear him right when he said there's only so much he can do or if she's been bracing herself for this news for a long time. "Where is he on the list?" she asks.

"Still second."

Anna winces and puts her head in her hands. Collins wraps his arm around her.

"But that's only two hearts, right?" Collins says. "Doesn't sound so bad, does it? How long does it usually take to move up that list?"

"An average of four months," the doctor says matter-of-factly. "Meaning the odds are Jason will have to survive another four to eight months to receive a heart. Could be less, could be more."

"Can he hang on that long?" Collins asks. "I understand what you said earlier, but is it possible?"

The doctor's eyes find the floor and I know we're not going to like what we hear. "Look, simply put, he has no chance to last eight months, or even four months. You can never tell—as I said, I'm not sure what's keeping him alive right now—but I'd be surprised if he lasts four more days. And it's entirely possible he could be looking at a matter of hours."

The words fall flat across the room. I would've thought words like that would bounce around and echo. Give you some time to comprehend. To understand. To digest. But he said the words, and then they were gone, as if the walls swallowed them whole. Leaving me wanting to ask what he just said. Maybe I heard him wrong. I must have heard him wrong.

"It's important that you understand this," the doctor says. "Because he's awake right now. The next time Jason falls asleep, I'd like you to make sure you've said everything you want to say to him."

Della lets out a quiet gasp, but Anna doesn't react. Not in the slightest. Collins wraps his arm around her more tightly, although she doesn't seem to notice. And me? I feel a fire flare up inside me like I've never felt before. Pure, clean rage, that's what. And I can't be quiet anymore. "Dadgommit," I say. "You're a doctor; you need to do your job!" He stares at me like he can't understand, so I keep shouting at him. "He's a kid, for Chrissake! A kid! How can you let him die?"

I stand up and the pain in my knee is nothing. Nothing compared to the fire in my chest. The rage in my veins. Jason was right. This is bullshit. And I don't even care if that's a curse word.

"There's a boy in there who needs a doctor," I say. "You go in there and do your job. Don't you dare let him die, you hear me? Don't you dare."

There are hands on me, holding me back. Collins, I realize. The Hands Man. But I can't help it. I can't control what's happening to me any more than I can control what's happening to Jason. So I continue to scream and shout until I run out of breath.

My world turns black yet again, and the last thing I remember is falling toward the floor.

CHAPTER 43

I wake up again, and my first thought is that a man my age shouldn't be able to lose consciousness twice in one day and live to tell the tale. And yet, here I am. Make of that what you will. Maybe I'm impossible to kill.

As my senses clear a bit, I realize I'm back in the same room as Jason, in a bed set up right next to his. He's sleeping soundly— at least I hope he's sleeping. Anna's holding his hand. Collins is holding hers. Della's in the corner chair and Tiegan, bless her soul, is on my side of the bed, keeping me company while I was out of it.

"Mr. McBride," Tiegan says. "How are you feeling?"

I take a quick inventory, but there's nothing I can find that doesn't hurt something fierce. "I feel like I'm a hundred years old," I say, and Tiegan's laugh clears away a good part of the pain.

"The doctor said to call for him when you woke up. He didn't seem very happy."

I recall the things I said to him before I passed out. Guess I wouldn't be very happy either, if I was him.

"We could just say we forgot," Tiegan says. But I shake my head, which makes my neck scream in pain.

"No, that's okay. I've dealt with scarier men than him." I'm surprised at how much effort it takes to talk. Never been this hard before.

Tiegan smiles and pushes a button on my bed. A minute later, the doctor sweeps into the room, a scowl on his face.

"I owe you an apology," I say before he can get a word in edge-wise. "I was upset, see?"

He waves it away. "Water under the bridge, Mr. McBride. Trust me, I understand."

"Then you're not upset with me?"

"No. Not at all." He takes a big breath. I guess this has been a hard day for him as well. Sometimes it's hard to remember that doctors are people too. "Mr. McBride, I'm afraid I have some bad news."

"About Jason?"

"About you."

He lets that sink in for a bit, but it doesn't really take that long. Forty years ago it might have come as a shock, but now? Only thing I can't understand is what took so long for the bad news to find me. "Okay then. Let's have it."

"When you lost consciousness—the first time—hospital pro-tocol dictates that we run some tests. Basic tests, but some of your results were out of the normal range, even for a man of your age. So we ran some more in-depth tests . . ."

"It's okay Doc, just spit it out. I can take it."

"I'm afraid you have late-stage bone cancer. From what we can tell, it started in the right knee. Lower femur actually, but it's spread to several organs, several bones . . . it's all over your body now."

"Okay," I say, because in all the time I've spent thinking about this moment, I never once considered what I'd say. I always figured the lungs would do me in. But all this time, cancer was sneaking up on me. I suppose most people would have caught it earlier, but when you get to be my age, aches and pains don't make you think "cancer." They make you think "old age."

"How much time, do you reckon?"

The doctor sighs. "Not much. Like Jason, the fact that you've been up and moving around recently is something of a medical miracle. It seems you two have been keeping each other afloat."

The spit in my mouth has all gone dry. "When you say 'not much' what does that mean? Is there anything to be done?"

"That's up to you. There are treatments available. We could start with a heavy dose of radiation and see how it affects the various tumors. There are also some newer, more experimental treatments you might be eligible for."

It sounds like he's got a whole lot more up his sleeve, so I cut to the chase. "What do you think I should do, Doc? What's the right thing to do?"

He looks around the room like he's searching for the right words. "The right thing is to accept that you've had a long, healthy life, and to die comfortably and with dignity, surrounded by those who love you."

A quick squeeze hurts my hand. It's Tiegan, with tears in her eyes. Anna and Collins are nearby, holding each other, looking at me with sympathy. That's different than pity. Pity makes me mad, but their sympathy? Well, I could swim in their looks of sympathy for years. 'Course, I don't have years.

It's an interesting thing, hearing your death sentence. Different than I would have expected. You get to a certain age and you think it won't be a big deal. That you'll be ready. Couple weeks ago I was ready.

Then I met Jason.

Still, there's something that lifts off my chest. A weight that's been there a long time now. Since my first boy died, near as I can tell. It's almost like I've been set free. I don't plan to die until Jason dies first. Maybe we'll die together. But when it's all over, then I'll be ready.

I take the doctor's hand and squeeze it tight. "Thank you, Doctor."

There's a little tear in his eye, which tells me right there he's a good man. An old codger hollers at you and his death still makes you sad? Then you're a good man in my book.

"We'll keep you comfortable until the end," he says. And I know by his tone that the end isn't far off.

CHAPTER 44

There's nothing quite like hearing you won't be around much longer. Really gets you thinking about what comes next. I can't help but wonder if everyone gets a chance to think about that, when the time comes near. Even those who die suddenly. Even if they don't see it coming. Maybe that's something the Good Lord gives us all. A moment, however brief, to really contemplate our mortality. Maybe it's just another way to explain the life-flashing-before-your-eyes thing.

Jason's still in the bed next to me. Every few seconds I look over, just to make certain he's still there. Make certain he's still breathing. One time when I look over I see a person standing in the doorway. My own flesh and blood. Chance McBride.

"Granddad," he says, and I have to admit there's a flutter somewhere in my stomach when I hear that word. Just something about being a granddad that's unlike anything else in the world, whether I remember everything that he remembers or not.

Chance comes over to my bed. He looks at Jason on the way by, but averts his eyes right quick. Makes me sad to think Jason's become something people feel uncomfortable around. That's how a fella's supposed to react to roadkill, not a kid like Jason. Then again, Chance is just like most of us—uncomfortable with pain and suffering and death. Makes it all the more meaningful that he showed up.

He doesn't say much for a good long while. Just holds my hand—something he's never done before, and which feels pretty damn good—and stares out the open blinds of the window. The only view is the roof of the next building, but Chance doesn't seem to care. I get the feeling he's not really looking at anything.

"There's something I want you to have, see?"

"What's that, Granddad?"

"My old baseball mitt. The one I let you use when we played catch. I want you to have it."

I've been racking my old brain, trying to remember playing ball with my grandson, but if the memory's in there it's lost, and lost good. But Chance doesn't need to know that. It may be true that honesty's the best policy, but it's a policy that compassion sometimes breaks in two.

"You mean it?" Chance says. "Because you don't have to do that. I mean, it's not why I'm here."

"I know it's not," I say, and I should be able to say more, but when I try to take a breath there's nothing there. For a long time—feels long anyway—I try to make my chest, lungs, and throat work, but nothing happens. I feel lightheaded and wonder if I'll pass out. If I do, I wonder if I'll start breathing again or if this is it. I clasp Chance's hands tightly and his eyes bulge. He seems to realize I haven't taken a breath in a long time and stands right quick.

"What's happening?" he says, saying exactly what I'm trying to say. "I'll call a doctor."

But just then whatever was blocking my ability to breathe breaks free and I suck in a long, full breath. It's not enough to feel comfortable, but it's enough to get me going again. Chance sits back down, but he looks at me differently. Like he's worried I'm going to die right in front of him and doesn't want to be here to see it. If that's the case, he might not want to stick around much longer. After another long stretch of silence in which the only sound is the whirring and clicking of Jason's machines, Chance speaks again.

"I want you to know, in case . . . you know . . . that I've always admired you, Granddad. I've always tried to be like you. I know I haven't succeeded. Not in any part of my life. But I always wanted to."

"No," I say, and I realize talking will never be easy for me again. I'll have to choose my words carefully and hope they convey more than I'm able to say. "Not like me. Be like you." My lungs are seized again by that same feeling. Like they're stuck and I forgot how to make them work again. But it passes quickly this time.

I look at Chance's eyes good and hard, and I can see that he's telling the truth. He has tried. And when it comes right down to it, what more can a person do? Sure, he's broken a few plates. But his intentions were good. I hope he hears more than the few words I can get myself to say.

"Proud of you."

CHAPTER 45

Jason and I both make it through the night, which isn't a given these days. Chance is gone, having said his goodbyes. Benedict, too. It's just me and Jason, with Tiegan and Della, and of course, Anna and Collins.

In the morning, a gift basket shows up, delivered by none other than Javier Candela. Jason and I are both awake. Sometimes we just lay quietly, sometimes we talk. Sometimes we reach across the beds and hold hands. Times like that, I know just how scared he is, behind his tough exterior.

"From the Cubs," Javier says, and he sets the basket down.

"What's in it?" Jason asks. His voice is devoid of excitement. His energy level is lower than a sinker ball.

Javier starts lifting items out. A baseball autographed by the entire Cubs ball club. A jersey with Javier's number but CASH-MAN embroidered on the back. He's even got two season tickets in there, for next year's season.

"They say to tell you, 'So we can fill your new heart with Cubs pride, too,'" Javier says.

Everyone thanks Javier over and over and over.

Nobody tells him that neither of us is likely to see next spring.

CHAPTER 46

Can't be sure of the time, but it's dark outside the window. Not the dark that comes with nighttime, but the dark that comes with a storm. No one's here but Tiegan. Jason's asleep, which is what he does most of the time now. Tiegan's sitting right next to his side, but when she sees my eyes flicker open, she comes over to me. She's like an angel, floating from one person in need to the next. An angel in pigtails.

"How are you feeling?" she asks. And then, before I can answer, "You look really good." She's been doing that recently—answering her own question before I'm able to give mine. And somehow it does make me feel a little better, even if I know I'm getting right close to the big kiss off.

I try to speak, but things are shutting down faster than I anticipated. The pain's worse, too, but that's just because I've been trying to lay off the morphine. But I click a little button the doctor gave me and another rush of peace flows over me. I try to keep my mind clear, but sometimes I can't help it.

"Nineteen twenty-seven," she says. "Runs batted in."

My mind immediately wakes up for the game she's been playing with me any time I'm awake—quizzing me on my baseball statistics. Nineteen twenty-seven. The boys would've been four and seven. Jenny was working in a factory to help pay the bills, so we didn't see each other much. Hard times. I felt pretty guilty that year, I remember that. My production was down, my mind not in the game.

"Sixty-seven," I say.

"Rats," Tiegan says, and she snaps her fingers. "So close. Sixty-three." She smiles like our little game gives her as much pleasure as it does me.

"I'm sorry," I manage to mumble to her. She brings her precious little face—freckled I realize for the very first time—inches from mine so she can hear.

"Why would you be sorry?" she asks.

I try to speak—I can feel my lips moving—but such little breath passes through that nothing audible comes out. I wonder if they gave me my pill. Must have though, if I'm still ticking. "Your wishes," I whisper. "You had five of them, too. I wasn't able to make them happen."

She pulls a box of Milk Duds from her pocket and tips the contents into her mouth. "Sure you did," she says. "Some of them, anyway. More than would have come true without you."

"I have more," I say. She chews her Milk Duds with a deep crease in her brow, so I force myself to continue. "Those candies of yours. Got a whole cupboard full of them. Got them from the grocery. Enough to last a good year."

"See," Tiegan says. "You made that wish come true. And the convertible, which was super awesome. And I didn't say anything before, but the reason J thought my wish to play every position in a baseball game was dumb is because I've already done it. So that's three. And that's pretty good, because I don't even deserve to have a list of wishes."

I try to move my head back and forth, but it won't move. Which saves me quite a lot of pain, come to think of it. "Of course," I say, and she leans in closer while I swallow and lick my lips with a bone-dry tongue. "Of course you deserve wishes."

"But I'm not sick. You should have been the one to have a list. You and Jason."

"Everyone deserves a list, way I see it. Everyone has one. Sometimes they're just too blind to see it." I think about Jenny, my two boys, a career playing the game I love, and the chance to meet Jason Cashman. In my book, that equals five.

I don't want to click the button again. I want to look at this precious kid's freckled face and pigtails, and I want to talk about baseball statistics with her for hours. I want Jason to wake up and play video games. I want to answer his questions about death, best I can anyhow. I want to make as many wishes come true as I can.

But that time has passed. And the pain is too great. I click the button again and my wasted muscles relax a bit. I tried to be sneaky about it, but Tiegan's eyes flick down to the clicker in my hand and her lips press together tightly. Smart kid, this one.

"Mom and I are going to go out," she says in her bright young voice. "I convinced her to take me to get some Milk Duds for Jason since they don't have any in the vending machines here. But I'll be right back, I promise. Can I get you anything while I'm out?"

"A pack of baseball cards," I say. "If you can find some."

"Great idea," she says. "We'll look through them together. And Mr. McBride?" She looks deep into my eyes like she's able to see through to my soul. To my thoughts. "Just hang on, okay? Something's going to happen for Jason. It's going to be okay."

"How do you know?"

"I can just feel it," she says. She looks straight into my eyes for a moment, then says, "SBK, Mr. McBride."

"SBK, kiddo."

She gathers up her sweatshirt from the chair beside Jason and pauses by his bed. She looks at him and touches his sleeping forehead, as if checking for a temperature. Della shows up in the doorway. Keys jingle in her hand. Tiegan turns to follow her, but something stops her. She looks back at me and seems to study me, real close-like. Like she's stripping away the years and seeing me as a young man. She rushes back to my bedside, leans over, and presses her soft little lips against my leathery cheek.

"You're beautiful, Mr. McBride."

And with that, she's gone.

CHAPTER 47

Sometime later, I startle awake. First thing, I look to Jason. He's awake, too, which is unusual. We haven't been awake at the same time much recently. Even more unusual, he's got a smile on his face.

"What?" I manage to ask after three or four tries. My voice takes a while to warm up.

"You farted," he says, and he actually starts to giggle. "You woke yourself up with a super loud fart."

His giggle turns into a laugh for one beautiful, brief moment. Then he stops right quick and covers his chest with his hand. I try not to think about it, but I get the feeling this here could be the last chance we have to talk.

"It's been a great ride," I say. "Me and the Fog Shadow."

A flicker of a smile, but then he shakes his head. "All the best superheroes—like Superman and the Hulk and Spiderman—even if their best friends don't know who they are, their family knows. Their family calls them by their real name. You're my brother," he says. "You can call me Jason."

I reach across my bed, over to his. Take his hand. He doesn't pull away. In the corner chair, Anna starts to cry.

"I was an old, washed-up man," I whisper, but the room's so quiet I know he can hear. "Had nothing to live for. Wasn't even really alive. Hadn't been for a year and a half. But then I met you, and suddenly I had a purpose. You brought me back to life, see? That's the best magic trick of all, in my book. The real thing. And by my count, that makes all five wishes."

It's not much, I know, for a kid who caught the worst of breaks. But it's something. Jason picks something up from his bedside table. His list, by the looks of it. I can tell by the way he moves that it took all his energy just to lift his arms that far. He stares at it for a good long minute, then looks at me through tears so thick I wonder if he can even see me.

"I'm really glad I met you, Mr. McBride."

This time I force my head to move back and forth, I don't care how much it hurts. "You call me Murray, you hear? You call me Murray." I try to force a smile but can't feel my face move. "That is, unless you prefer 'Dude.'"

The smallest of movements twitch at the corner of Jason's lips. We lay on our hospital beds, heads turned toward each other, hands intertwined, and listen to Anna's muffled sobs from the corner of the room.

CHAPTER 48

Next time I wake up, Jason's bed is empty. I think back on what the doctor said last time.

Make sure you've said whatever you need to say to him.

I try to bolt upright with the help of a shot of adrenaline, but halfway to sitting I scream in pain and fall back. My mind is in complete panic. I'm not sure I said everything I wanted to say. Not sure I could have no matter how long I had. It's just not that easy to empty your heart to someone, no matter how much you might love him.

There's someone in the room, but my eyes aren't working so well. My old body's shutting down, real quick-like. But when he leans right over top of me and bends just a few inches from my face, I see the thick black hair and the priest getup, and I exhale nice and deep because Father James has come to see me.

It's hard to know exactly what's going on because my mind is as foggy as my eyesight. And to think, at one time I had such clarity of focus and such keen eyes I could hit a ninety-mile-an-hour fastball right out of the stadium. But now, it's not until the good father drips oil on my forehead that I realize he's giving me my last rites. Must have skipped right over the penance part, seeing as how I can't seem to talk anymore. But I figure that's okay. I've asked forgiveness plenty of times in this life, and if the Good Lord can't understand why I wasn't able to ask it recently, then he's not the Good Lord I thought he was.

"You did it, Murray," Father James says when he finishes his prayers. "I have to admit, I wasn't sure you had it in you, when you came to the church and told me about the list. But you did it. You should be proud."

It gives me a flutter, those words. Everything's muffled now. Nothing's very clear. But I feel something jump in my chest, just a little bit.

I know perfectly well what it means—Father James being here, giving me my last rites. Saying nice things about me. But I can't seem to think of anything but Jason. I try to stay awake. Maybe they just took him somewhere and he'll return soon.

But no, I know that's not true. There was no need to take him to the restroom. Or to get food. They'd already done all the tests. And he was still months away from getting a heart. There's only one thing that makes sense. My little friend has died.

In case I needed confirmation, Father James grabs my hand and squeezes it tight. "You can go now, Murray. You're free." His voice cracks. Father James is a good man. Good enough to care about an old codger like me, anyway. "Go be with Jenny," he says. And the tear I feel trickling down my cheek matches the ones on his.

I click the morphine button, then click it again. The pain washes away and I feel sleepy. I click it several more times, in rapid succession. Then I drift off into an empty sleep.

CHAPTER 49

My body is shaking. Hands on my face. My name. Over and over, I hear my name. Slowly, I awaken. It's Anna. Leaning over my bed. Her eyes are wild, her face smeared with makeup and tears. When I open my eyes fully, she falls back into the chair next to my bed and weeps. I dread what she will say.

"He's alive."

She comes back to my bed, like she can't decide where she should be. Her face is buried in the sheets near my arm. Her voice sounds like the public address system at a small-town ballpark. Garbled and warped. It sounded like she said he's alive. I try to ask, I need to know. But the ability to speak has left me. I can only hope she repeats it.

"He's alive, Murray. He's going to make it. It's so wonderful, but . . . I can't even say it. There's so much to tell you."

There's so much I never noticed before. A clock on the wall ticks seconds away. How is it possible that those seconds have been ticking my entire life? And that, for me, they will soon stop? A ray of sunlight slants through a window blind. How is it possible that, with all the sunlight I've felt on my skin, I've never been able to explain why the warmth is so comforting?

"They went in, Murray. They took out his heart, can you believe it? Took it right out of his chest and put the other one in. They said they'd never seen anything like it, not in someone who was still alive. And they said I needed to tell you. You can't go, Murray, not until I tell you. Can you hear me?"

Hear? I can hear. The words are strange. They sound so joy-ous, and yet she cries. Tears of joy, to be sure, but something else right along with it. A sadness. An agony.

"I hope you can hear me, Murray. They said there was no physical way his heart could have kept his body alive. Medically, it should have been impossible. They say they don't understand. But I do. I understand perfectly.

"It was you, Murray. You kept him alive. You and his wishes. Making them come true. Without you he would have died."

She looks at me through a sparkle, a shimmer. Full of an emo-tion I can't even recognize. She puts her palm on my cheek. "You saved my son's life," she says.

Jason has a heart. He's not going to die after all. Not for a good, long time, anyhow. Not until after a long, happy life.

Way I see it, I can rest in peace now. I can die knowing Jason will be okay. I close my eyes, and I feel like I'm soaring. There is no pain. No worry. No hurt. I see Jenny. I see my boys.

And I am happy.

I stop my story and look around backstage. My eyes are tearing up. I take in the bustle, the excitement; only moments before show-time now. I look at the scuffed wooden floorboards, the black satin curtain, the dust motes floating between me and Miles. My biographer stares at me with eyes wide as silver dollars. It's a history he never knew. A story beyond anything he could have expected when he set out to write a biography of his favorite magician. He's been silent for a long time. Smiling and gasping and sighing at all the appropriate times, but never interrupting. He seems to know the importance of this story.

"When I woke up," I say, "there were only three people I wanted to see. First was my mother, and she was holding my hand when I awoke. The second was Murray. But I was told that he had passed away peacefully while I lay in my hospital bed recovering. To this day, my biggest regret is that I never had a chance to thank him.

"And the third . . ."

My voice cracks when I say the word *third*, as if my body is warning me it won't be able to talk of her. To this day, I never have. But it's a story that needs to be told. To my biographer. To the world. I just have to figure out how to do it without breaking down in tears.

"Let me tell you a story about a girl," I say, because that's the only way I can tell it—to distance myself from the hurt. "The sweetest girl you've ever met. Such a good person, with such a good heart. She befriended an old man and a young boy. She joined them in their adventures. And when things were difficult, she told them it would be okay. She made them feel better. Maybe even more than the boy, she made the old man feel young again.

"She was there at the hospital when both of them were very sick. She stayed next to their beds almost the entire time. Almost, but not completely. There came a moment when she knew there was nothing she could do there, and she wanted to do something. It was in her nature. So she convinced her mother to take her to the store for candy, because she knew the boy would like that and she wanted to have a gift for him when he awoke. If he awoke.

"So they drove, this girl and her mother, despite the rainy skies and the slippery roads. They shouldn't have done it, but that's how this girl was. She was willing to put herself at risk for the simple happiness of her friends.

"It wasn't her fault. Not her mother's fault. No other driver was at fault. It wasn't anybody's fault at all. But how can something so terrible be no one's fault? How can nobody be responsible for the world's worst tragedies?

"The car hit a puddle and began to hydroplane. It slid off the road. Just the tires on the right side at first, but the girl's mother lost control. There was nothing she could do. The car plowed into the ditch. It's something that happens every day, and drivers are pulled from the ditch and they go back to their normal lives. But on this night, with this girl and this mother, there was a light pole. The car could have slid into the ditch before the pole, or it could have slid past it. But it didn't. It hit the pole squarely, right where the girl sat.

"I can only imagine what happened next, and in truth I don't want to imagine it. I don't want to think about what happened to that girl, or the terror her mother must have felt. The horror, the paralyzing fear, and then the sadness. The immense, all-consuming sorrow. Her daughter was gone. Moments before, this beautiful girl had been alive and talking and smiling in the back seat. She had been looking forward to the look on the boy's face when she gave him his candy. And then, in the blink of an eye, she was gone.

"The mother, of course, was devastated. It would have been perfectly understandable if she had been too wrapped up in her shock and grief to function. But the mother was no ordinary woman. She was strong. She was brave. And she was kind. So, to the boy's everlasting gratitude, the mother was able to summon a level of strength almost beyond comprehension. Because she knew the boy. And she knew of his problem. His need.

"So she pulled out her cell phone, and with her beloved daughter lying dead in her arms, she made a life-saving call. Within moments, a helicopter departed the hospital. The mother and girl hadn't made it far. It didn't take long. Soon, the lifeless girl was on the operating table at the hospital.

"The doctors worked diligently. They too, had to put aside their sorrow for the girl. They had to do their job. And they did. They made certain that in death, the girl would continue what she had always done—she would give life."

My biographer has tears rolling down his cheeks, dripping from his jaw. I hear the stir of the audience. When I peek around the curtain, I see a full theater. Every last seat is taken, with the exception of the two right in front.

"I don't understand," my biographer says. "If the girl was Tiegan, and the boy was you, then that would mean . . ." He tries to finish, but can't. Instead, his eyes bounce from one of mine to the other, and then down to my chest.

"Tiegan's heart, yes. She went out to buy me candy and ended up giving me her very life."

He's speechless, my biographer. He looks shell-shocked—like his view of the world has been changed forever, just as mine was as a ten-year-old boy when I awoke with a new, strong heart beating in my chest. The heart of my very best friend.

So much has changed since then. So much has happened. I am living a life. A life given to me by Tiegan Rose Marie Atherton.

"I decided right away, despite my youth and immaturity, to devote my life to making Tiegan's last wish come true. I grew up quickly, after what happened. I threw myself into magic. Just toys and books at first. But when I grew old enough, I moved away to study magic all around the world. Slowly, I became a master. I began performing. I began making money.

"I lived as sparsely as possible, saving every possible penny, determined to raise a million dollars for the homeless. For Tiegan. It became my obsession. I didn't make friends. I kept family at a distance. As you know, I never granted an interview. Until now."

"Now" is a time I never thought I'd see. A time when I'm a thirty-year-old man, with many more years still in front of me. A time—a night—when I'll reach one million dollars and complete my friend's wishes. Tiegan's five wishes.

I feel a tap on my shoulder. Standing in front of me, for the first time in years, is Collins. Gentle Collins. My fourth wish, come true far beyond my expectations. "Jason," he says. "I mean, Prospero."

"No, no. It's Jason. Of course it's Jason. You came," I say. "I was beginning to worry you wouldn't." I stand and hug him, hoping the tightness of my embrace will convey the gratitude I feel.

"Are you kidding? We wouldn't miss this for the world."

"Is Mom here?"

He moves aside so I can see behind him. There's a man standing awkwardly by himself, looking around backstage as if lost. My father. Here. Supporting me. As he always has, I suppose. In his own way. His hand flicks in a small wave but then he moves quickly toward the audience to take his seat.

"There," Collins says, pointing.

An usher strides through a hallway and into the backstage area. Two women follow him. One is my mother. When she sees me in my tuxedo, her entire face spreads into a grin and she runs to greet me. She squeezes me wordlessly, the urgency of her embrace saying more than words ever could.

When she pushes me to arm's length to stare at me, I see the tears in her eyes. She simply nods and turns toward someone with a flowing dress and purple streaks in her hair.

"She wasn't going to come," my mom says. "Said it was too painful. But something changed her mind."

I rush over, unable to believe it might actually be her. But when she turns to me, despite twenty years, there's no doubt. "SBK, Jason," she says. I crumble into her arms, try to hold back a sob, but then completely break down. I owe my very life to this woman. My very heart. "Thank you for this," she says. "Tiegan would be so very proud of you."

My mother joins our embrace, then Collins. We huddle together, arms wrapped tightly around each other.

"You don't have to stay away anymore," Della says. "What you've done is beautiful. But you're free now. You can come back to your family."

I nod hard through the tears. A boy, saved from death, finally returned home.

A loud voice booms from the other side of the curtain. It's the stage manager, introducing me right on time, oblivious to the drama taking place backstage. I try to pull myself together so I can perform.

"This," I say, nodding to each of them. "All of us here, together, this is real magic. Who would have thought the last of my five wishes and the last of Tiegan's would come true at the very same moment? I think, more than anything, it's what Murray would have wanted. Our wishes . . . they were always his, too."

I straighten my bow tie and take a deep breath to steady myself. "I have to go," I say. "But stay, please. Watch the show from back here. After the performance, we'll be together. After this, everything will be how it should be."

To my left, Miles is listening in, staring at me like he's seeing me for the first time. "Prospero," my biographer says. "Magic. This show. It's all so, so secondary. So meaningless in comparison to your story."

"No," I say. I take his hand in mine, amazed as always that I'm alive, that I'm able to touch another human. That blood continues to flow through my body. "This show means everything."

I'm not sure where Tiegan and Murray are right now. And I used to be unsure if they even knew about those of us here on earth. If they cared about us and watched over us. But now I know. They're here with us. At this moment and always.

I know, because I can feel it in my heart.

My biographer can only stare as I walk away. I step to the center of the curtain and close my eyes. When the announcer says my name, I walk through the part in the curtain and straight into a puff of smoke. The audience erupts in applause. I bask in it for a moment, wondering what Tiegan would think of it all.

"I'd like to thank you for coming," I say, and silence immediately blankets the entire auditorium. A spotlight is the only light in the building. Pointed directly at me, it makes the lapels of my tuxedo shine. Dust motes hover in the still air.

I have their complete attention. The audience. My family. And somewhere, an old man and a young girl, looking down and smiling.

"It's impossible for me to articulate how happy I am that you're here. Rest assured, you will not leave disappointed. Tonight you will see things that defy possibility. Things that can only be attributed to mystery and miracle. Tonight, my friends, you will join me in witnessing things beyond the realm of this universe."

My eyes are drawn to the banner above, and to the waiting stares of thousands of people. I close my eyes, and focus on my old friend Murray, and on the young girl who saved my life. *Thank you,* I say to them. *Thank you for making wishes come true.* I open my eyes, feel the warmth of the spotlight, and spread my arms wide. I yell, with all the love and energy and passion I have in my healthy, overflowing heart.

"I am Prospero, Master of the Impossible! And tonight, I bring you . . . Magic!"

The End

AFTERWORD

Six years ago, with the release of *The Five Wishes of Mr. Murray McBride*, my life changed dramatically. But I wouldn't realize it for many months.

The Five Wishes of Mr. Murray McBride was first released by a small publisher (Black Rose Writing) with very little fanfare. When release day arrived, along with my "author copies" in the mail, I didn't celebrate a momentous accomplishment and start a book tour. Since no one but my closest friends and family had purchased the book, I held back tears and put the books—still in the box they arrived in—into my basement storage space and tried to forget about them. I tried to pretend Murray, Jason, and their wishes had never existed. To let go of SBK and Tiegan Rose Marie Atherton. Because it was obvious that no one wanted to read the story you now hold.

But I would soon realize the difference between no one wanting to read it and no one knowing about it.

The change was slow. A contest here, an award there. A good review here, a batch of sales there. There was something satisfying about the organic nature of it. This story had to prove itself over and over again. About a year after the book was released, I could go onto Amazon and read new uplifting reviews daily. There was the elderly woman who said she read the story and found a reason to continue living, and the mother of a heart transplant recipient who thanked me for making her feel the presence of her son, who had since passed, and countless others who were touched by the story. These reviews made the whole thing worth it, even when the number of copies sold was only in the hundreds. But eventually, through little more than word-of-mouth and advertising, the story began to find its legs. And then it began to run wild.

I wrote this story shortly after my dad died. I wish he could have lived to read it. I was very close to my dad and his death came as a heart-wrenching shock that I was ill-equipped to deal with. I realized I had regrets about how little I had seen him in the years immediately before he died—due to my decisions, not his. In many ways, I found myself wishing I had been a better son. Writing this story was my therapy and my penance. Several people have asked me how I, as a forty-year-old, could write convincingly in the voice of a one-hundred-year-old. I think it's because my dad's death aged me. My soul, if not my body.

I miss him every day. It felt meaningful to dedicate this specific story to his memory. I like to think he would be proud to say his son wrote it.

This book will never be confused with a work by William Shakespeare or Walt Whitman, and I couldn't write the beautiful, literary works of our best writers of today even if I tried to be like them. But, undeniably, something about this simple story has connected with many people.

Maybe it's the fact that it's authentic and written from the heart. Maybe it's that we're inundated with negativity and hate these days and people are looking for a little bit of love in their lives. Maybe I just stumbled upon characters and a storyline that "work." Whatever it is, I feel incredibly grateful.

I hope you, too, can allow yourself to be immersed in the lives of Murray, Jason, and Tiegan. I hope you get to know them and feel like you're a part of their lives for a couple hundred pages.

Most of all, very simply, I hope you enjoy the story.

—Joe Siple, 2024

ACKNOWLEDGMENTS

I've heard the creation of a book is a team effort, but I'm not sure I truly believed it until I wrote *The Five Wishes of Mr. Murray McBride*. So many people helped this story become what it is that I can no longer see it as exclusively mine.

First, a big thank-you to my original publisher, Reagan Rothe, at Black Rose Writing. I'll be eternally grateful for the opportunity.

One of the most exciting days of my life was when I received an email from Barbara Berger, executive editor at Union Square & Co. Thank you for making this dream come true, and for being so professional along the way. It has been a pleasure to work with you.

To the rest of the Union Square & Co. team, my sincerest gratitude for the beautiful cover, the polished manuscript and design, and the smooth production of the Murray McBride books: Alison Skrabek, project editor; Patrick Sullivan, cover designer and art director; Erik Jacobsen, cover design production; Richard Hazelton, interior designer; Kevin Ullrich, creative operations director; and Sandy Noman, production manager. You all did wonderful work and I'm proud to be partnered with you.

My local writer's group provided important feedback as well as creative brainstorming that led directly to some of the best parts of the story. I couldn't have done it without you guys.

And, most importantly, my family provided me with support and encouragement throughout the peaks and valleys of writing. A special thanks to my wife, Anne. When I wanted to quit, you told me you saw me as a writer and bought a bottle of La Folie to toast this success before we knew it would happen. I can't thank you enough.

Lastly, I'd like to thank you, the reader. I hope you enjoyed Murray, Jason, and Tiegan as much as I enjoyed creating them. May we all live life as if we had a limited amount of time to make our wishes come true.

After all, we do.

BOOK CLUB QUESTIONS
FOR DISCUSSION

1. Death is not only the main antagonistic force in the story, but also a main theme. The intent was to deal with death seriously and honestly, while still leaving the reader feeling a sense of redemption. Was this accomplished? Why or why not?

2. Regret is another major theme, especially for Murray. Is it possible to live a life free of regret? If it is, do we risk missing out on opportunities to learn and grow? Can regret be a good thing?

3. "Second chances" is another theme. This is where redemption comes from. Which characters in the book are given a second chance, and how do they take advantage of the opportunity?

4. What did you think about Murray's age as it relates to his abilities as well as his motivations to accomplish his goals? Do people tend to become more careful and reserved as they approach the end of their lives, or more carefree and spontaneous?

5. Jason can be disrespectful and maybe even a bit obnoxious. He's able to get away with more than a normal character because of his illness, but does it ever go too far? Did you ever find yourself not liking him?

6. Tiegan is meant to be a "perfect" character, free of the flaws that most characters need in order to be interesting. Does this work for her? Why or why not?

7. There isn't a typical "protagonist vs. antagonist" to keep the plot moving. Instead, the story is structured around the five wishes

and relies on them to propel the story forward. What are the benefits and drawbacks of a story that focuses on "character vs. situation" as opposed to "character vs. villain"?

8. Tiegan has a unique relationship with her mother. Do you think their relationship would have been as close if they hadn't been through hardship together? Is there value to creating personal greetings, like SBK, as a constant reminder of shared history and worldview?

9. What did Murray's relationship with Chance illustrate regarding assumptions and miscommunication in close relationships? Who was in the wrong, and who was responsible for their reconnecting? Is there anything to learn from their struggles and ultimate reconciliation?

10. Murray played baseball at the highest level, and yet Jason couldn't imagine that a man so old had ever been athletic. What assumptions do people make about older people, and how do those assumptions change as we age?

11. What did you think of the ending? In what ways was it tragic? In what ways was it hopeful? In what ways was it redemptive?

Turn the page for an exclusive sneak peek
of Joe Siple's second book in
the Murray McBride trilogy

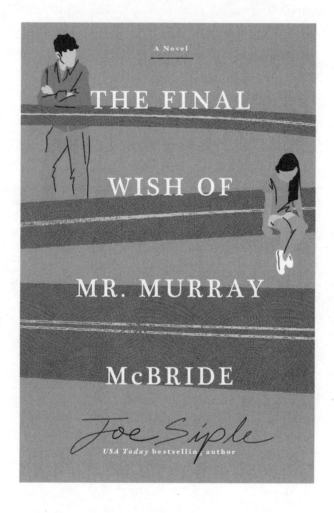

A Novel

THE FINAL
WISH OF
MR. MURRAY
McBRIDE

Joe Siple

USA Today **bestselling author**

Available from Union Square & Co.
in February 2025

I'm starting this silly thing because Father James said I should. Ridiculous, if you ask me. Not that anyone would ask my opinion these days. But I respect the good father, and Jenny had one of these journals, so I guess it can't be all bad. Don't plan to write much, though.

The only thing I'm going to say today is that young folk don't understand how much emptiness hurts. They think if you have pain, there must be a cause. Something real and substantial and . . . what's the word I'm looking for? Tangible, that's it. But they don't understand that what hurts more than anything else in the world is nothing at all. Pure emptiness. Sometimes I think I'd pay good money for a little pain. Give me something, anything, except for this confounded emptiness.

—From the journal of Murray McBride

CHAPTER 1

JFK Center for the Performing Arts

The stage curtain closes in front of me. A puff of dust billows off the thick fabric, and the three thousand people seated in the theater disappear from view.

Under my perfectly pleated tuxedo, my slicked-back hair, and a bit of stage makeup is an amazing amount of pain. My heart hurts. Figuratively, sure, but that's not what I mean. I'm talking about the squeezing in my chest. The physical ache that has grown into much more than discomfort.

It reminds me—as if I needed a reminder—that my heart is not my own.

I ignore the pain and heave a sigh. After twenty years of studying, practicing, and traveling from one show to the next—each seemingly bigger than the last—I've finally given my best friend, Tiegan Rose Marie Atherton, her fifth and final wish.

I know she's watching, wherever she is. Right along with Mr. Murray McBride, most likely. Chewing on some Milk Duds or hitting heavenly home runs with that beautiful swing of hers, just like when we were kids.

The excitement of the moment makes my heart thump, and I squeeze my eyes shut, focusing on the ache, embracing the pain. Tiegan's heart sends the blood of life through my veins. It's a concept I doubt I'll ever fully wrap my mind around. It's a debt I'll certainly never fully repay.

My mom is here, walking backstage from the wings with tears in her eyes, holding Collins's hand and beaming. Her embrace feels warm and familiar, despite the time that has passed. But I can't focus on it because of what I see over her shoulder. Della—Tiegan's mom—staring at the floor, unable to meet my eyes.

I recognize the confused furrow of her brow and the vacant stare, pointed at nothing. It's a mirror image of what's inside me. Something I didn't anticipate but now realize I should have.

Emptiness.

Since that day twenty years ago when I awoke in a hospital bed in Chicago with Tiegan's heart pumping in my chest, I've been laser focused on one thing. If I could become a well-known magician, I could earn enough money to make Tiegan's final wish of raising a million dollars for the homeless a reality. If that singular focus and determination also helped me deal with the loss of my two best friends—one an old man and the other a young girl—so much the better.

And it worked. Until now. Until the distraction is gone, and all I'm left with is a gaping hole and an uncertain future.

Funny that I would think of my goal as a distraction. The truth is, it's been my entire life's meaning. But I'm finding the old saying is right: the road is better than the inn. And now I'm faced with a question, so soon after reaching my goal: What comes next?

I have no answer, and it paralyzes me.

Forget the questions about the future of my career, or my relationships, or any other big picture things. I can't even figure out where to move my feet. Standing here behind the curtain, I hear the loneliest sounds I've ever heard.

The fading of the crowd's applause.

The clicking of seats folding into position.

The shuffling of feet as they exit.

The silence that covers the theater like a plague.

"Jason?"

It's my mother's voice. The fear and sadness in her eyes make me feel even worse, so I try to smile. "How'd I do?"

"Amazing," she says. "It was truly amazing." But after watching me stand motionless for several long moments, she touches the shoulder of my tuxedo gently. "What's wrong?"

Staring straight at the backside of the curtain, I shake my head. "I'm lost, Mom."

There's a squeeze of my shoulder. I can tell she wants to hug me again and I wonder if she's holding back because of the distance I've created in the name of focusing on my goal. "If you're lost, you can always come home," she says.

I want to ask her: What home? I haven't had a home since I woke up in that hospital bed twenty years ago. The last time I had a home, I snuck out of it and into Murray's car in the middle of the night. Together, we journeyed. We adventured. We lived.

And we lost so very much.

But I've caused my mother enough pain as it is. First, she had to live with the uncertainty of my health, then, she surely believed she'd lose me to a failing heart. After that, I surprised her by surviving—only to disappear on a quest as soon as I was old enough, the motivation for which I could never adequately explain.

So I nod, give her a hug, and kiss her cheek. "Okay, Mom," I say. "I'll come home."

The heart is such a mystical thing. It's so much more than an organ. So much more than a muscle that pumps blood through the body, delivering oxygen and nutrients. Over the years, it has come to symbolize love itself—thanks to the combined ideas of a philosopher and a physicist.

Aristotle once described the heart, not quite accurately, as having three chambers with a small dent in the middle. Then, in the fourteenth century, Italian physicist Guido da Vigevano drew the shape he imagined from Aristotle's description: the modern "heart" shape we see on Valentine's Day cards.

Needless to say, I've spent a lot of time thinking about the heart.

It's been years since my heart and I (which I think of as two separate things) have set foot in my hometown of Lemon Grove, Illinois. I returned for a while after the transplant. Long enough to finish elementary school, middle school, and high school. But it's amazing how little of those years I remember. With all the hours I spent reading about magic, practicing magic, even performing magic the last few years I was there, I barely remember anything after Murray picked me up in the middle of the night and drove me to Chicago, where so many of my wishes came true.

Along with my worst nightmares.

It's the nightmares that haunt me. I wish I could remember the feeling of kissing Mindy Applegate, or watching the baseball sail over the fence at Wrigley Field, or punching that bully to defend Tiegan's honor. But all I can think about is what happened to Murray and Tiegan in the end. All I can remember is waking up with them gone. All I can feel is guilt.

I suppose this is how Murray must have felt before he met me—worn out and washed up, having outlived what should have been his life. If he hated himself for living when others died, if he had a void that felt too big to fit inside him . . . well, then I guess I'm getting to know Murray better now than I ever did during our adventures together.

I can't get out of DC fast enough, so I take a red-eye to O'Hare, then rent a car and drive up to Lemon Grove. But I don't go home. My mom wouldn't be there anyway. Everyone who was in DC for the show is still in DC, except for me. So despite it being the middle of the night, I drive straight to the old house where Murray McBride used to live.

I never actually visited his home when Murray was alive, but I used to take the city bus to this neighborhood and walk by when I was in middle school, after he was gone. I'd look in the windows and try to imagine him eating his bran flakes. I'd crack up at the thought of him getting ready to go to his art class, where he was a nude model, although in his case, *nude* only meant removing his top shirt. It was one of the few things that could make me laugh in those days.

It doesn't make me laugh now.

At some point, I must have fallen asleep in the rental car because when I wake up, the sun is up. The driver's side seat is fully reclined, which I don't remember doing. I must have been exhausted from the adrenaline of the performance followed by the flight here and car rental. I probably didn't even get here until 4:00 a.m.

I glance at my phone: 8:48 a.m.

For all the times I visited Murray's house in the years after his death, I never knocked on the door. I don't know why. Fear that the people who live there now might feel intruded upon? Fear that the memories of Murray would be too much? Whatever the reason, it doesn't affect me now. So I step out of the car, straighten my wrinkled tuxedo as best I can, and walk straight up to the door.

And I knock.